AFTER DEATH

A *Blue Bloods* NOVEL

AFTER DEATH

A *Blue Bloods* NOVEL

MELISSA DE LA CRUZ

HYPERION
Los Angeles   New York

First Edition, July 2023
10 9 8 7 6 5 4 3 2 1
FAC-004510-23139
Printed in the United States of America

This book is set in Baskerville MT Pro/Monotype
Designed by Marci Senders

Library of Congress Cataloging-in-Publication Control Number: 2023930338
ISBN 978-1-368-06700-3
Reinforced binding

Visit www.HyperionTeens.com

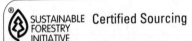

For my Blue Bloods fans,
thank you for everything

Child of blood and bless'd—
Upon the return of darkness,
The Sons of the Star light the Way.
Blade of flame thy brand,
Go forth. Be not afraid.
With the right hand of the Fallen,
Usher upon thy deed.

—Prophecy of Paladin Morgana, c. AD 650 (translated)

BEFORE

Max Force was a prisoner.

Of all the places he'd imagined he'd wind up one day, strapped to a cold table and unable to move even an inch was not high on the list. The ironic part was that he'd been the one who had designed this particular prison for traitors. Now that *he* was the traitor himself, it was kind of funny in a hysterical way. His cell was reminiscent of an operating room, with stark white-brick walls and harsh fluorescent lighting that made his eyes water.

A handful of Silver Bloods—corrupted vampires who had once followed Max's orders—moved around the room. They inserted needles and tubes into his skin, connecting him to a huge metal machine at the foot of his table. With all the tubes sticking out of it, the machine looked like it had grown long spider legs. It was about the size of a car, the metal shiny and polished, etched with Enochian script—the ancient language of angels. A glass chamber was at the heart of it, and light slowly thrummed inside as if it were beating. As if it were a living heart.

Max had no idea what his captors were planning to do to him.

He strained against the straps holding him down, fought against the gag across his mouth. Even he, Azrael, the angel of death, couldn't break free of Enochian bindings.

"Think it'll work on him?" one of the Silvers asked.

"Do not speak your doubts aloud. Aldrich will cut out your tongue if he hears."

On the outside, Aldrich Duncan was the mayor of New York City, beloved father to Max and his twin, Jack, but in reality he was the Morningstar, the fallen Prince of Heaven, Lucifer returned to earth.

"All the Red Blood test subjects died before. The machine needs more souls to—"

"We're not dealing with a Red Blood now, are we?" Max recognized this Silver, an agent formerly under his command. Max never bothered learning their names, and this one was no exception. But it looked like the agent had gotten a promotion. He sneered down at Max, his silver eyes catching the low light. "Besides, this is just a trial run."

The machine clunked and whirred like a ferocious beast yawning to life. The tubes connected to Max's arms and legs lit up, and he felt pain he'd never thought was possible. He almost forgot what not being in pain felt like; it defined his existence, unspooled what made him Max. The Silvers cut the power within seconds, but it felt like it lasted lifetimes.

His brain felt like it had been scrambled, inundated with images of memories that didn't belong to him. Layers of visions overlapped one another, superimposed like transparent photographs, and he didn't know what was real. He felt like he'd lived not only a thousand lifetimes in this world, but in a thousand other worlds too. Was Aldrich trying to make him go mad?

Max's breath was hot against the strap. He choked on his own panic, eyes rolling in their sockets. They removed his gag, but still he couldn't speak. He couldn't even form a coherent thought.

"How was that, Azrael?" The men's laughter echoed all around the chamber.

They didn't stick around to wait for an answer. They slammed the cell door behind them, leaving Max alone with the machine and his fear.

When next they came to him, he had lost track of time. It could have been hours, days, or months since they'd been there. All he could do was snarl as they checked the tubes and needles, ensuring the machine was connected and ready to go again.

"You think torture will work on me?" Max asked. "It won't. I won't talk."

The Silver lieutenant leaned over him, looking down at him like he was swamp scum. "You really believe this is just a torture device?" He huffed, amused. "And you always thought you were so smart."

They gagged him again. Max didn't even have time to brace himself as they flipped a switch and the machine roared to life. Pain. Eternal. Fathomless. Memories of other worlds, piling on him, threatening to melt his brain. And it was over in seconds. Through his tears and the pleading of his body to die already, he heard the Silvers laughing again.

They removed his gag once more, as if wanting to hear his pitiful cries more clearly.

"What's he saying?"

"I think he's saying, *Kingsley, Kingsley!*"

Kingsley Martin, a reformed Silver. Max's bondmate. Max hadn't realized he'd been saying his name aloud. He thought he'd been repeating it in his mind like a mantra, something to focus on to get through endless agony.

The lieutenant shook his head, amused. "Kingsley Martin is dead, Max! Thanks to you. He can't save you now. No one can."

The Silver wasn't wrong. Lucifer's brother, Leviathan, had snapped Kingsley's neck, and just like that, Max's future with Kingsley was over before it began. Unlike Max and the other Blue Bloods, Kingsley was enmortal, and he would never return after death. No rebirth, no reincarnation. Gone. Forever. A life stolen in an instant. The image of his dead body had been burned into Max's brain like a brand. His one true soul mate, staring at him with lifeless eyes, right before they threw a bag over Max's head and dragged him away.

Max was selfish. He wanted their future back. He wanted *Kingsley* back. It was a cruel irony that even though he was the angel of death, he couldn't stop the people he loved from dying.

"Shut him up," the lieutenant said. "It's pathetic."

They secured the Enochian gag over his mouth again before they left, leaving him to lie in silence. All Max could do was shiver in the dark, drifting in and out of consciousness.

Hunger marked the passage of time. No one came to give him blood. His stomach twisted and turned with cravings. If he didn't feed on human blood soon, he would fall asleep and never wake up.

It was apparent that his jailors didn't intend on keeping him around long enough to bother. He used Kingsley's name to stay focused. He refused to die.

Max must have drifted off because the next minute he realized the door had opened again.

He braced himself for another round of torture, but something far worse appeared at the foot of his table: his identical twin, Jack.

No, Jack! Get away from here!

"Max!" Jack gasped, breathless. His blond hair was swept back from his face, and his eyes were bright with excitement. "There you are! Hurry! I've come to rescue you."

Max's cries were muffled behind his gag. His heart raced, and his thoughts rushed like a hurricane. How had Jack found him? How did he get in without alerting anyone? Max was so relieved to see his brother he wanted to cry, but he had to warn Jack that this was a trap. He tried, but with the muzzle on, all he could do was howl.

Jack pulled at the straps holding Max's arms, but they wouldn't budge. Max reached out to him in the glom, to tell him to run and save himself, but there was no answer. Jack's glom was dark as a void. Why wasn't he replying?

Suddenly it all made sense. Max's breath hitched in his chest and he got very still. Jack noticed. "What's wrong? Come on, I'm here to save you."

Max was seething. Rage pumped in his veins.

Jack stopped trying to break the straps and smiled down at him. But it wasn't Jack. His eyes weren't right. They should be warm and soft; instead they were cool and sharp. Max should know. The eyes that looked back at him were identical to his own . . . but they weren't Jack's.

The thing that wasn't Jack puffed out his cheeks as he sighed, disappointed that the fun was going to be over so soon. The *mutatio* melted away and in Jack's place stood Lucifer's angelic brother, Leviathan.

Only the most powerful vampires had the ability to fully transform their visage, an old hunting technique to get close to their victims. And being one of the oldest and most powerful vampires on earth, Leviathan was a master shapeshifter. He could look like anyone. Most recently he had masqueraded as May Woldock, a political figure whom Aldrich killed so Leviathan could replace her in order to trick more humans into trusting their plan. In his usual form, Leviathan looked much like Aldrich—they were brothers after all. But Leviathan was greasier, oilier, his smile wide and hungry.

Leviathan snapped his fingers and leaned on Max's table. "I really had you there, didn't I? I was wondering when you'd notice," he said, smiling wickedly. "Oh, don't look so angry. I need to have a little fun around here. Come on, lighten up. It'll be over before you know it." He tapped playfully on Max's bare feet.

All Max wanted to do was lash out, grab Leviathan around the throat and squeeze, watching the light go out in his eyes. Just like Leviathan had done to Kingsley before snapping his neck. But the best he could do was ball his hands into fists.

Sitting alone with his thoughts for so long, Max had imagined the myriad ways he wanted to kill Leviathan: tear out his throat with his teeth, jam his fist down his gullet, push his thumbs through his eyeballs. Given some time, he could get creative. Thoughts of revenge had kept him alive for the same amount of time as he'd been kept imprisoned.

But even if Max could resurrect Leviathan and kill him in every one of the million ways he wanted to, it would never bring Kingsley Martin back.

Leviathan just smiled at Max.

The door creaked open again and Aldrich Duncan's face appeared, smiling down upon Max with all the warmth of a winter night. "Hello, Max."

Max's whole body went cold. This was the first time Aldrich had visited him since he'd been captured. Fear and anguish and hatred bubbled up to the surface, and it felt like the air had been sucked out of the room. Max forgot how to breathe.

For so long, he had thought of Lucifer as a father, a sorry replacement for the one he'd lost as a child. How foolish he'd been, he'd thought as he watched a Silver Blood in a lab coat tend to the machine, making adjustments. Max's heartbeat quickened. Leviathan took up a spot at the far side of the room, his arms folded across his chest, his eyes gleaming excitedly like polished stones in the dark. If Leviathan looked excited, it was wise for Max to be terrified.

"Deep breath," Aldrich said, patting Max on his bare shoulder. His hand was cold. "There are other matters to attend to before we get started on you. Tell me, where is Jack?" Aldrich clicked his tongue. "Oh, someone, do take off his muzzle. He can't answer me with that thing strapped over his mouth." Hands appeared in Max's vision and pulled the enchanted gag away from his face.

Max croaked, "I don't know." His throat hurt and his tongue felt like sandpaper in his mouth. But there was also a bloom of hope in his chest. If Aldrich didn't know where Jack was, that meant Max's brother had escaped. He could still be out there.

"Your brother abandoned you," Leviathan said. "He left you here to die alone. How does that make you feel?"

Good, thought Max. His twin was unshakably resourceful. He hoped Jack wasn't planning to do anything as stupid as try to rescue him for real, though. *Don't do it, leave me be*, he sent through the glom. Being twins, they were particularly connected, like no other Blue Bloods. *Save yourself*, he sent. But Max couldn't sense a reply or even an acknowledgment of his message. Maybe Jack had shut himself off to avoid detection.

Or, Max thought with a sinking unease, *he's already dead.*

"Lost track of your best and brightest?" asked Max. Jack had always been Aldrich's favorite. For good reason too, as he was the golden boy, the apple of Aldrich's eye, practically perfect in every way. Max smiled, because Jack had betrayed Aldrich just as he had. "How much did it hurt when your most beloved son stabbed you in the back?"

He could only follow Aldrich with his eyes as he circled the table. "That bravado of yours will get you nowhere."

"It's a shame Jack's not here," Leviathan said, sneering at Max from his dark corner. "Torturing him in front of you would have been a good motivator."

Max's lip twitched. The Silver Blood lab tech pushed a button and the device started warming up, the inner workings grinding to life. Max couldn't help the fear that knifed through his heart. He didn't want to be tortured, but he didn't want to see Jack tortured instead. He'd rather die. "Motivator for what? You could just kill me. Why wait?"

Leviathan said to Aldrich, "He's right. Let's just kill him and take it. It'll be so much easier."

Take what? Max wondered.

"No. It doesn't work that way," Aldrich said. "And without it, we'll just keep running into the same results we've been running into up to now. If all goes according to plan, I won't need Jack anyway."

In his hand, Aldrich held a small quartz crystal that, when it caught the light, gleamed like gold. It looked special. He handed it to the Silver Blood, who loaded it into the heart of the machine.

"What do you need me for? I won't work for you anymore." Finally saying it out loud made Max feel stronger.

Aldrich didn't seem to care. His gaze landed on the machine, then he looked at Max. "Do you believe in parallel universes?"

For a moment, Max thought Aldrich had truly lost it, but then he remembered Kingsley had once mentioned something about many worlds. And every time they used the machine, he was inundated with new memories, memories that didn't belong to him, not entirely. But in some ways, it felt like they did. It couldn't be a coincidence, could it?

Aldrich pressed his hands to his chest, smoothing out his bright white dress shirt. "Long before I was born in this body, I was fascinated by secrets beyond our universe. Time travel, string theory, many worlds, knowledge of reality that could be mastered. I built this machine here in Montauk in an attempt to tap into that potential, harvesting power from subjects willing to open the barrier to the other side. Sacrifices were made, and unexpected visitors came through to our world. Power begets monsters."

Max wondered if he meant that literally.

"Even though I saw an opportunity, I knew we weren't ready. I shelved the project, and only recently I saw something that renewed my interest. That girl at city hall. Her aura was not entirely of this world, like it had been touched by memories of another. Dimensions had collided without my doing anything to bring it about and the only way that could happen was through power—archangelic power.

"Her existence proves that there are worlds beyond our own."

"I don't know who you're talking about," Max lied. No way was he going to tell Aldrich about Schuyler Cervantes-Chase. Until that day in the Repository when he tracked down Kingsley and the other rogue vampires, and Schuyler had tried to protect Kingsley with a well-aimed book to Max's head, he'd always thought she was another mortal at Duchesne, barely anyone worth paying attention to. Max still wasn't sure who—or rather *what*—she was, but he knew that she did something no one else had ever done before: She scared Aldrich. Max had known him too long not to see the fear in his eyes. Aldrich didn't like it when he wasn't the one in control.

That meant Schuyler was more important than anyone could ever have imagined and needed to be protected at all costs. This was one secret he would keep, even if it killed him.

Aldrich walked around the table. "With Michael and Gabrielle dead in this world, twin angels of the Apocalypse are the only ones strong enough to shatter the barrier between worlds. Present company excluded." He tipped his head toward his brother. "The celestial sword is the key."

Leviathan scoffed. Not being able to kill Max was putting him in a sour mood.

Max snarled. "I'm not giving you Michael's sword. You'll have to kill me to get it." The same way Azrael had killed Michael to claim ownership of the sword, Aldrich would kill Max to obtain it now.

"See? I told you," Leviathan said.

But Aldrich just smiled knowingly. "There are other ways."

Aldrich clasped his hands behind his back, tipped his head down, and asked, "Was it worth it?" When he looked up again, Max saw a glimmer of pain sparkling in his icy-blue eyes. "My top lieutenant, my one true heir, betrayed me. Only to wind up here at the end of all things."

At one point not too long ago, Max would have done anything to make Aldrich proud of him. He would have destroyed the whole universe had Aldrich asked him to, no questions asked. And he would have done it gladly too. He'd been a different person then, angry, and with a heart full of lead. But Aldrich's guilt trip wouldn't work on him any longer. "Now my family has turned against me. The twin orphan boys I so graciously brought into my care, raised properly, to be powerful, to inherit the world I built for them. And this is how you repay me. What did I do to deserve it?"

It was a question that didn't need an answer. The machine had warmed up, the Enochian markings across its surface glowing with power. The crystal inside it shone like a million stars. The hair on Max's arms started to stand on end, a mixture of static electricity and white-hot fear. He was already bracing himself as best he could for what was to come. This was different.

Aldrich's blue eyes danced in the light from the machine. "I don't want this world anymore; I want them all. And I've finally figured out what I need to do to get them, even without my sons at my side. I'll find another who will not disappoint me."

"Whatever you're trying to do, it won't work," Max said. He knew he sounded desperate, but he didn't care.

"It will be more difficult now, without your cooperation, I admit. With your sword, your power would have been able to tear open the gates to other worlds. Permanently. You would have been a god of more than one reality. But you chose to turn your back on me. Where would we be if you had made better choices?"

Max's chest tightened. "I won't help you."

Aldrich's smile was soft, tender even. Like a father might do, he reached out and brushed a lock of Max's blond hair away from his forehead. His eyes were filled with pity. "Oh, my child. I'm not asking you to. I'm sorry it had to end this way."

Aldrich stepped back and Max's heart hammered in his chest. He strained as hard as he could against his bindings, but they refused to budge. Struggling was useless, but Max fought anyway. His vampire fangs sprang out as he summoned the last bits of his strength; sweat beaded on his forehead, and he gasped with the effort. Aldrich simply watched him, detached, as if Max were making him torture him. Leviathan appeared gleeful.

But, if nothing else, Max would die fighting, just like Kingsley had done.

Aldrich nodded to the Silver Blood assistant at the control panel and didn't even watch when he flipped the switch. Max refused to give up and tell Aldrich what he wanted to hear as the machine roared back to life.

"Come along, brother. Even you don't want to see this," Aldrich said. Leviathan looked disappointed that he was going to miss the show, but he did as he was told. Aldrich paused at the door to look over his shoulder at Max one last time.

"You will serve your purpose soon enough, Azrael," Lucifer promised. Then he was gone.

Pain.

Agony.

Suffering like nothing he had never experienced.

Max didn't exist anymore.

All that was left was torment.

His eyes bulged as his life force, all the blood in his veins—blue as the morning sky—drained out of him, down the tubes and into the crystal, and only then did he scream. . . .

PART ONE
FRIENDS IN NEED

ONE

SCHUYLER

"Sassy Pants! You're going to be late for school!"

Schuyler Cervantes-Chase was already scrambling to get ready when her father called to her through her bedroom door. She pulled her favorite oversize sweater over her rumpled black dress and called back, "I know! I know!" Then she cursed when she realized she had put her sweater on backward. Once it was fixed, she tossed her neon-green water bottle full of donated human blood into her backpack, barely checking to see if the lid was screwed on.

She couldn't believe she had overslept—at least that's what she would tell people who didn't know about her secret life as a Blue Blood vampire. She had slept through her alarm—that part was true—but they didn't need to know that it was because she'd spent the night before searching all over Manhattan for Jack Force.

After the battle of city hall, when she and Jack had interrupted Lucifer's plans to impose the Silver Legacy to wipe out all mortal Red Bloods on the island under the guise of a deadly pandemic, Jack had left to find his twin brother, Max. He'd been worried that something terrible had happened, and he was right. Schuyler's human Familiar, Oliver Golding-Chang, had seen Max and Kingsley get caught and Kingsley killed. Max was taken prisoner. Schuyler could only guess what had befallen Jack. Why else would he still be missing after all this time?

Every night she went out looking for him, searching for some sign, but every night she came home alone and exhausted.

Two months had passed since she'd last seen Jack. Two months come and gone, and she was worried sick about him. But she couldn't tell anyone about it, not even her family.

She ran her fingers through her curls as she raced out of her room, backpack flying behind her. Mornings in the Cervantes-Chase household were almost always loud and coffee-scented. Schuyler's father, Stephen, already in the kitchen, had brewed up a second pot while her mother, Aurora, sat at her piano in the living room, rehearsing for a gig that weekend. The TV murmured quietly in the background, recounting a story about a man who had gone missing—the third one this week.

"No leads so far on the mysterious disappearances," the newscaster said, "and the police are asking for any information related to the case. On a more uplifting note, Unity Fest, a post-pandemic charity event, is scheduled to happen later this month on the Great Lawn in Central Park. Proceeds from the festival will go toward helping those affected by the plague that has ravaged our city. All are encouraged to attend. Tickets for the event will go on sale starting—" but Schuyler was too in a hurry to pay any attention.

She dashed to the table to grab the toast and a banana that had been set out for her before kissing her mother on the cheek.

"Have a good day at school, mi cielo," her mom said. She played a chord on the piano, a chord of encouragement to get Schuyler out the door. Schuyler had inherited her mother's dark brown curls and tawny complexion, but she hadn't inherited the full range of her musical genius. She guessed that wasn't a thing that could be passed down. While she looked like her mother for the most part, she had her father's bright blue eyes.

Stephen ran through his usual checklist before she headed out. "Do you have your phone? Wallet? Keys?"

Schuyler answered yes to every question around a mouthful of dry toast, tying her boots so quickly she might have tied her fingers together in the process. Her father was wearing his usual painting clothes, a tattered eighties rock band T-shirt and pajama pants, dappled with paint. The outfit looked like it could sell in a boutique clothing store for thousands of dollars to wealthy clientele. His fingers were stained blue from working on a painting that morning. She did a double take, at first thinking it was blood, not paint. But only vampires had blue blood, like her, and Stephen was mortal— she was certain of that.

Her parents had no idea about her Blue Blood nature, however, and Schuyler planned to keep it that way. For their own safety.

"Bye!" Schuyler downed her breakfast in record time, threw on her red scarf, and bounded down the stairs of her family's loft in SoHo. She jogged down the street toward the subway, which she would take all the way to the Upper East Side.

The deadly illness that had brought the city to its knees had vanished just as mysteriously as it had appeared, and slowly but surely life was getting back to normal in Manhattan. A "new normal," anyway. As if anything could ever be any sort of normal again. Schuyler was the only person who knew the truth. Mayor Aldrich

Duncan had been building an army of Silver Bloods from Blue Blood vampires who had broken their vows not to harm humans in exchange for extraordinary power—killing mortals for sport and planning to harvest them as an ultimate power source in Duncan's plans to crush the world and bend it to his will.

The media had been silent about what had happened that night at city hall. Not one newspaper or news channel, or even a nut-job conspiracy website, talked about the mayhem Schuyler had caused when she unleashed Lucifer's own hellhounds on his Silver Bloods and disrupted his scheme. She wasn't surprised. Aldrich Duncan would make sure that no one would ever know his real intentions. His administration backtracked on its version of events overnight, the clinics closed, and the mysterious and deadly disease that was killing humans would soon be forgotten. Life went on.

Except Jack was still missing.

He had turned his back on his father, just as Max had done. Jack and Max Force had been raised as Lucifer's heirs, but they had chosen to fight for the Light. In doing so, they had betrayed the darkness inside themselves.

Schuyler kept Jack's note tucked in the pocket of her skirt, the paper wrinkled and limp from opening it and refolding it so many times. His note was the only thing she had left of him. The last lines of his letter were the ones she reread the most.

Please. Don't try to find me.
    My heart is yours,
    Jack

Of course she wasn't going to sit at home and do nothing. But with no leads, no way of knowing where Jack or Max was . . . Not knowing was the worst.

When she wasn't scouring every inch of the island in her search, she waited for him. To keep from biting her nails to the quick with anxiety, she'd picked up her old hobby of weaving bracelets, ones she used to craft when she went to theater camp in the summer. She'd wind the knots from embroidery thread, creating multicolored chevron patterns in long bands, thinking of Jack and wishing he was home, hoping he would knock on her window like he did when he decided to help her save Kingsley. She'd made half a dozen bracelets already and had no intention of slowing down. She would wait for him no matter what.

The subway station was packed with commuters from all walks of life, adults on their way to work or home from a late shift, students heading to school, tourists making their way to the overpriced hot spots across town. Bodies overflowed the turnstiles and an announcement overhead crackled on the P.A. speakers. It was hard to make out the words, but the collective groan from the other subway goers indicated that the trains had been delayed. It wasn't too surprising for a regular MTA rider, but it was the last thing Schuyler needed to hear when she was already running late.

She was going to have to do this the vampire way.

She turned around and wove her way back through the crowd and up to the street once more, hurrying into an alley between a bodega and a gym, checking to see if the coast was clear. Once she was sure, she jumped onto a fire escape and scaled up to the roof of the building. With a leap, she ran with extraordinary speed across the rooftops, the wind rushing through her hair as she picked up the pace. Even though she was a vampire, she wasn't immune to after-school detention.

Oliver Golding-Chang was waiting for her at the entrance to Duchesne. He wasn't just her human Familiar. He was also her best friend in the entire world. She leaped down from above and landed next to him just as the first bell of the school day rang.

Startled, Oliver let out a yell and jumped away, arms wheeling. "Sky! Don't *do* that!" he exclaimed.

"Sorry, Ollie," she said, breathless but thankful she'd made it to school on time, and glanced around. No one was watching them, most of her classmates having already headed inside. People didn't pay a lot of attention to the two of them in the first place. Schuyler and Oliver were outsiders in a lot of ways.

Duchesne was an elite private school for the academically and financially privileged members of society. The building was a former mansion turned into a school, but it still had the same air of prestige as it did when it was built in the Gilded Age. Its beaux-arts style had been featured in several magazines and on architecture tours, and its extraordinary façade hinted at the very serious endeavors happening behinds its double-height doors. The future leaders of the country studied among John Singer Sargent paintings, performed orchestral concerts beneath real crystal chandeliers on terraces that overlooked Central Park, ate lunches in sitting rooms completed in the same beaux-arts style, with satinwood tables in the lounge and reupholstered Schastey chairs. Though students didn't wear uniforms anymore, there was a special cachet about attending Duchesne that made anyone lower their voice as they entered the building, as if they needed to pay respect to its history.

It was a bright, sunny morning, and spirits were high. Most students were glad to be back after Duchesne had closed its doors during the pandemic, and Schuyler should have been glad she could be back too. She had liked the idea of studying from home, but nothing beat sitting with Oliver at a reading desk in the library and sharing snacks while they texted each other in study hall, silently giggling over stupid posts shared online. Oliver and Schuyler joined the rest of their class in the fleur-de-lis–wallpapered hallway as students gathered their things from their lockers. Schuyler was still breathless from her run halfway across the island and Oliver noticed.

"Cutting it a little close, don't you think?" he asked, his lilting British accent taking on an edge of teasing. "Overslept again?"

"Trains were late. Barely had time to eat."

Ollie pulled out a foil of Pop-Tarts from his hoodie pocket. "Are you hungry? Breakfast is the most important meal of the day. Wait, maybe the second most. Not counting the . . ." He trailed off and pulled the collar of his T-shirt down, hinting at Schuyler's blood-sucking habit.

"Ollie," Schuyler warned, looking around for lingering stares. Everyone was too busy, yelling or laughing in their own conversations to notice.

Oliver laughed. "No one's listening! It's *us*, remember?"

Schuyler huffed.

But Oliver was right. Even if someone did overhear what they were talking about, they wouldn't care. She and Oliver didn't fit in with the rest of the crowd, but Schuyler didn't mind. They had each other.

The treat Oliver offered was tempting, though. Schuyler broke off a corner of the pastry and nibbled on it. "I've got something to drink in my water bottle. The run took a lot out of me, but I'll be fine for the rest of the day."

"Just say the word, we can sneak off to some broom closet and you can get your fang on." He grinned, his tongue poking out of the corner of his mouth.

Schuyler laughed and slapped him on the arm. When they'd first performed the Sacred Kiss together—the special bond created when souls are spiritually connected from direct feeding—he had opened his heart to her, showing his true feelings for her. It had changed their relationship and taken it to a whole new level. It scared her. She felt how much he loved her, but she couldn't reciprocate. She was in love with Jack; she *still* loved Jack. But when Jack disappeared and Max was captured, Oliver had been there for her. He'd witnessed Kingsley's murder and comforted her in her darkest moments. She let him hold her and it felt right. Being close to him had always felt right.

He still delivered lunch coolers full of donated blood packs in the interim, maintaining his duties as Conduit, ensuring that Schuyler never went too long without the sustenance she needed. Since their Sacred Kiss, she hadn't taken any more blood from his veins. Even though it didn't hurt him, she didn't want to take the risk. He was too important to her, and if she lost control and took too much blood, she couldn't bear to lose him. Until they had no other choice, the packs of blood would have to be enough.

The pair of them wove through the halls of the school, heading to first period. "Did you hear about the concert they're throwing in Central Park?" Oliver asked.

"The what?" After a moment, she remembered. "Oh, yeah, I think I heard something about it on the news this morning."

"It's going to be incredible. And the money they raise is going to do a ton of good. They've already booked huge headliners. I even heard that Snap and Pop are getting back together for a reunion show."

In the wake of Lucifer's fake virus, there were still a lot of people in need, especially kids. In order to help, Duchesne had organized an after-school charity club called Duchesne for Change, and Schuyler and Oliver joined immediately. They helped organize silent auctions to raise money, and clothing and food drives for families in need. Although the club had over fifty members, it still didn't feel like there were enough volunteers. Schuyler knew that no matter how much money they brought in or how many families they made meals for, as long as Lucifer was still in power, nothing would change. There would be more families destroyed, more suffering, more pain.

"I was thinking," Oliver said, with a gleam in his honey-colored eyes, "maybe you'd want to go with me? Like old times?"

The idea of going to a concert with Oliver after everything that had happened still felt out of reach to Schuyler, like she was stuck in cement while everyone else seemed to be moving forward. She wanted those "old times" with Oliver back, and now that the rest of the world was returning to a state of normalcy, all she wanted to do was believe that things could be normal for her also. But how could that happen when everything still felt askew?

The best Schuyler could do these days was wake up every morning, get dressed, kiss her parents on her way out, and head into school as if she were an average, almost sixteen-year-old student and not some vampire running around in the night among demonic hellhounds and sucking blood from her best friend.

"I don't know, Ollie," she said, stepping out of the way of a horde of rowdy basketball players.

"Come on, we've been working so hard. With all we've been doing for Duchesne for Change, we deserve a little break."

Schuyler hummed. She had to admit, getting lost in a crowd with Oliver by her side didn't sound so bad. "I'll think about it," she said, smiling.

Oliver smiled back.

Dr. Perkins, their European history teacher, was busy writing on the chalkboard when Schuyler and Oliver entered the classroom and took their spots as usual in the back near the windows. They were the last students to arrive. While everyone else was mingling in clusters around the room, talking and laughing, Oliver slid the rest of the Pop-Tart they'd been sharing toward Schuyler. She gave him a grateful smile and opened her textbook, ready to start the day, when the door to the classroom opened and a girl Schuyler had never seen before walked in. She stood out from the rest of the prep school kids in her nineties grunge aesthetic, sporting layers of flannel, ripped jeans, and a choker necklace, but that wasn't what made the hair on the back of Schuyler's neck stand on end.

"Oh! You must be the new student!" Dr. Perkins said, greeting the new arrival with a warm smile.

The girl didn't answer. She just handed Dr. Perkins a sheet of paper and glowered as she looked around the classroom, scanning the faces staring back, her backpack clutched tightly over one shoulder. Her hair was bright purple, cut straight at her chin. When she pushed her round wire-frame glasses up her freckled nose, Schuyler noticed that her hands and wrists were wrapped in white bandages.

Schuyler didn't know how she knew it, but there was something different about this girl. The atmosphere in the classroom felt like a shift in the wind before a storm, and Schuyler's whole body tensed.

The girl's gaze moved about the room before her dark eyes narrowed, glaring right at Schuyler.

Whatever Schuyler sensed about her, it seemed that the girl sensed it right back.

Was there another vampire at Duchesne?

Two

SCHUYLER

*T*he new girl's appearance was causing a different kind of stir among the students, most whispering behind their hands as they passed judgment, until Dr. Perkins clapped her hands to get everyone's attention.

"Class, I'd like to introduce you to our newest student at Duchesne, Ay . . . Ay-oh . . ." She squinted at the piece of paper the girl had handed her. "Aoife."

The girl sighed. Apparently people butchering her name was old news. "It's pronounced like 'EE-fa.' Would you like me to spell it out for you as an interpretive dance?"

A few people laughed nervously, but most were shocked at the girl's brazen attitude.

Dr. Perkins cleared her throat. "My apologies. Aoife Hayward, everyone. Can you tell us a little about yourself?"

"No."

More nervous laughter.

Dr. Perkins balked. "Okay, then. Please." She indicated an empty desk a few rows away from Schuyler and Oliver, and Aoife took her assigned seat. It was the seat that Jack would have occupied had he been at school. But it had remained regretfully vacant. Until it wasn't.

Schuyler couldn't help but stare at the bandages on Aoife's hands. She didn't mean to be rude, but she couldn't help wondering if there were any telltale blue veins of a vampire hidden beneath them. Aoife must have sensed that someone was staring at her and turned around, locking eyes with Schuyler, who promptly lowered her gaze to the open book in front of her.

Kingsley had drilled it into her head that she needed to avoid trouble wherever possible. As the last remaining light of Gabrielle, Schuyler was too important to lose. Like her, Kingsley had remembered another world, memories of an alternate reality, a phenomenon he called *Superimposition*, and he knew that she was destined to defeat Lucifer here, just as she had in her original timeline. Without Kingsley or Jack at her side, though, any plan to do it needed to start from scratch. But if Aldrich Duncan was expanding his search for her, sending one of his loyal vampires to Duchesne was well within the realm of possibilities. The perfect opportunity for a sneak attack. The mayor had a whole army and she had . . . no one. She couldn't help darting her eyes to the exit. The urge to run and get away from this new girl was overwhelming, but Schuyler stayed, her fists clenched. She needed to be vigilant and keep her head down, avoid trouble whenever possible, and not draw attention to herself. So far she was doing a terrible job of that. She was not acting normally. Even Oliver noticed.

"What's wrong?" he whispered, leaning in close to her.

Schuyler shook her head. *Not now.* Aoife gave Schuyler a thorough looking over, taking in her whole body from head to toe before turning to face the front of the classroom as Dr. Perkins started the lesson.

Schuyler tried her best to focus on the class, but it wasn't easy. Aoife's stare was as sharp as broken glass.

After class, Schuyler was one of the last students to leave the room. Aoife was already speaking with a few of their classmates and Schuyler's ears perked up at the mention of Jack's name.

"Jack Force," Aoife said to the girl next to her, Julie Bradford, who was one of those helpful student-council types. She worked with Schuyler on Duchesne for Change. "Where is he?" Aoife certainly had a way of getting to the point.

Julie hugged her books close to her chest and glanced at her friend Mina, as if looking for backup. "I don't know. He's been absent."

Mina chimed in. "Probably on some holiday. His family jet-sets everywhere."

Aoife pinched her lips together like she was sucking a lemon. "When will he be back?"

"How should we know? Jack and his brother are always doing their own thing."

"His brother . . ."

Mina scoffed. "Max. *Duh.* He goes here too. But he's not here either, in case you're wondering."

Julie raised her eyebrows at Aoife. "Are you, like, obsessed with them or something?"

Before Aoife could do or say anything, Mina said, "Of course she is; they're only the hottest guys in school. But Max is way hotter."

"Are you crazy? Jack is the hot one."

"Can one identical twin even *be* hotter than the other?"

It took everything in Schuyler's power to hold her tongue, but she kept her head down. She was the only one who knew the truth about why Max and Jack were absent. A roiling, bitter guilt in her stomach made her feel like puking. She could only hope that the twins were still alive and unhurt. Schuyler considered herself an optimist, but even she had a hard time convincing herself that Max was okay, having been captured. How would Lucifer punish a traitor? She didn't want to know.

Meanwhile, Aoife looked unimpressed with the conversation unfolding between the two girls. Without another word, she turned and disappeared into the crowd of students clogging the hallway.

Schuyler furrowed her brow in thought as she made her way to her next class. Why was Aoife asking about the Force twins? Did she know who they really were?

Throughout the day, Aoife appeared in the same classes as Schuyler. Every chance she got, she asked people where Jack and Max had gone. Everyone had the same answer. They didn't know. Aoife was clearly on a mission, but as the day progressed, she seemed to get more and more agitated.

In second-period physics, Aoife had started writing in a large bound book. Schuyler couldn't help but notice a missing person poster wedged between two of its pages. Before she could get a proper look, Aoife noticed her gaze and snapped the book shut, burying it beneath a stack of worksheets. Schuyler's skin prickled. Who carried around missing person posters?

In gym class, Aoife refused to join the rest of the group swimming laps in the pool. She sat on the bleachers overlooking the Olympic-size pool, her bandaged hands folded as she rested her elbows on the knees of her torn jeans. Schuyler too sat out from swimming, claiming she was sick. She didn't want to get distracted and accidentally show some of her superhuman speed or strength. She had secrets of her own to keep.

Fourth period, they watched a film in civics class. It was a terribly boring and cheesy video, and Schuyler probably would have dozed off, but she was focused on Aoife, who was furiously writing in her strange book. Schuyler suspected she wasn't taking notes on the video.

At lunch, Aoife sat at a table alone, barely touching the catered meal on her plate. She kept glancing around, looking over her shoulder, as if she expected someone to sneak up on her.

"What's going on with you?" Oliver asked.

Schuyler tore her gaze away from Aoife and said, "Nothing." She helped herself to some of his fries, a tried-and-true symbol of their friendship. He sensed she was lying, though. She could see it in his eyes.

"I'm fine. Just thrown off my rhythm today." Schuyler couldn't help but glance at Aoife again, but only because Aoife had stood up suddenly from her table and left the cafeteria, her book tucked under her arm.

Oliver watched her go, then stabbed a fry with a fork before dipping it into some ketchup. "Leave her alone. She doesn't look like she wants to make friends."

———

"All right, everyone," Mr. Donovan said, standing at the podium at the front of the music room. Duchesne for Change met here every Tuesday after school, the only room big enough for making posters and organizing other large projects that needed lots of floor space. Mr. Donovan, their sociology teacher, was the club sponsor, and he commanded everyone's attention, even Schuyler's.

Schuyler had, of course, been watching Aoife since she walked in. She hadn't expected the girl to join a club so soon. It was only her second day, and for Schuyler it had been much the same as her first. All through classes, she had felt nothing but pins and needles crawling all over her skin whenever Aoife was around. She'd hoped to feel some respite at Duchesne for Change, but her hopes had been dashed.

"We're looking for some new ideas for fundraisers," Mr. Donovan said. "Anyone?"

Oliver's hand went up, and Mr. Donovan called on him. "We could co-op with the city's charity concert. Maybe get some back-stage passes and we can auction them off? I've got some contacts that might want to work with us."

"Excellent idea, Mr. Golding-Chang. How about you take the lead on that?"

Oliver looked at Schuyler, beaming proud, and she smiled back as best she could. She could feel Aoife's eyes on her and her gaze made her skin itch like a sunburn. Oliver was blissfully unaware. He had stepped up to help with Duchesne for Change, offering to host several events at his house, and Schuyler was proud of him.

Ruby, a quiet girl with a shy smile and a swoop of dark bangs shadowing one eye, raised her hand next. She'd been the new girl before Aoife came along. "I'd love to help Oliver," she said. Her cheeks flushed when she glanced at him. "My cousin works for Snap and Pop."

Mr. Donovan nodded. "Oh, wonderful! You two can work together. In fact, let's pair off and come up with some ideas to complement the charity concert event."

"Like what?" asked Julie Bradford.

"Maybe a carnival attraction," the teacher suggested, "or a booth of some kind. Something to get people excited."

Someone at the back of the room said, "Like a kissing booth?"

The club members erupted in giggles and jeers.

Mr. Donovan quieted the group by clapping his hands. "Let's see what you come up with. I'll put you into pairs. Get creative."

The teacher started assigning pairs and groups broke off to discuss the assignment separately. Schuyler felt dread as the number of potential partners dwindled until there was only one choice left.

"And, Schuyler, you're with Aoife," he said.

Schuyler's stomach dropped. Aoife stared at her with a look of bewilderment mixed with contempt. Schuyler swallowed her nerves.

Aoife crossed the room, looking as if she was tensing every muscle in her body. She was shorter than Schuyler, but it didn't take away from her imposing manner.

"You're Schuyler," the girl said.

Schuyler cleared her throat awkwardly. "Yeah." Oliver caught her eye, checking on her. He was sitting in the far corner of the room with Ruby now, but Schuyler could handle this on her own. She pointed to the chair beside her. "Want to sit?"

Aoife's gaze dropped to the empty chair. She picked it up and moved it so she and Schuyler were farther away from each other, as if Schuyler smelled bad or something.

Aoife watched her carefully for a beat, then asked, "Jack Force. Know him?"

Was this some sort of test? Schuyler needed to choose her words carefully. "Not really."

"You seem super interested every time I ask people about him." Her accent was Midwestern. She definitely wasn't from around here, but that didn't rule her out of being Lucifer's scout. His reach was long and far. And clearly Schuyler wasn't playing it as cool as she had hoped.

Schuyler needed to stay in control, so she shrugged. "Who wouldn't be? He's the most popular guy in school. People pay attention when he's absent. How do you know him?"

Aoife took a moment, then said flatly, "Business."

A shiver ran down Schuyler's spine, but she kept her composure. *What kind of answer is that?*

Aoife's eyes narrowed ever so slightly. Then she pushed up her glasses and sighed. "So. This concert."

If Aoife had bought the lie, Schuyler couldn't tell. As far as she could hope, Aoife thought she was just a normal girl like everyone else. There was no small talk between them as they jotted down ideas for the charity concert. Aoife definitely wasn't like the others: She was up to something, and Schuyler knew that it was nothing good. If she really was a Blue Blood, like Schuyler suspected, she *had* to be working for Lucifer. There were none left who weren't loyal to him. He'd made sure of that, down to the last rebel: That had been Kingsley. The only vampire Schuyler could trust was Jack, and he was nowhere to be found.

If only she knew where he was . . . and if he was alive and whole . . . the not knowing made everything worse.

THREE

JACK

Jack Force's life was perfect.

Every morning, he spent time on the porch, leaning against the railing, watching the warm sun rise through the forest trees around his little cottage. He'd always dreamed about owning a place like this, and now that dream was a reality. It was a small, white cabin with gables and wide eaves, like something printed on a postcard. It was his own little slice of heaven, tucked away beneath the shade of grand pine trees and hugged on all sides by a perfectly maintained garden, abundant in vegetables, as well as snowdrops and lilies. The wind danced over the forest floor, kicking up leaves like little dancers, and he could smell the ocean, which was only a short walk down the dirt path to the rocky shore. Birds called cheerfully to one another overhead, invisible in their nests atop the branches, and sunlight dappled through the breaks in the trees. If he was lucky, which was often, he spotted a fawn and its sire, a buck with a towering set of antlers.

Jack smiled. He didn't have a care in the world. He was happy, he was free. He was so happy, in fact, he couldn't remember ever being unhappy. He didn't know of any time before this place. The only thing that mattered was this cottage in the forest, and it was bliss.

Of course, he knew there had to be a time before this. He'd been trying to find his brother, Max. . . .

Where did that come from? It struck him all of a sudden, as if he was remembering a dream he'd had last night. But the name faded, like sand through an hourglass, trickling away until it became nothing. Did he ever have a brother? he wondered. No, of course not. He had all the family he ever needed right here with Harmony, the girl of his dreams.

Harmony sang softly in the kitchen, her voice carrying through the open window as she made breakfast. When she was happy, she would sing, and she was always singing. Jack couldn't think of anything more perfect than waking up every morning next to her, her soft golden hair gently draped over one shoulder, the way she smiled at him with sparkling blue eyes. He would do anything for her, anything to protect her, and she cared for him, just as he cared for her. Her voice grew louder as she joined him on the porch, wrapped her arms around his waist, holding him close. Her voice filled the air with warmth and the heat of her breath tickled the skin on his neck.

She was his soul mate, his one true love.

But she's not Schuyler. . . .

Schuyler? The sound of the name had a familiar ring, like the start of a memory. But then it faded, just like everything else, and was replaced by Harmony's gentle touch as she traced his forearms with her hands.

"What are you thinking about?" she asked, pressing her lips to his neck. Her body was so soft and warm, and he leaned into her. She felt like home.

He smiled and answered, "Nothing."

"I can tell when you're thinking. . . ." She came around to his side, watching him with those incredibly blue eyes, as blue as the ocean beyond the woods, and the corners of her lips turned upward. Her fragile beauty took Jack's breath away. She traced a slender finger from the center of his forehead down his straight nose. It felt good. His breath steadied and his muscles relaxed. She always knew how to calm him. "You get a crease when something troubles you. You have nothing to worry about here, my love. Let go."

Jack's shoulders relaxed. He was so tense, and she eased his mind so effortlessly. She was perfect, as if she had been designed just for his pleasure. "It's nothing, truly."

"Tell me," she said. "I want to make you happy."

Jack couldn't keep anything from her. "I was thinking about my family . . . thought I needed to do something." The names escaped him, like a song he'd forgotten the lyrics to.

Harmony's laugh was as pretty as starlight. "Family? But I'm right here."

"I know." He pressed his lips to the back of her hand and she smiled. "I don't know why. It came to me all of a sudden. There was a name. Something I've forgotten to do . . ."

"You're not leaving, are you?" When she pouted, Jack felt like he was disappointing her.

"Of course not! It was merely a thought."

"I see." She clasped her hands around his wrists. "If it will ease your mind, they'll be here soon. Your family."

"They will?"

"Yes, don't you remember? We're having them over for tea."

Jack blinked. Of course. How could he have forgotten? And there they were!

Behind her, walking up the earthy path, were Jack's father and mother. Jack had been foolish to think he had somewhere else to be. His parents had come to visit! They smiled, carrying baskets of food fit for a feast and waved to him, calling his name. He had inherited his father's golden-blond hair, his mother's eyes. Their appearance made him feel so at home, so safe. They looked so alive, after being dead for so many years, and—why did he ever think they were dead? Of course they were alive. Nothing bad ever happened in this place.

They ascended the steps to the porch and greeted Jack and Harmony. Harmony and Jack's mother kissed cheeks. Jack's mother had always said she wanted a daughter. Now she had one.

"My boy!" His father grinned as he came in for a hug. When Jack embraced him, he felt like he hadn't done it in forever, which was ridiculous. Jack buried his face in his father's shoulder, breathing him in. With a squeeze, his father pulled away. "I'm proud of you, son."

Jack almost didn't want to let go, but his mother was waiting expectantly. When he hugged her, he barely managed to let out, "I missed you so much."

His mother smelled like the sea. "Oh, Jack. We only just saw each other yesterday!" She cupped the side of his face with a soft, warm hand and looked at him with such tenderness, Jack almost cried. The tears pricked hot in the back of his eyes, betraying the fact that he was happy.

He was in paradise.

FOUR

SCHUYLER

nce Duchesne for Change let out, Schuyler followed Aoife outside, watching from behind clusters of other Duchesne students. Most of her classmates were picked up by their chauffeurs, whisked home in a procession of black vehicles, but Aoife was further proving herself not to be like the rest. She walked around the block, listening to music with large over-ear headphones. That made it easier for Schuyler to follow her without being obvious, but she nevertheless kept a healthy distance between the two of them. Schuyler hadn't told anyone that she was giving in to her paranoia, but she needed to find out who Aoife was and if she was working for Aldrich Duncan. She needed to know what Aoife was up to and how to stop her from doing . . . what was it that she was doing exactly? It wasn't illegal to ask where the two most popular boys in school had disappeared to, but Schuyler couldn't shake the feeling she had in her gut. Normal people didn't give her a full-body static shock simply by entering a room. And what kind of business could the girl have with Jack?

Schuyler had told Oliver that she needed to get home to do chores. She knew he'd insist on coming with her, as was expected of a Familiar, and he'd already done enough—risked his safety too many times to count. Schuyler needed him to stay home. Then she'd called her parents to tell them she was going out with him for boba tea and wouldn't be back until later. A white lie.

She followed Aoife for an hour as she walked from Duchesne through Central Park, where crews were already setting up a large stage for the charity concert, then circled back all the way through forest paths. She stopped to get a pretzel at one of the food carts near the west side of the park, and paused to watch a trio of musicians busking for change. Schuyler started to wonder if what she was doing following Aoife was all totally pointless. Aoife seemed to be getting used to her new city, stopping in the most touristy locations. The most suspicious thing she did the whole time Schuyler followed her was wait for the crosswalk signal at the intersection of Eighty-First and Central Park West. Most city folk would just cross whenever it was clear. Following her was actually kind of boring.

Schuyler almost called it quits when night fell. She was getting cold and hungry (regular hungry—it was supposed to be taco night at home), and a more rational part of her brain was pleading with her to get a grip already. Then Aoife stopped in front of the American Museum of Natural History. It was a sight to behold for sure, all lit up at night, the building emitting a soft white glow— something Schuyler took for granted, walking past it as often as she did. Aoife took off her headphones and seemed to admire the face of the museum. Huge banners advertising the latest exhibit billowed in the slight breeze: *Empires: A Rise and Fall*. Schuyler blended in with a crowd of people waiting at the nearby bus stop as Aoife crossed the street and entered the building.

Schuyler had come too far to turn back now.

Hardly anyone else was in the museum at this hour on a Tuesday. It was a few minutes before closing, and some of the stragglers had small children to wrangle, others were attempting to squeeze in one last view of the T-rex or get their last-minute souvenirs in the gift shop. Aoife, however, seemed to be on a mission. She didn't linger or look into any of the wings. She paid for her ticket and entered quickly, forcing Schuyler to hand over the couple dollars she'd been planning to spend on actually getting boba with Oliver for real sometime later in the week. Hurrying to catch up to Aoife, she almost lost her in the mass exodus of a school field trip and took the stairs to the second floor. Thankfully, she spotted Aoife on the floor below, heading deeper into the museum. Schuyler kept an eye on her all the while, quieting her footsteps as best she could. Aoife seemed otherwise oblivious to her presence, her headphones playing a throbbing drum beat that Schuyler could hear. It was so loud she imagined that even if she didn't have enhanced vampire senses, she'd be able to hear it in the quiet of the quickly emptying museum.

Aoife had stopped at the exhibit about empires. It was full of different artifacts from throughout history, like Mongolian riding saddles, daggers from the Ottoman Empire, a goblet that was said to have been used by Alexander the Great—thousands of years of human history in one place. Aoife paused in front of an illuminated display case containing a metal shield with a dragon's face imprinted upon it. As far as she could tell, she was now alone. Everyone else had left the museum, and Aoife didn't seem to be in any rush to do the same.

Schuyler took cover behind a large suit of armor on the mezzanine level. Trailing Aoife was getting ridiculous. Clearly the girl was just enjoying the sights. Schuyler was about to give up and head home when a figure entered the exhibit behind Aoife.

At first, she thought it was another patron, but something about their movements was off. They walked with jerky steps, their arms scrunched up to their chest, and their head cocked to the side. Aoife didn't seem to have noticed them come in. She was still listening to music, reading the plaque in front of the display case. But the hairs on her arms were standing on end. That same magical energy she'd felt when Aoife appeared in class washed over her skin now.

Something was happening.

The person who entered the exhibit made a low groan, the sound reminiscent of sand scraping on stone. It took a few shuffling steps toward Aoife.

That was when everything clicked for Schuyler. This wasn't a person at all. Or rather, it used to be a person. It was a mummy. An actual Egyptian mummy, its wrappings trailing behind it as it stalked forward, its dried hands clenching and unclenching as it reached out to Aoife. Its eyes were covered in wrappings, but it didn't seem like it needed to see. It moved forward, gnashing its rotten yellow teeth. Schuyler had never seen anything like it before. She was used to demons and vampires, but this was a first. It took her brain a good second to process what she was seeing, and by the time her wits returned to her, it was too late. Other mummies were lumbering into the room.

Aoife was in trouble.

But before Schuyler could cry out to warn her, the girl sprang into action. She whipped her headphones off, resting them on her shoulders, and leaped to the side. When she spun around, the bandages around her hands unraveled, twining together into a long rope she snapped like a whip. The end of the whip glowed with magical power.

"There you are," Aoife said to the mummy, smirking. She circled it, expertly keeping a healthy distance between herself and its reach. She snapped the whip again, and it cracked like lightning.

The mummy rasped at her, its jaw hanging loose. Schuyler could almost swear it was smiling. Gray, thin-as-newspaper flesh tightened on what was left of its cheeks, revealing more teeth. Behind Aoife, two more figures appeared, rasping and moaning. One was a man dressed like a security guard, the other an old woman in a floral dress, but their skin looked like dried husks, their bodies desiccated, mummified too. Had the first mummy done this to them? It was now three against one, and Aoife was surrounded. They had her trapped.

Aoife glanced over her shoulder, noting other mummies closing in on all sides. All of them moved with that same stiff gait as the first one, but Schuyler knew they were faster than they looked. A dark, evil magic seemed to course through their limbs, commanded by the oldest mummy. A mortal would never stand a chance against these things, but Aoife grinned and snapped the whip again, in time with the rhythm of the song coming from the headphones wrapped around her neck.

The mummies charged, quick as a blink, on all fours like animals.

The mummy in the dress leaped at her and Aoife dodged. She cracked the whip, and it flashed with bright white electricity, smacking what used to be the old woman in the chest. The mummy burst into flames, desiccated skin catching as easily as paper, and the creature screeched like nails on a chalkboard as she attempted to scramble away before turning into a pile of ash.

Aoife moved with such speed and strength, Schuyler almost couldn't keep up with her. She was as fast as a Blue Blood, for sure. She used the whip like a lasso, wrapping it around the security guard mummy's arm and, with a great tug, pulling it clean out of the socket. She caught the arm in midair with an outstretched hand. Even though it was detached, the disembodied hand continued to claw at her face and she flung it to the side, where it slammed into the wall, disintegrating in a cloud of dust.

Aoife's lips moved, saying something under her breath, and her whip ignited again, crackling with lightning. She swung the whip up and smacked it down, striking the one-armed mummy across the head. It went flying into a heap twenty feet away. She let out a satisfied "Ha!" but the lead mummy crept up behind her and slashed the back of her leg. Schuyler could see the creature's heart glowing beneath its rib cage, growing brighter by the second, like it was charging up for another attack. Aoife cried out in pain, and when she turned to fight, Schuyler spotted three deep gouges, her torn jeans already turning a shade of deep crimson red.

So, Schuyler reasoned, she was mortal after all. But still she moved like a vampire.

Who are you, Aoife Hayward? Schuyler thought, dumbstruck.

The crack of Aoife's whip was deafening, but the mummy was quick. It dodged the strike and lunged at Aoife, knocking her off her feet. She landed on her back with a yelp. She was hurt, but she didn't give up. On shaking legs, she stood, despite the blood darkening her jeans, only to realize her whip was lying on the floor on the other side of the hall. Now empty-handed, she cringed in pain, but stared down the mummy with fire in her eyes.

Schuyler couldn't sit by any longer.

She vaulted over the mezzanine railing and landed on the floor between Aoife and the mummy.

So much for keeping a low profile.

Aoife stared at her with wide eyes. "Schuyler?"

There was no time to explain.

Schuyler's heart pounded as she stared at the place where the mummy's eyes should have been. It tilted its head curiously. The air smelled like burned paper. The mummies were susceptible to fire, that much was clear. But Schuyler had no weapon of her own, let alone one that could start a fire. She looked around desperately for something, anything, she could use.

"Schuyler! Get out of here!" cried Aoife. "That mummy has the power to turn you into one of them!"

Schuyler ignored her. She had to think quickly. The mummy sneered at her, and a normal person might have run. The creature seemed to be sizing her up, pleased at the fear that was visible on her face. But Schuyler wasn't going to leave Aoife here alone, especially not when she was hurt. She pointed to the whip and screamed at Aoife. "Go!"

Aoife didn't need to be told twice. She leaped for the whip and Schuyler rushed the mummy.

It lunged at her, its broken, clawlike nails snatching at her head, but Schuyler dodged every one of its attacks. It was doing exactly what she wanted it to do—go after her, not Aoife. Out of the corner of her eye, she saw Aoife take up the whip.

Schuyler lured the mummy out into the open and Aoife attacked. The whip cracked overhead, the air around Schuyler's head crackled with energy, but the mummy dodged at the last second. It landed on all fours and charged Aoife, bounding at full speed. Aoife snapped the whip again, but missed. The mummy was too quick— they needed to stop it.

Aoife tumbled out of the way of the charging monster. At that range, she couldn't use the whip. She needed space.

Schuyler had an idea, but in order to carry it out, she had to time her actions just right.

The mummy skidded on the marble floor, resetting itself for another charge. Its gaping mouth hung loose, its voice nothing but a rasp of dust and death. It charged Aoife again.

Now!

Schuyler smashed her fist through the glass of the display case with the shield in it, and museum alarms blared all around them, so loud they vibrated in her skull. The mummy didn't seem to realize what was happening until it was too late. It looked up and let out a shriek of surprise just as the security gate came crashing down on its body, smashing it to the floor. It struggled and writhed on the marble, trying to get free, reaching out to Aoife in a desperate attempt to seize her, gnashing its teeth and shrieking, but Aoife snapped her whip and it exploded into fire and then to dust. The battle was over.

Aoife and Schuyler caught their breath, panting heavily.

Schuyler's fist was covered in her blue blood. She'd cut it when she broke the glass of the display case. Her secret was out, but a lot of secrets had come to light now, hadn't they? She hissed in pain, tore off a part of her maxiskirt, and wrapped her hand tightly.

Aoife's whip transformed back into bandages, snaking into place on her wrists. She stared at Schuyler in amazement.

Aoife spoke first. "Who are you?" Then she gasped in pain and collapsed.

Schuyler caught her before she could hit the floor and held her close. The gash in her jeans was wet with blood.

"I'll be okay." Aoife squeezed her eyes closed, as if she were concentrating on the pain. Her skin was pale; she'd lost a lot of blood already. She squinted with one eye open. "Nice moves back there."

"I'm taking you to a hospital." The alarm was still wailing. The museum would be swarming with security in seconds; Schuyler needed to get them both out of here.

Aoife's eyes shot open. "No. No hospital."

Schuyler heard shouts approaching from down the hall. The guards were coming. "We're running out of time! I can't leave you here."

"I need to get to the Warehouse. There's a healer there."

"The Warehouse?" Schuyler repeated.

Aoife mustered up the strength to stand and picked up the

shield from the display case Schuyler had smashed. She brushed off the glass bits. "Thanks. Actually, this is what I came here for." She strapped the shield to her back.

Schuyler balked. "You're a thief?"

"Harsh. I mean, yeah, I disabled the security cameras and all, but does that really make me a—" She cut herself off. The rushing footsteps were close. They'd be caught any second.

Schuyler looked around for a way out. The absolute last thing she needed today was to be accused of stealing, let alone vandalizing a museum, and she wasn't done with Aoife just yet. There were too many questions that needed to be answered, and Aoife was in no condition to be on her own. Schuyler lifted her eyes to the skylight in the ceiling above them.

Aoife wavered on her feet and Schuyler steadied her with a hand on her shoulder. She had another idea. "I'll help you, just . . . trust me."

With an eyebrow raised in curiosity, Aoife didn't protest.

When the guards opened the security gates they found three piles of dust, a smashed display case with a missing artifact, and didn't notice when two shadows disappeared through the skylight window, vanishing into the night.

FIVE

SCHUYLER

"This is it?"

Schuyler had helped Aoife walk all the way from the American Museum of Natural History to the Warehouse, which was aptly named. It was a run-down four-story storage unit on the corner of Thirty-Sixth and Ninth that looked like it had seen better days. In fact, at the moment it looked abandoned.

In the wake of Aldrich Duncan's pandemic, a lot of buildings had been vacated and reclaimed by nature, including this one. Ivy grew out of one of the broken windows a few floors above and a nest of pigeons had made their home in the holes in the red-brick wall. A sign over the door read *Condemned*, but Aoife assured Schuyler this was the place.

"How about you start telling me what is going on here?" Schuyler was tired and wasn't in the mood for any more surprises.

"Come on, we can talk inside."

Schuyler couldn't begin to think why a healer would be in a dump like this. Images of backroom surgeons came to mind as she helped Aoife through the door and down a long, dark passageway.

She wasn't afraid, but she started to think maybe she should be. "Where are you taking me?"

"Technically you're the one taking me."

Schuyler huffed. Now wasn't the time for an argument about semantics. "What kind of healer is this anyway? Do you trust them?"

Sweat glistened on Aoife's upper lip. "If I can't trust Theo, I can't trust anyone."

She smelled so strongly of blood, Schuyler's head swam. Being close to her blood was overwhelming. Schuyler hadn't fed in a while, and she hated to admit how hungry she was. She'd left her water bottle of blood in her locker at school.

"How did you know that mummy could turn me?" Schuyler asked, trying to focus on asking questions instead of on the saliva gathering on her tongue.

"It's sort of my job to know. Almost there, I promise."

Schuyler wasn't sure how far she could trust Aoife, but she'd come too long a way to turn back now. The air felt close, and it tickled like sheer fabric on Schuyler's face, but a light at the end of the passage guided the girls forward.

Schuyler's jaw dropped when they emerged into a wide-open space stacked high with wooden crates and boxes. Sunlight beamed in from skylights above, signaling that they weren't in any time or place remotely close to Manhattan anymore. Only a minute ago it had been the middle of the night. It was like they'd stepped into a whole new world. Symbols and markings in hundreds of different languages, some of which Schuyler didn't recognize, were branded onto the sides of boxes, a chaotic collection of wooden towers.

"Where are we? It was nighttime . . ."

"It's night in New York, sure," Aoife said. "But we're not in New York, not really. We're on the cusp, between ley lines, a pocket of sorts. It's the best way I can explain it."

"Aoife!"

A boy their age with copper skin nearly dropped the cup of noodles he'd been blowing on when he saw them. He wore a galaxy-print T-shirt and a backward baseball cap over curly dark hair, and looked concerned as he rushed to Aoife's side.

Aoife removed herself from Schuyler's shoulders and smiled through the pain. "Theo! Just the guy I need to see."

"I knew you shouldn't have gone on that case alone," Theo said, shaking his head. He inspected Aoife's injuries with all the disapproval of a fussy parent. "I just knew it! Mummies are too dangerous. I should have been there with you. Who is this?" He looked at Schuyler with a furrow in his brow.

Aoife said tersely, "Heal now. Talk later."

"Please be careful, Theo. You're a butcher." Aoife was lying on her stomach on a wooden table, more suited for a carpenter's bench than an operating table, while Theo cut away her jeans with scissors.

"They're already covered in holes!"

"You sound like my aunt. Come on, these are my favorite jeans."

"Then I guess you shouldn't have worn them on a job."

They bickered like siblings, Schuyler noticed. Theo had a Southern drawl, so Schuyler guessed they weren't really related, but it took her off guard. She had expected the healer to be someone older—maybe someone who had a degree. He barely looked old enough to drive, let alone dispense medical advice.

Theo said to Aoife, "You don't have to do everything alone, you know."

"I wasn't alone. Schuyler was with me."

He glanced at Schuyler, who had a million questions burning on the tip of her tongue, but they got tangled up before she could ask them. Theo looked back at Aoife. "Does Jasper need to make her forget?"

To Schuyler, his words sounded like a threat and something inside her snapped. "I've had enough of my memories messed with; it's not happening again. What is this place? What is going on? Who are you?"

Theo didn't answer. Instead he clapped his hands together, rubbed them as if warming up, and then pressed his palms into Aoife's leg. When he did, a soft glow came and went and the pain across Aoife's face seemed to ease. When he pulled his hands away, her wounds had vanished.

Schuyler stood, amazed. He'd healed Aoife with a touch. "What is this . . . magic?"

"It's not magic. It's a gift," said Aoife.

"What's the difference?"

"You should know. Anyone who can go toe-to-toe with a mummy must have a patron. Who's yours?"

Schuyler squeezed her eyes shut. So many things were happening at once, she didn't know where to start. "My—my *patron*? What are you talking about?"

Aoife and Theo glanced at one another, eyebrows raised. Then Aoife sat up, swinging her legs over the edge of the table. "You're not a Paladin?" She unwrapped the bandages on her left arm and revealed a tattoo on her wrist. It depicted two circles, interconnected like an infinity symbol. Theo had the same design on both his wrists.

Schuyler had never seen the symbol before. "A Paladin? What? No. I'm not. I'm—" She caught herself, then took a step back. They weren't Lucifer's agents. They were something else entirely, and that scared her more. In this world or the memories of her last, she'd never encountered anyone like them. She thought she'd known how the rules of this world worked, but new factors were at play, and she wasn't sure what was going on.

"Are you injured?" Theo asked. "Hardly anyone walks out of a mummy fight unscathed."

Aoife said, "She cut her hand on some glass."

Quickly, Schuyler put her hand behind her back, squeezing her makeshift bandage so tight it hurt. The cuts in her palm were still bleeding. If Aoife or Theo saw her blue blood, they would know she wasn't like them.

"Let me take a look. It won't hurt, I swear." Theo had warm, dark eyes, and he smiled at her. Schuyler's heart raced. She wanted to run, but she didn't know where to go. She didn't pull away as Theo gently brought her hand toward him and peeled back her makeshift bandage. Schuyler held her breath, waiting for the inevitable.

Her blood, blue as sapphire, glistened in the light.

Theo gasped and stumbled back. "What—what are you?"

Aoife jumped down from the table and put a hand on Theo's chest. "Hold on."

"She's a monster!"

"If she were a monster, why would she save my life?"

Schuyler held up her hands. "I promise . . . I won't hurt you."

Theo stared at her with wide, frightened eyes, but Aoife looked more curious than scared. To Theo, she said, "Maybe our definition of *monster* needs an update. Help her, like she helped me. I'd be a mummy right now if it wasn't for her."

Theo looked at Aoife pleadingly, as if begging her to see reason. But the girl didn't back down. So, with a deep breath, he approached Schuyler again, watching her warily. He took her hand into his and furrowed his brow in concentration. Nothing happened.

"It's not working," he said. He tried again. Still, the cuts remained. "That's never happened before."

Schuyler took her hand back and curled it against her chest. "Maybe because I'm not entirely human."

"Who are you, then?" Aoife asked.

Who, not what. Schuyler felt that was a start. But it was still the dreaded question. Schuyler clamped her lips shut. She wasn't sure how much to say, but her secret was already halfway out. It was now or never. "I'm a vampire." Her breath hitched on the last word.

Silence. No one spoke, no one moved. Schuyler felt like crawling into a hole. Only a handful of people knew her secret, and now that secret club had expanded its numbers. Theo and Aoife glanced at each other, like they weren't quite sure what to make of her confession.

Schuyler lowered her hands. "Now," she said, her heart still hammering in her throat. "I've told you the truth about me. It's time you did the same. Who are you and what is a Paladin?"

"We're monster hunters," Aoife said.

Theo asked, "How do you know Aoife?"

Aoife answered for him, "She goes to school with me."

"What kind of bloodsucker goes to school?"

"I'm half-vampire," Schuyler said. "I'm not like the others. I . . . I don't hurt people."

"You don't work for Lucifer? The OG vamp?"

Aoife's question took Schuyler by surprise, like a sucker punch to the face. "No, of course not. H-how do you know about Lucifer?"

Aoife gestured to herself. "Monster hunter, remember?"

"I thought *you* were working for Lucifer," Schuyler said, pointing for emphasis.

"Me?" Aoife looked offended. "You think I'd work for the devil?"

"How else would you know Lucifer is a vampire?"

"It's our job, duh," Theo said. "Did you get hit in the head or something?"

Schuyler decided not to take this as a personal slight. Her head was pounding with all the questions she wanted to ask.

Aoife said, "I'm sorry. I've never met a vampire who didn't want to kill us before. We figured they all worked for Aldrich Duncan, Lucifer incarnate, but . . . This is a first."

"I'm only a half-blood. I tried to stop Lucifer once, but I'm the only vampire left who wants to kill him. Besides Jack and Max Force."

Whatever she said made both Aoife and Theo exchange another look.

"But you already knew that . . ." Schuyler said, figuring it out. "That's why you were asking about the twins at school."

"Are you ready to stop lying to me about not knowing them now?" Aoife asked, folding her arms over her chest.

Schuyler flushed. "I'm sorry. I thought I needed to protect them. Did you know they were vampires?"

"All vampires are on Lucifer's team, all except a few foretold. But if you're telling the truth, it changes everything. What do you know about the Force twins?"

Foretold? Schuyler had to answer one question at a time. Keeping the twins' secret was pointless now. "They're not simply absent, they're missing. Last I heard, Max was captured by a creature named Leviathan, Lucifer's brother. Jack went looking for Max and now they're both gone. I'm worried something terrible's happened."

Aoife clenched her jaw. "Okay," she said, nodding, thinking. "Okay. This still leaves us with one big question. Who are you if you're not working for Lucifer?"

"I'm the only one who can stop him."

Theo said, "Aoife, she's the . . ."

Aoife's eyes widened. She pointed at Schuyler. "You're the one from city hall. You're the girl who commanded the hellhounds."

Schuyler's heart leaped. Someone outside of her friend circle knew about the evil walking the streets of Manhattan. It was like a weight had been lifted from her shoulders. "How did you know that?"

"We have eyes everywhere. So it's true?"

"Yeah, that was me. I made Lucifer's day a lot worse."

"You did more than that, that's for sure," Theo said, grinning.

Aoife's jaw dropped as she was struck by a sudden thought. "Half-blood vampire. Oh," she said, then louder: *"Oh!"*

Schuyler started. "What?"

Aoife was too worked up to hear the question. "Theo, stay put.

Don't tell anyone about this, not until we know for sure. I'm taking Schuyler to her."

Schuyler asked, "To who?"

But Aoife was already rushing off into the depths of the Warehouse. "Follow me!"

Schuyler did as she was told. Aoife's pace was quick, and her eyes blazed with renewed energy. "I can't believe I didn't realize! It all makes sense now!"

"You're going to have to fill me in here, because I'm genuinely lost."

"There's someone you need to meet!"

SIX

SCHUYLER

*A*oife hurried deeper into the Warehouse. Her pace was quick, and Schuyler barely had time to take in her surroundings as they wove through the mazelike aisles of towering wooden boxes. It reminded her of the Repository, the library for all things related to vampires, but instead of books it was home to thousands of innocuous-looking objects being packed away into the wooden crates by kids who looked just like Aoife. They handled the objects with such care, Schuyler wondered if the items were dangerous or fragile or both.

As they moved on, Schuyler saw a lot more people around her age, some a bit younger and some a bit older, but all of them had the same marks on their wrists as Aoife and Theo. The group reminded Schuyler more of an after-school club than a warehouse full of mysterious objects. She thought she saw a huge claw-foot mirror standing in a cleared alcove that sparkled with light, and beyond that was an elephant statue with jewels for eyes standing halfway in a wooden crate, and another area had a mask of a human face in midscream locked away in an iron cage.

"Aoife, wait," Schuyler said, hustling to keep up.

"Walk and talk. How does a half-blood vampire like you exist?"

Once Schuyler got talking, she almost couldn't stop. She showed Aoife the dark blue veins stretching up her forearms, and explained that every Blue Blood had them, and that she was no different from the rest, despite being the first-ever *Dimidium Cognatus*, a new soul born into a vampire's eternal reincarnation cycle. She had no past lives, and she didn't count the memories she had of being another Schuyler in a different dimension of reality on a nearly identical Earth.

"Superimposition?" Aoife asked.

"Memories of another world. I know I killed Lucifer in a parallel universe, and I have to do it again."

"Wow. That's . . . a lot. So being a vampire . . . How'd that happen?"

"No idea. I just woke up like this one day. In my old world, my mother was a vampire and it passed down to me. I was half-vampire, half-mortal. Here, I'm not sure what exactly I am. My life isn't the same as it was. My parents are . . . achingly normal."

Aoife asked, "No one turned you?"

"It doesn't work like that. No one can turn into a vampire. We just are."

"It all makes sense. Lucifer is a fallen angel. Lucifer is the first vampire."

Schuyler nodded. "Exactly. How did you know Aldrich Duncan is a vampire anyway? He doesn't exactly go around proclaiming it."

"I read. I'm definitely adding this to the book." Schuyler remembered the book Aoife had been writing in. She wondered if she meant that one, but before she could ask, Aoife said, "You don't hurt people, though, right? You do drink blood, or is that an urban legend? Anti-vamp propaganda?"

"Drinking human blood is how I survive and heal. A friend brings me donated blood pouches. But I don't hurt anyone."

Dozens more people, mostly other kids in their teens, appeared, shouting information to one another, labeling crates, and nailing them closed. Schuyler had to dodge out of the way of a forklift that had come whizzing by carrying a stack of wooden pallets. Not everyone in the room was working, though. A small group of kids was playing a pickup game of basketball in a cleared alcove, all moving as fast as Aoife had in the museum. A couple more were flipping through tabloid magazines on lawn chairs in the kinds of outdoor furniture displays that reminded Schuyler of things she might see in a department store display, complete with Astroturf grass and a hammock. A small table was laid out with dozens of different kinds of metals and objects, a handful of kids doing what could easily have been mistaken for arts and crafts. They were chiseling symbols into brass knuckles, and knotting necklaces with silver beads, and assembling ammo kits full of salt, all while gossiping and laughing with one another.

"They're making relics," Aoife said, as if reading Schuyler's mind. "Objects with innate power, like protection from evil. Similar to a lucky charm. They come in handy a lot more than you might think."

"What is this place?" Schuyler asked.

"This is the Warehouse. It's where we store supernaturally significant artifacts recovered from all across the world and keep them out of the hands of those who intend to use them for evil. Some are cursed, others are possessed, some aren't of this world."

"What's to stop anyone from just walking in here and taking something?"

"We're very good at hiding," Aoife said with a wink. "The Warehouse exists in a little pocket of reality. Only people who know what they're looking for will find it. You were with me, so you could enter the fold. If you weren't, you'd just be spit out the entrance, right back where you started, even if you are a vampire. The place is pretty good at keeping out the bad guys. Come on, this way."

Aoife took a hard right. She was a lot more talkative now than she had been at school. It might have been relief at the realization that Schuyler wasn't planning on killing her, and the knowledge that Schuyler was relieved for the same reason.

"As for us"—Aoife gestured to the kids playing basketball—"we're called Paladins."

"Paladin, like a knight?"

"Exactly. All of us have been chosen to fight against creatures of darkness, marked with a blessing and granted the special powers of the Paladins who came before us. Some of us can heal, like Theo; some can create illusions or shapeshift; others can manipulate the mind to make people forget we exist. We've been around for generations."

"Like reincarnation?"

"No, not really. We don't have past lives. Our gifts are energy, and that energy never goes away. It just transfers to the next chosen mortal. When I die, it'll pass on to someone else."

Schuyler had often wondered what would happen to her when

she died. Blue Bloods were reincarnated after death. But since she wasn't a normal Blue Blood, and especially now that most of the Coven would want her dead forever, those rules might not apply to her. She'd always felt like an outsider because of it, on this world and the last.

"How does a Paladin get chosen?" she asked.

"The marks on our arms usually appear when we're teenagers, kind of like your veins. But anyone can become a Paladin. At some point, we showcase a trait the patron in Paradise values and they choose us. My patron is the Maid d'Orléans."

Schuyler knew that name from history class and her jaw dropped. "Joan of Arc? As in, *the* Joan of Arc? The famed lady knight who was burned at the stake for witchcraft?"

"Most powerful women in history are accused of witchcraft at one time or another," Aoife told her. "But yes. No one remembers that she fought an entire army of undead English soldiers after the king used necromancy against her."

The secrets of the world never stopped unfolding. Aoife was proving that the world was a lot bigger and scarier than Schuyler could ever have imagined. "How did you become a Paladin?" she asked.

"I had a run-in with a wraith haunting the woods where I lived in Wisconsin. There'd been rumors about a monster in the forest and I thought it was just a dumb ghost story and decided to take a shortcut anyway. I had no idea what I was up against. I thought I was going to die, but the Maid had other plans. I killed my first monster that day."

Schuyler was suitably impressed. "So she gave you her power?"

Aoife nodded. "Strength, speed, my Banner—my gifted weapon." She gestured to the bandages wrapped around her wrists. "A few days after I first got my powers, another Paladin found me and introduced me to all this. The rest is history. Over here." Aoife made another turn down another aisle lined with wooden crates.

"It's a pretty ingenious idea to keep your weapon on you at all times," Schuyler said. She wished she had that ability. Even Jack and Max could summon a weapon instantly, out of thin air. They both had magical swords that once belonged to the archangels Gabrielle and Michael, taken when they defeated them in battle. Schuyler wasn't so lucky. "I always have to fight monsters the old-fashioned way."

Aoife said, "If a monster made the stupid move to attack me, I'd be ready, but you've proven you can think on your feet, so any monster would be a fool to underestimate you."

Schuyler appreciated the compliment. "What kinds of things are we up against?"

Aoife smiled. "We?"

"I thought I was alone. It's nice to know that there's others out there who haven't given up."

Aoife seemed pleased with that. "Anything you might read about in a fairy tale or spooky ghost story, we track down and eliminate. Fae, poltergeists, sirens, you name it . . . we hunt anything that hurts or kills people. We had a few reports of people going missing at the museum. We traced it to a traveling mummy exhibit and it was pretty easy to figure out from there. Mummies are always trying to come back to life. Once they find a victim, they absorb the person's life force"—she snapped her fingers—"leaving behind dried husks, and new mummies."

"And the shield you stole?"

"Thanks for that, by the way. Two-for-one special. The shield had been sold to the museum—'donated,' as most folks incorrectly call it. You can't donate something that was stolen in the first place. I was there to get it back, and figured I'd kill some mummies while I was at it."

"How do you know all this?"

"Paladins keep meticulous records of every monster we've ever faced throughout history. I keep a book on me for reference. Learning about monsters is part of the job."

"I had no idea any of this was happening."

"That's sort of the point, isn't it? If everyone knew what we did, it wouldn't be a secret anymore."

"Have there always been monsters to fight?" Schuyler asked.

"That's the thing—not really. When I got my powers, there was apparently a huge surge of cases. There used to be a lot more in the first few centuries AD, but the activity dwindled over time to almost nothing. We don't know what happened or why, but the monsters we thought were extinct are coming back and hunting people again. It's like they've been . . . set free somehow. With the rise of darkness, Paladins were called back to Earth. At first, we only had to deal with a few monsters a year, but since Aldrich Duncan's rise to power, there's been a huge uptick in reports. More and more monsters are attacking people. There's a handful of us here in Manhattan dealing with all of it, even more across the world."

"And this whole time I thought you were an agent of Lucifer . . ." Schuyler said, mostly under her breath. "When I saw you, I felt that you were different."

Aoife's eyes brightened. "I know! Me too! I was about ready to exorcise you in the middle of class. I should be thanking you for what you did back there. Even if you were following me . . ."

Schuyler sighed. "I had to know what was going on. There are no vampires left who aren't trying to kill us. When you came into class, there was this energy about you. I always felt it when I faced monsters."

"I know. I felt the same way about you. That's why I was so standoffish. I thought you were a monster."

"You're not totally wrong," Schuyler said, with a smirk. "Halfsies."

The girls laughed. And for the first time in a long while, Schuyler felt like it was a real laugh. She'd been hiding every day, trying to put on a brave face for the world while the odds mounted against her, keeping her identity a secret from everyone she cared about to keep herself safe and her family from harm. Being able to laugh about it was freeing.

Aoife sighed, sounding relieved. "And here I thought I knew everything."

She led Schuyler even deeper into the Warehouse. Aoife wasn't messing around when she said that this place existed in a pocket of space. It felt like the building extended a lot farther than Schuyler initially realized.

They came upon a series of metal shipping containers converted into small apartments, similar to tiny fashionable homes Schuyler had seen in magazines and online. Aoife entered one that was painted a deep shade of green, the inside decorated like a thrift-store show-room. Most of the furniture was mismatched and frayed, and the covers faded on the stack of tabloid magazines on her messy bed. A row of random mugs on the kitchen shelf meant that she was a fan of tea, or coffee, or other hot drinks. The space looked cozy, the vis-ible equivalent of the smell of old books and their soft pages. The whole room was aglow with fairy lights and electric candles. In the very middle of the room was a kid's fort made of sheets and pillows, like Schuyler used to build when she was little. Aoife crawled inside the tent and Schuyler followed.

Inside, a pale-faced girl, probably no older than five, sat cross-legged on a stack of pillows, surrounded by a haze of lavender incense burning in a copper pot at her feet. She wore a plastic prin-cess crown atop her black hair, and she had a few Barbies strewn about the blanket in front of her. Her eyes were closed, her hands carefully folded in her lap, and Schuyler thought she was asleep.

Aoife gently put her hand on the little girl's shoulder, singing softly, "Meggie. Hey, Megan."

The girl's eyes slowly eased open. She looked dazed, as if she was still half-asleep. Schuyler would be sleepy too if she were sitting in a cloud of lavender incense in a warm, cozy tent made of pillows.

"Megan, this is Schuyler. Schuyler, meet Megan."

"Hey," Schuyler said softly, with a smile. Megan still looked tired, blinking. She rubbed her eyes hard and it seemed to wake her up a little more. Schuyler spotted the telltale ink on her wrists, marking her as another Paladin. Aoife had mentioned most Paladins were chosen when they were teenagers, but Megan was apparently an exception.

Aoife said, "Schuyler might be someone you want to read a little closer. I think she's the one."

Megan's sleepy eyes went wide. She reached out and grabbed Schuyler's hand, holding it tightly with tiny fingers. Schuyler didn't pull away, but she looked at Aoife, who explained, "Megan is our seer, with the grace of Morgana. She's got the gift of prophecy."

Megan held Schuyler's hand. She traced her fingers over the lines in her palm, closed her eyes, and took a deep breath. Her mouth went slack and she looked like she had fallen asleep again, but her grip on Schuyler's hand was like a vise. Anxiety swelled in Schuyler's gut.

"What's she doing?"

"Reading you. Past, present, and future."

Schuyler took a calming breath. Having her fortune told was scarier than she liked to admit. Knowing the future might be comforting to some, but to Schuyler it felt like more things beyond her control.

"She's so young," Schuyler whispered. "Where are her parents?"

The skin on Aoife's face pulled tight and she leaned in, keeping her voice low. "Wendigo attack. Her parents didn't make it. That was the day she became a Paladin. We're trying to find a new home for her, but it's been tough. . . ."

Schuyler swallowed thickly. To lose your parents so young . . . In her old world, she had a life much like Megan's. Her mortal father was dead and her mother was in a coma. Here, in this world, it was different, but her heart still ached for Megan.

Megan's lips moved silently, her eyes flicking around behind her lids. Disembodied voices surrounded them outside the tent, seeming to come from nowhere and everywhere at once. Schuyler's skin crawled.

Megan breathed deeply and sighed. "Schuyler Cervantes-Chase. You are multitudinous," the little girl said, dreamlike, as if someone were talking through her. "You're a daughter of two worlds, of many worlds. There's much you've done in this one and the last. You are a warrior, stronger than you know. But you've lost people close to you. I sense a name. Kingsley, he's—"

"Is he alive?" Schuyler interrupted hopefully.

"No, he's far from here. Beyond the veil. He's in the void of Purgatory."

Schuyler's heart went cold. "Do you see anyone else?" She hoped the child wouldn't mention Jack or Max. But if they were gone too . . . at least she would know.

"No," Megan said. "There's no one else. His spirit is alone."

Somehow, to Schuyler, that felt worse than Kingsley being in Purgatory. He was dead—alone in some void—and it was all her fault.

"I know who you are," Megan said. Schuyler noticed her eyes were a deep, dark purple. "You're the one we've been looking for."

SEVEN

JACK

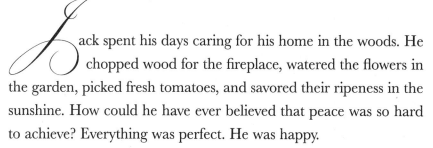

Jack spent his days caring for his home in the woods. He chopped wood for the fireplace, watered the flowers in the garden, picked fresh tomatoes, and savored their ripeness in the sunshine. How could he have ever believed that peace was so hard to achieve? Everything was perfect. He was happy.

Despite all that, a small voice in the back of his head tried to tell him that something was off, that something was missing from this life, but the thought always faded away before he could catch it. Nothing could be wrong here. It was impossible. But the voice of warning spoke more frequently as the days, weeks, and years passed, even though time felt like it was at a standstill. The weather never changed, the seasons never shifted, there was only the cottage in the woods by the sea . . . nothing more. Every day was the same, and it was as it should be. Nothing else mattered in this place. He could be free.

Jack raised the ax he was holding and brought it down with a heavy swing, chopping the wood into smaller logs to stoke the fire in the kitchen, when a voice carried through the trees, calling out to him. He stilled, listening.

Jack . . . Jack . . . Be careful.

He knew that voice, somehow, from somewhere, but he couldn't place it. It was like it came from beyond the woods. It was the same voice that he'd been hearing, a woman's voice, lyrical and soothing. It had a message for him, but it was too far away for him to discern what the message was.

He waited, listening as hard as he could, trying to focus on it, but the voice faded, blending into the rustle of the trees that were being nudged by the ocean breeze. Someday he'd visit that ocean. He couldn't remember ever having done so before, even after all this time . . .

He gathered up the pieces of wood for the fireplace and went inside.

There, he found Harmony in the kitchen, standing at the dining room table Jack had built for them, a mountain of flowers piled before her. She had picked them from the garden earlier that morning, humming softly as she worked. She smiled at him, her whole face brightening at his entrance. She dipped the petals into wax and pressed them flat, creating colorful and elaborate landscapes depicting their cottage, using the flowers as if they were paint, her art born from the paradise around them. Her favorite flower, the snowdrop, was nestled behind her ear, pinning her hair back from her lovely face. She looked more radiant by the day. As time passed, she remained as youthful and beautiful as ever. Jack couldn't remember how long it had been.

"What's wrong?" she asked suddenly, watching him as he moved to her side.

His gaze went out the window over the kitchen sink, peering through the trees as if he would see what it was that troubled him.

"I'm not sure I can explain," he said. "I feel like I'm supposed to be doing something, supposed to be looking for someone, but I can't remember who." He could have sworn he saw a woman standing in the woods, but she melted into the sunlight. A figment of his imagination.

Harmony touched his hand. "I know just what you need." She draped her arms over his shoulders and tilted her head up, looking at him with those lovely blue eyes, deepening, darkening, like a whirlpool in the middle of the ocean. She sang him a song as she traced her delicate fingers up and down the length of his neck, sending shivers down his spine that reached his toes. The air filled with a pink haze, and Jack's face relaxed. He sighed with relief. He couldn't remember what he'd been so worked up about. All his worries disappeared.

"Nothing's wrong," Harmony said.

"Nothing's wrong," he repeated.

"You're with me."

"I'm with you."

"Forever?"

"Forever."

Harmony smiled and leaned in. When Jack kissed her, nothing else mattered. She was his everything, his whole world, and nothing could tear them apart.

EIGHT

SCHUYLER

$\mathcal{M}$egan recited a prophecy for Schuyler:

"Child of blood and bless'd—
Upon the return of darkness,
the sons of the star light the way.
Blade of flame thy brand,
Go forth. Be not afraid.
With the right hand of the Fallen,
usher upon thy deed. . . ."

Even when she stopped speaking, the air in the tent felt heavy with the weight of her words.

Schuyler waited a beat. "Is that it? I feel like there should be more."

Megan looked tired and let go of Schuyler's hand. "That's all there is."

Schuyler had never been one for prophecies. They were often too vague about the truth, but there was one part of this one that stood out for her. *Child of blood and bless'd.* Aldrich Duncan used those exact words in the dream she'd had when her memories of the other world first manifested. In that same dream, she had a vision of Jack in his angelic form as Abbadon, the angel of destruction, standing in the middle of New York City as it burned around him. The dream had felt so real, but she thought it was just a nightmare. Could it really have been a warning of what was to come?

But no. Jack had come back to her side. When she had that dream, he'd still been under Lucifer's shadow. He had changed his own fate when he chose her. But this prophecy still predicted that Lucifer's return would bring about darkness. That alone made Schuyler's stomach churn.

"All this time I thought it meant a Paladin, someone like . . . well, different," Aoife said. "Don't you see, Schuyler? You're of two worlds, of blood and of the blessed angels, half-blood vampire."

"How do we know for sure it's about me?"

Megan explained, though she looked like she would have preferred to take a nap. Her eyes were half-closed. "This prophecy has been passed down through the ages, from my forebears, carried through time to reach us now." She sounded so much older than she looked. Schuyler couldn't help but wonder if something really was speaking through her. "I read it in your palm. You are the one."

Schuyler felt it was no use arguing with an all-seeing psychic. She thought about the other lines of the prophecy. "So . . . the sons of the star. It's the Force twins. Aldrich adopted them, Aldrich is the star Lucifer."

Aoife nodded. "Exactly. That's why I was looking for them. If

Megan is right, which she always is, the Force twins will help us in some way."

"Jack would, but Max . . . I have no idea where he is, or if he's even alive. Max used to be fully committed to Lucifer's cause."

"What are they exactly? What makes them so special?"

"Jack is the reincarnation of the angel of destruction, Abbadon. His twin brother, Max, is the angel of death, Azrael. Some of the oldest and most powerful beings in the universe. Aldrich Duncan planned on using them to kick-start the end of the world, but that was before . . . It seems like whatever he's planning now, he's shifted his focus. What do you know about the surge in monster attacks, Megan?"

Megan fiddled with one of her Barbies' hair, winding it between her fingers. "I think Lucifer is trying to open all worlds into one. Like dumping all kinds of toys into a toy box."

"Except his toys are evil," Aoife added.

"How do you know this?" Schuyler asked Megan.

"I've seen it. In my dreams. Falling stars of fire. Mirrors in the sky. Creatures of the night. Then nothing at all."

Schuyler was well acquainted with dreams that felt all too real to simply be dreams. She didn't consider herself clairvoyant, but could her dreams really be more than dreams?

Megan curled up in Aoife's lap, nestled there like a cat, and dozed off. Aoife patted her head gently, with all the affection of a big sister.

Aoife explained, "Lucifer is trying to break the multiverse. He's opening the passages to other worlds, letting monsters through from other realities, releasing chaos on Earth. That's why the Paladins have been so busy lately. We think he's only able to do it a little at a time, though. Megan has seen visions of it happening, and it's happening more frequently."

"He would need a lot of power to combine worlds." Schuyler remembered when she'd first woken up in this world during the height of a swirling purple storm. She'd had a dream in which her other self reassured her that everything was okay. Her mother, Gabrielle, the archangel, had used her power to smash realities together so Schuyler in this world could defeat Lucifer again. The only other beings who came even close to Gabrielle's kind of power were . . . "He needs Azrael and Abbadon to fully break reality again. Death and destruction, doing what they do best."

Aoife's face went grim. "And you're sure Max and Jack aren't helping Lucifer?"

"They're the sons of the fallen, like the prophecy said, right? They can't be helping him. If they were, we would know it. But with Gabrielle and Michael gone in this reality, they'd be the next-best thing, and Lucifer would be looking for Jack and Max. He needs their power."

"To bring more monsters to earth."

"The monsters are just a side effect. Lucifer is all about the big picture. Monsters are too small. We can fight monsters, and he knows that. Maybe he doesn't have the amount of power he needs yet, or he's missing something he doesn't realize he's lost. All these monsters are squeezing through the cracks in reality, worlds colliding, but only for fractions of a second. He needs more power to make the changes permanent. Before he died, Kingsley told me that if Lucifer lived in any world, no universe was safe."

Schuyler's thoughts raced so quickly, she felt like she was going to explode. Maybe after the battle at city hall, Lucifer had realized she wasn't entirely of this world. When he'd looked at her that night, it felt like he was looking into her soul. Maybe he'd figured out what Gabrielle had done.

Schuyler stood up. She didn't feel like she could sit still anymore. "The ultimate way to destroy the world is to destroy all of them. The Apocalypse."

Those two words sent a shiver down Schuyler's spine. She had hoped it would never come to this. And yet, at the same time, she'd always expected it. "If we don't stop him once and for all, he's going to keep trying. He'll keep releasing more monsters into this world, and more people will die, people like Megan's parents. If he really plans on bringing about the Apocalypse, it's up to us to stop him."

"Then we need the Force boys."

"I have no idea where to start looking, though. Jack and Max risked everything to turn against Duncan. It's killing me not to know what happened."

"You said Max was captured when Kingsley died. But so far, nothing has changed. Maybe Lucifer needs both of them for it to work. If Jack is still out there, there's time."

It was a solid theory, but it didn't make Schuyler feel any better. Her stomach churned with worry. "But where could he have gone?"

Aoife looked Schuyler dead in the eye. "Don't worry. We'll find him."

This time it was Schuyler who picked up on the plural pronoun. "We?"

The corner of Aoife's mouth lifted, her eyes bright behind her glasses. "Yeah. We."

Schuyler looked at the little girl asleep in Aoife's lap and sadness struck her heart. She felt like she had failed somehow. She was supposed to be a prophesied chosen one and she had already let people die without knowing it. She had lost the game without even realizing that it had started.

"We need a plan," Schuyler said. "We can't waste any more time on hypotheticals. We need to know exactly what Duncan's doing. Now."

Aoife's smile spread. "Funny you say that. I've already got someone on the inside."

"A spy?"

She nodded. "We don't just rely on Megan's visions for the truth. We have Paladins hiding in plain sight. Now that you're able to fill in some of the blind spots, we can get a better picture."

Schuyler still felt like that wasn't enough. She couldn't sit by and wait. She took a deep breath and stood taller. "I'd like to help the Paladins any way I can," she said. "I'm not as powerful as Max or Jack, but I can hold my own. I can fight."

"Clearly. Based on what I saw at the museum today, you'll fit in nicely around here." Aoife gently laid Megan down on her tower of pillows and stood up to meet Schuyler's gaze. She held out her hand, and Schuyler shook it. "Welcome to the team."

NINE

JACK

*J*ack had no reason to want to leave this place. Everything had been designed to satisfy his heart's desire—every tree, every animal, down to every blade of grass. This was his home, and he would die here.

He would give anything to stay. He'd convinced himself of that, shutting out the little voice in his mind that gave way to doubt. He could spend eternity here with no regrets. Wasn't that what he always wanted, what he'd longed for deep in his soul? What more could he ask for?

Jack spent his days with Harmony and her songs, and her voice was intoxicating. Like this place, she was perfect.

He wanted for nothing. Once he thought fondly about having a dog for a companion, and one appeared. Of course, his dog—a black Lab named Buddy—had always been there! And he had a library that never seemed to run out of books, new ones manifesting on the shelf every time he looked. And Harmony cooked his favorite meals every day, as if reading his mind and learning what he craved. He sketched the wildlife he encountered from his front porch, drawing in his notebooks the various deer, and rabbits, and sparrows that came to say hello every day.

But then something changed. A hawk was circling overhead, high above the treetops. He heard its shriek before he saw it and moved out quickly from the porch's overhang to get a better look. He'd never seen a hawk here before and it sent a thrill down his spine. Nothing ever changed in this place. Could this be something new?

He lost sight of it once, but then it appeared from behind some branches and shot straight across the sky into the bright sunlight.

Jack shielded his eyes against the sun. It was so bright, brighter than it should be. Black spots appeared across his vision, but then faded as the hawk's shriek diminished as it flew farther away and disappeared into the forest. But the trees had grown thick, clouding most of the blue sky. The mossy path Jack was on darkened, cast in shadow by branches too thick to see through. No way could he follow the hawk to see where it landed; he'd surely get lost. The sound of the hawk resonated in his mind, though. It was like a tap on the shoulder from a ghost.

He shouldn't recognize that call. That Light had been put out. Or at least he thought it had.

For some reason, he felt as if he were a shipwrecked sailor, floating out to sea on a piece of driftwood, watching helplessly as the sails of a rescue ship disappeared over the horizon. Fear gripped his insides like a cold claw.

"Jack." Harmony stood behind him with her arms folded across her chest. Her lovely face had lost some of its luster as disappointment hardened her eyes. Jack immediately felt the need to apologize for his state of distraction, to make her happy, but he couldn't. Dread seeped into his bones, screaming for him to run, but Harmony reached out a hand and calmed his mind with a song as she stroked his cheek. "What are you doing?"

Waves of purple smoke enveloped him, dancing with the sound of her voice. "I thought I saw something from my past," he said dreamily. There were no secrets he could keep from her. He swayed on unsteady feet, drunk on the sound of her voice.

"Your past doesn't matter here. Not anymore. Why would you want to leave this place? Leave me?"

The haze swirled around Jack's head and he sighed as he drank her in. She was right. Of course she was right. She loved him, she could never lie to him. But his eyes drifted to the place where the hawk had disappeared. The call was farther away, and it seemed to say: *Jack* . . .

He snapped his head to the side, listening. "Did you hear that?"

Harmony grasped his chin and made him look at her. "My love. You're imagining things. Relax. You're just tired," she whispered. Despite her words, the lavender haze grew stronger. "You should rest your eyes. You work too hard."

Jack's eyelids drifted closed, like weights were pulling them down. "Yes, I'm going to rest my eyes."

Harmony took him by the hand and brought him into the cottage, to their bed. Jack fell onto the mattress, floating on bliss and drowning in Harmony's voice as she sang.

He wanted to believe her. He wanted to ignore the call of the hawk. It urged him to return, to go back, but to where?

Home. Something in his stomach shifted, a deep unease that made the saliva in his mouth taste bitter. Something was terribly wrong. He shouldn't be here.

Schuyler.

Max.

What was he doing? He shook his head and sat up. The sunlight in the cottage dimmed, like a storm was coming.

A woman stood outside the window, looking down at him through the glass. Her aura was blinding, shimmering like the northern lights. He couldn't mistake it anymore. The hawk had been Gabrielle— Gabrielle the messenger. The archangel . . . uncorrupted . . . alive.

"Jack . . ." Gabrielle's voice drifted toward him. "Come back! Wake up! Your family needs you. Your real family."

Harmony threw out her hand and the woman vanished in a cloud of purple smoke. Harmony smiled, though her blue eyes remained as cold as the bottom of the ocean. "Don't listen to her, Jack. Stay here. You're safe and happy here. You can't leave. You can't leave me."

When she touched him, her hands were cold, and clammy, and scaled, like the body of a dead fish.

Jack lurched back in fear, scrambling to get away, but Harmony put her hands on his chest with unnatural strength, pinning him down. He was too weak to move. He blinked, and for a moment he saw that he wasn't in a cottage anymore, that he wasn't lying on a quilted bed, that he wasn't in Paradise. He was lying in a dark, damp room on a hard wooden table stained with blood. A monstrous shape crouched over him, licking its lips clean of blue blood it had just drunk, his blood. The monster's hideously disfigured, humanlike features caught the light, a far cry from the beautiful face of Harmony. The smell of briny water and rotting fish and death made him gag. She sang again, the purple smoke choking him. He tried to fight, but the song was too powerful.

She smiled down on him, her teeth sharpening. "Don't fight it, my love. We are together now. You were looking for 'Max, Max, Max' and you found me. Just like all the rest. I'll make you forget. I'll make you mine."

Jack struggled to stay awake, thrashing, but her spell was strong. He blinked again and he was back in the cottage, drifting to sleep on the melody of Harmony's song, his fear melting away like candle wax.

"Your blood is unlike anything I've tasted in my whole existence," Harmony said, inches from his neck, her eyes hungry with want. "When I crossed the boundary into this world, I had no idea something as magnificent as you existed. I can't let you go. I'll keep you happy forever and ever. You're mine now."

"Yes, I'm—" Jack's eyes rolled up into the back of his head. "Yours."

Even the great Jack Force was no match for a siren's song.

TEN

SCHUYLER

chuyler wished she could stay with Aoife longer, learn more about the Paladins and the prophecy, but as was the case with most half-vampire monster hunters, she had school the next day. Just because she had another world to save didn't mean she could abandon her normal life. College had always been important to her parents, both of them encouraging her to go— unfortunately, dropping out of school to fight demons was not a viable career option. She and Oliver were already planning which universities they wanted to go to, intending to apply to the same ones. He'd major in business and she'd major in performance art. Even though they were two vastly different fields, a lot of Ivy League schools offered prestigious programs in both. She couldn't bear the thought of being separated from him anyway. Graduation was still years away, but she imagined meeting him for coffee at a small café before a lecture, staying up late in their dorms to cram for midterms, going to parties and charitable events. She could picture her future so clearly, and she wanted to hold on to it. If Lucifer won the upcoming battle, neither Schuyler nor anyone else would have a future at all.

Even though she had memories of a different world, she felt like this one was hers. And this one still had Jack in it, even if he was missing. To have Jack at her side at school too would be better than anything she could imagine. The life they'd had together in the other world could still be duplicated in this one, and she wanted that so badly, she ached. Any future with Jack in this world was a future worth fighting for.

She was walking home alone with renewed energy and checked her phone. It was almost midnight and there were three texts from Oliver. One was a waving-hand emoji, another was a GIF of a person falling asleep at their desk—he must have been bored doing homework—and the last was a message: *Why does math hate me?*

She felt bad about lying to Oliver earlier so she could follow Aoife alone, but at least tomorrow she'd be able to explain everything. He'd want to be kept in the loop, especially as her Conduit. Seeing his messages put a smile on her face. Even though it was late, she started to type a response, knowing he'd still be up, but she almost leaped out of her skin when a trash can nearby tipped over with an echoing clang. The culprit, an alley cat, glared at her, its eyes flashing silver in the streetlights, before it darted away.

It took a moment for her heart to stop jackhammering in her chest. The cat's eyes reminded her of the way Kingsley looked whenever his Silver Blood power manifested. Even something as mundane as seeing a cat's eyes made her miss him so much, and it hurt. What would Kingsley have thought about the Paladins? Schuyler hoped he would think she was doing the right thing in teaming up with them, but . . . he was in Purgatory. And it was all her fault. She took a steadying breath and kept walking.

It wasn't just the cat that had made her jumpy. Knowing that there were monsters in the world again made her slightly more paranoid than she would normally have been as she continued her way down the street, keeping an eye out for trouble. What kinds of creatures had come through to this world from other dimensions? Aoife made it sound like they were creatures who'd been long extinct in this world. What terrors would seek revenge for their annihilation?

Since the pandemic ended, people had returned to the city, so there were many more walkers out late that night. The streets had come back to life, but Schuyler couldn't help but wonder how many monsters lurked in the shadows. Silver Bloods and hellhounds she could handle, she'd faced them before, but she'd never faced a poltergeist or a fae or any of the creatures of lore Aoife had mentioned. How would she know what to do, how to fight them? She was glad that people like Aoife were out there, protecting the city. It made Schuyler feel like she wasn't entirely alone in her duty anymore. The hope that Aoife engendered in her was one of the things that could keep her going.

Schuyler walked all the way from Hell's Kitchen to her family's loft in SoHo. The lights were off, as they should be, her parents asleep and blissfully unaware of their daughter's nocturnal life fighting evil. Keeping her movements quiet, she entered the alley behind her building and scaled the fire escape then crawled into her bedroom window. She'd done it so many times now, she was becoming an expert.

Her body ached with fatigue, and she would have undressed and thrown herself into bed if not for the prickling sensation crawling across her skin that something was wrong.

The room felt . . . off. Much the way she might feel if she sensed eyes upon her from across a subway platform. It unnerved her.

Something was here.

The hairs on her arms stood on end as the smell hit her nose. It reeked, like the river after a storm. A shadow moved across the floor and Schuyler took a step back, fists raised. A hand lashed out and icy-cold fingers wrapped around her wrist in desperation. It took everything not to scream. A face caught the light from the window.

Schuyler gasped. She couldn't believe it.

"Max!"

There was no mistake. Max Force, found at last, barely alive and sopping wet, stinking like the Hudson. His grip was weak and his face strained with pain. "Help me . . ."

He collapsed into a heap on her floor, hurt and covered in his own blood.

His bright red blood.

PART TWO
TWIN MOTIVATIONS

ELEVEN

MAX

One minute Max was on the floor of Schuyler's bedroom. The next minute, the sidewalk was scrolling by, his arm swinging limply above his head; he had a vague understanding that he was being carried upside down. The minute after that, he was in a long, dark hallway. He fought to keep conscious, but he was losing. He thought, stupidly, that he'd sprung a leak. Wet. Pain. More wet, sticky. Red. So much red.

Schuyler's voice was high-pitched and panic-stricken. "Aoife? Aoife! Theo!" The names echoed in his head.

The world tipped and darkness took him again.

Squares of light. A ceiling. Lamps. Max was on his back. His eyelids were so heavy, he could barely keep them open, but he needed to see. An unfamiliar face appeared above him. Purple hair. Glasses. Breathless. "Is this him?"

"His brother, Max."

"But you said he was—"

"I know!"

"Okay. Hang on, Max. You'll be okay. Theo, get over here now!"

More light. Different light. Glowing. Warm hands on his chest.

A male voice telling him he was going to sleep. Max's eyes rolled into the back of his head. A deeper, darker blackness swallowed him.

Max was alone.

When he sat up and looked around, he was surrounded by towers of wooden boxes that looked like they were about to teeter over and crash to the floor. Sunlight streamed in from skylights above, and the space was accented with random assortments of house lamps, Christmas lights, and even the kind of tungsten lamps one might see on a movie set. The air smelled like iron and sawdust, and he shivered in the cold. He realized he was wearing an oversize T-shirt that read *Grandma-tittude. Mess with my grandkids and learn the definition!* in a truly horrendous font. He didn't know who'd given it to him. Max might have been mortified if he'd been in any other situation, but there were bigger things to worry about than his fashion sense.

For a gut-wrenching second, he thought he might be dreaming, still strapped to the table, Aldrich's prisoner, tortured. But no dream could feel that real, could hurt that much. He remembered the reality of it, bits and pieces, and it washed over him in waves until he was drowning in the memory.

He didn't know how he'd survived. One minute he'd been in agony, his blood draining out of him; the next he was floating in the Hudson, choking on rancid city water. They'd dumped his barely conscious body in the river, like garbage—less than garbage. They probably thought he was dead. He *should* be dead.

His mouth still tasted like the river, like a rotten fish smeared on the bottom of an old shoe dipped in gasoline, and he leaned over and puked his guts out in a nearby trash can. The river water was worse as it came back up. Tears burned his eyes as he heaved and gagged until his stomach twisted like a still-wet, wrung-out towel. Once he was done, he moved to hold his head in his hands, but he realized his right arm was tied to the table by a a rope. He pulled at the knot, but it wouldn't budge. Some kind of magic was at play. He tried biting at the knot and pulling with all his strength, but he realized something was off. He attempted to summon his strength, his speed, but try as he might, he couldn't even extend his fangs.

Max looked at his hands. They were covered in rusty, dried blood. His blood. His stomach swooped up like he was going to puke again, but he didn't. It almost didn't feel real.

Max thought he would see something different in the lines of his hand as he flexed his fingers, testing their movement, but he couldn't. They were the same as they'd always been, only now red blood flowed beneath his pale skin. The only real sign that anything had changed was that the blue veins on his forearms had vanished. He had gotten so used to them, their absence made him freeze. They had been a symbol of his destiny, his potential, a visual cue that he was special. Now that they weren't there, it was a symbol of what he'd lost. Of what had been taken from him.

Lucifer had stolen his power.

He was mortal.

"Max."

With a start, he looked up to see that Schuyler had appeared from behind one of the towers of boxes. She held herself close, watching him carefully. Her hands were stained with his red blood. The expression on her face was a mixture of confusion, fear, worry, and shock. "Are you okay?"

The last time Max had seen her was in the basement of city hall. They'd run into each other, crossing paths on two simultaneous attempts to break Kingsley out of his cell, only Max had gotten to him first. And it had gotten Kingsley killed.

"No, I'm not okay," Max said. "But let me go right now and I'll think about not killing you."

Schuyler sighed. "Aoife, he's awake."

Max tried chewing at the rope again, but the girl with purple hair appeared next to Schuyler. "My Banner won't release unless I tell it to," she said. "You're not undoing that knot anytime soon. Not until you answer some questions."

He snapped, "Let me go! Now!"

Schuyler and Aoife glanced at each other. Schuyler turned back to Max and said, "As a sign of good faith." Then she nodded at Aoife.

When Aoife said, *"Renodo,"* the rope around Max's wrist unwound and turned into bandages that snaked up Aoife's wrist.

As soon as he could, Max leaped down from the table, ready to run, fight, do something, but his head felt light and he wavered. Nausea swept over him.

"Whoa, slow down," a boy with a galaxy-print T-shirt said, coming over and putting a hand on Max's chest and another on his shoulder, steadying him. Max remembered the glow of his touch, and that his name was Theo. "You lost a lot of blood. You still need some time to fully heal."

The world stopped spinning long enough for Max to shrug him

off. How dare a mortal think he could touch him? Then he realized the irony of that thought, and seethed.

A cluster of kids his age peered at him from around one of the crate towers, whispering behind their hands to one another. Aoife shooed them away. "Paladins, leave him alone." They vanished around the corner, still whispering.

"You need something to eat," Theo said. His brown eyes were kind. "Sit. Do you like noodles?"

Max didn't reply, but Theo disappeared somewhere within the maze of crates, presumably to get some food. Max sat back on the table. "What is this place? Who are these people?"

Schuyler said, "They're Paladins. Mortals. They healed you."

Max glanced at Aoife, looking her over, seemingly unimpressed by what he saw. "Why did you tie me up?"

Schuyler answered for her. "I told her to. We didn't know what to expect. Besides, last time I checked, you were still working for Lucifer."

"Funny how things change," Max said. He dragged his fingers through his hair. It was greasy and damp, the worst combination. All he wanted was to take a shower and have a good, long sleep.

"What happened to you?" Schuyler asked. He hated that he saw pity in her eyes.

He took a moment to find the words. His throat felt tight. "After we met that night at city hall, I got Kingsley streetside, but we were ambushed by Leviathan. He killed Kingsley and they took me captive. I was being held by the Coven somewhere, experimented on, hooked up to this machine . . . I can't really remember much before that. My brain feels like it just went through a meat grinder."

He put his hand to his head again. He felt like he was forgetting something, but every time he tried to remember what it was, it slipped away like fog. Whatever they'd done to him, it had messed with his head too.

"And they just let you go?" Aoife asked, eyes narrowed.

"They didn't let me go. They dumped a body. They didn't need me anymore."

Schuyler's eyes went wide. "They took your power," she said. "They took the power of Azrael."

Max's eyes blazed. "How do you know that name?"

Schuyler stared him down defiantly. "There's a lot you don't know about me."

Max raised an interested eyebrow. The last time they'd seen each other, she'd been with Jack. His brother had come to help rescue Kingsley too. Never would Max have thought he himself would betray Aldrich, but Jack . . . ? Aldrich's best? Jack was full of surprises. Though so too was this girl, this nobody, and yet Max had known he could trust her. He'd crawled out of hell to get to her because they had Kingsley in common.

He should have known something was special about her when he saw her in the Repository that first time, when he went to fight Kingsley. No normal, overprivileged Duchesne girl would be swept up in all this. It killed him not knowing the full story.

"You can't use your powers at all?" Schuyler asked.

"I have my memories of being Azrael, thousands of years of lives in my head, but no. I'm . . ." He couldn't finish the thought.

"Where were they keeping you? What were they doing to you?" Schuyler asked.

His temples throbbed, but he struggled to remember. "Aldrich mentioned something about Montauk. That's all I know. But Aldrich was talking about how he needed my power to shatter worlds. I told him I wasn't going to help him and so he . . . took it. He took my blood. Stole it. I don't know what he'll do with it now."

"What do you mean he took your blood?"

"They drained me and stored the blood in a crystal. But I don't know more than that."

"What about Michael's sword? Where is it?"

Max decided he wasn't going to ask how she knew about that either. All these questions were becoming tiresome. His head pounded and his stomach was threatening to revolt again. He reached out with his thoughts, trying to summon the celestial blade to his hand, but it wouldn't come. "It's stuck in the ether. I don't have my power, so I can't get it. They took my claim to the sword."

"How do we get it now?" Aoife asked.

"Why do you need it?"

Schuyler said, "A prophecy. I need a blade of flame."

"What prophecy?"

Schuyler recited the prophecy, then repeated one line. "'Blade of flame thy brand.' If I'm destined to stop Lucifer, I need Michael's sword. It's the only angelic sword that's made of fire."

"Well, good luck with that. I have no idea how to get it back." He was more surprised that the prophecy had mentioned him and Jack, the sons of the star. Had he always been destined to be this much of a screw-up? Did he have a choice in anything at all? Plus, why would a nobody like Schuyler be at the center of a prophecy? All these questions were bringing on a migraine.

Aoife asked, "How did you get Michael's sword in the first place?"

Max heaved a sigh and massaged the bridge of his nose with his thumb and index finger while he gathered his thoughts. "When we first fell from Paradise, my brother Abbadon and I battled Michael and Gabrielle. I killed Michael and laid claim to his celestial weapon, same as Abbadon did with Gabrielle's. If someone were to kill me, they'd have rightful claim on the sword next. But since my power is gone, it's in limbo."

"So you're saying so long as you don't have your power, you can't summon the sword out of thin air?" Schuyler asked.

Max rolled his eyes, feeling the migraine intensifying "You don't have to rub it in. I get it. Thanks for the reminder."

Aoife huffed. "So it's lost. Great!" Her sarcasm was not helping.

Schuyler asked, "How will Lucifer use Azrael's power next?"

Max was stumped. He let out a breath and shook his head. "I have no idea. All I know is, I have to get it back."

Schuyler looked like the weight of the world was on her shoulders.

Max stared at her. He didn't know what was so special about her. Jack had betrayed Aldrich when he stole Max's hellhound whistle to help her. Why would Jack do such a thing? And why would she know about a place like the Repository of History? Without his power, he wasn't able to sense anything about her at all. This whole human thing was getting really annoying.

"My turn to ask a question," Max said. "How do you know Kingsley?"

Schuyler took a moment to find the right words. "We're old friends. *Were* old friends."

Past tense. Right. Kingsley was dead. A lump formed in Max's throat. He wasn't sure he'd ever get used to talking about Kingsley in the past tense. Even though their bond was new to him, it was intense and real, and Max had betrayed Duncan in order to create it. Now Max didn't have a future with Kingsley that would let him know what they might have had, could have had, should have had. Leviathan had not only taken Kingsley's life, but he'd also taken Max and Kingsley's potential together. Righteous anger heated Max's face. First Kingsley, now his power—he was not used to losing things. "How long have I been gone?"

"Two months," Schuyler said. "I thought you were dead."

Max sat with the fact that he'd lost two months of his life. He only wanted to see one person next. "Where's Jack?"

The color drained from Schuyler's face. "He wasn't with you?"

"I thought he'd be with you."

Schuyler shifted her weight from one foot to the other. "He went looking for you right after we escaped. I haven't seen him or heard from him since you got captured."

Max swallowed thickly. "He went looking for me?" He didn't want to think the worst, but his day was already bad enough, so what was one more devastation? "They tortured me to find out where he was, but I didn't know. He shut himself off from the glom and now I . . . I don't have a connection with him anymore. We're not connected because I'm . . ." He couldn't bring himself to say it out loud. *Mortal.* "I can't."

"We'll find him," Aoife said.

But Max jumped to his feet again and said, "I have to find him, I need to . . ." His vision tunneled. He should have listened to Theo. The world slipped sideways and he passed out in a crumpled heap.

The last thought he had before darkness consumed him was that he hated being human.

TWELVE

SCHUYLER

"Now what?" Aoife asked.

She and Schuyler had stepped away while Theo tended to Max, putting a glowing hand to Max's head. The former Blue Blood had pushed himself too far, and Schuyler felt like she was partially responsible. She'd asked him too many questions at once. She had allowed her overeagerness to get her hands on the sword to overwhelm his need to rest. Now Max was waking up slowly, and Theo handed him a steaming cup of noodles.

"Without the sword, we're treading water," Schuyler said, watching him. Max scrunched his nose at the noodles, and she got the distinct impression that someone like him wouldn't go near microwaved food even if he was starving on a desert island. Everything had been taken from him—his family, his fortune, and now his power. It might have been easy to hate Max for everything he'd done before he stood up to Aldrich at the battle of city hall. It was his fault that Kingsley was captured in the first place, but it was Max's bravery that got him out. That had to count for something. He had a lot more work to do to win Schuyler's favor, but it was a start.

They had to find a way to get the sword back.

What would Kingsley do? Schuyler asked as she held herself closely, her fingers still sticky with Max's blood. So much had changed. She knew Kingsley would have had a plan. He always had a plan. But now she felt like she had more questions than she had answers. How could Lucifer have possibly stolen Azrael's power from a human host?

"Can you clue me in on the whole vampire thing?" Aoife asked. "How can a vampire's power be taken from them? You'd said you're born this way."

"Vampires have a literal bloodline, tracing back through time. Power in our blue blood. It's what gives us our memories, our abilities, and is used again and again to reincarnate the eternal soul. I've never heard of it being . . . *extracted* before."

With Aoife close behind, Schuyler marched over to Max, who was force-feeding himself ramen while Theo looked on. She asked, "Where would Lucifer be keeping your power?"

"I have no idea." Max clenched his fists. "But I have to get it back."

"Is that even possible?" Aoife asked.

"It has to be." He made it sound like a promise.

"Just how powerful is the blood of Azrael, this angel of death?"

"Like the power of a million nuclear bombs. Pure energy. In the wrong hands, it's absolute annihilation."

Schuyler's stomach twisted. "So, if they capture Jack, they'll try to do the same thing with Abbadon. They'll take his power, and his celestial sword—"

Aoife finished for her: "Then we'll be royally screwed."

"You put it nicer than I would have," Max said.

In that moment Schuyler's desperation to find Jack grew tenfold. Life was starting to feel like a race now. But the sooner she got her hands on Michael's sword, the sooner she could end this problem once and for all. They had to get it before Lucifer did. "We can't let him use Azrael's power. We need it. It's the only way we can get the sword."

"You mentioned Montauk," Aoife said to Max. Schuyler could see her mind working behind her eyes.

"Yeah, so what?"

Aoife blushed. "Don't judge me, okay, but I'm really into conspiracy theories. Most of the time it's fun nonsense, but sometimes there's real supernatural things happening beneath the surface of ordinary life. You've just got to be on the lookout for the right stuff. I've read about the Montauk Project on the dark web. It's this secret government operation most people suspected involved an effort to discover time travel and dimension hopping."

"What do you know about the multiverse?" Schuyler asked Max.

"That it's something Lucifer is interested in," Max said. "That's about it. Why?"

Schuyler let out a shaky breath. There was a lot Max needed catching up on, but where to start? "I think Lucifer is planning to use the power of Azrael somehow as a vector to merge the parallel universes, colliding dimensions together," she said. "He needs to use the power to bust through. It's the ultimate scorched-earth tactic, isn't it? All Earths, all of creation in every conceivable reality, destroyed at once."

"The end times. The Apocalypse," Theo whispered.

A grim realization settled on the room, and it felt like the air temperature had dropped several degrees.

Aoife asked, "But how would he use it? Azrael's power? If it's stored away, maybe it's like a key, or something."

Max added, "I honestly don't know. That's why I need to get it back."

"It's up to us, then," Schuyler said.

"But how will we get it?" Theo asked.

Everyone looked at each other, as if waiting for someone to step forward with a plan, but they all looked as overwhelmed as Schuyler felt.

"We need the sword," she said, grasping at the one thing she felt she knew for certain. "The prophecy says the blade of flame is how I can defeat Lucifer. And Max needs to get his power back before Lucifer can use it. Getting Azrael's power back is our number one priority."

Max's eyes flashed. "I won't stop until I have it."

"You need to rest," Theo said. "You're going to kill yourself if you don't listen to your body."

"Rest is for the weak. Besides, my brother is out there somewhere and he needs me. I'm useless to him like this."

Schuyler understood his anger. He was scrambling for solid ground to stand on. She had been feeling the exact same way for months.

"You won't be any good to anyone if you're dead," Schuyler said.

Max glowered at her but snatched up his noodles and ate some more. Either he was feeling light-headed again or he was smart enough not to snap back.

Schuyler said, "Aoife, you said you have a spy . . ."

She nodded. "I'll see what they can find out. Now that we know to be on the lookout for some . . . crystal, right, Max? I can pass on the info. What about in the meantime?"

"Gather our strength. Jack's still out there somewhere. I know he is. We have to make sure Lucifer doesn't capture him as well."

"If they use him to break open the fabric of the universe . . ." Aoife said. "It would complicate everything."

Schuyler nodded. "For now, we have to lie low. If we make ourselves known to Lucifer too early, we could miss our chance at getting Azrael's power. Business as usual. Let's regroup tomorrow."

"If there is a tomorrow . . ." mumbled Theo.

Aoife put a hand on his shoulder. "Hey. It's not fate until it happens." She looked around at the rest of them, standing tall and confident. "We can do this. We're Paladins. And now there's more of us." She looked at Schuyler and smiled. "We're stronger than ever."

THIRTEEN

SCHUYLER

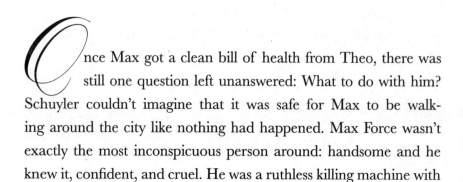

Once Max got a clean bill of health from Theo, there was still one question left unanswered: What to do with him? Schuyler couldn't imagine that it was safe for Max to be walking around the city like nothing had happened. Max Force wasn't exactly the most inconspicuous person around: handsome and he knew it, confident, and cruel. He was a ruthless killing machine with a catty attitude. Someone like him didn't blend in and he seemed to like it that way.

Aoife led Max through the Warehouse and Schuyler followed.

"Good news is," Aoife said, "Lucifer probably thinks you're dead."

"At least I've got that going for me."

Schuyler expected that Aoife would set him up with a place to stay—something similar to where Megan lived, but Aoife had other ideas. "We don't get a lot of visitors, so we're not flush with amenities right now. We can buy some supplies later, but for now we can only make do with what we have."

Aoife paused at a cleared-out alcove between towers that looked more like a storage closet than part of a room, with a mop bucket and a couple of rags piled in a corner. Pushed up against a wall was an old army cot and a moth-eaten blanket. "Home sweet home," she said.

"It's . . ." Max started to say, but the mop fell onto the cot with a short *clack*. "Terrible."

"Well, excuse me for not rolling out the red carpet, Mr. Force. How may I be of more service to you next time, Mr. Force?"

She gave him a little bow, and he wrinkled his nose and spun on his heels.

"I'm out," he said.

Schuyler imagined Max was used to sleeping in a four-poster bed, with servants delivering his breakfast in the morning and taking care of his every need. Now he was offered merely a cot and a humble blanket. How far the mighty had fallen. Even Schuyler could see the sleeping arrangement was a little rough.

"Where will you go?" she asked, hurrying after him.

Max didn't break stride. She doubted he even knew where he was going. "I don't know. I'll figure something out." He straightened his shoulders, making himself taller, but Schuyler saw through his false pride.

She stopped in her tracks and groaned loudly. "Would you cut the act?"

"I'm fine. I don't need your help or anyone else's."

Aoife snorted. "Sure, buddy."

Schuyler pressed her lips into a line and glared at the back of Max's head. She was more upset that he was still putting up a front that he was this unstoppable, powerful being—that he was too proud to admit he needed them. "You can't go home, you don't have any money. So . . . what? You'll just sleep on the street?"

Max slowed to a stop, then spun around to face her. He tipped his head up ever so slightly to look down his nose at her, but he didn't say anything.

To believe he could be trusted so quickly and so easily was an act of pure faith. She knew this. But she had to believe that his effort to save Kingsley was the start of real change. Schuyler took a deep breath and asked a question she hoped she wouldn't regret. "Do you want to stay at my house?"

Sure, Max may have hated her, but would he really be stupid enough to decline a roof over his head, a hot shower, and some food other than instant noodles? He looked at her for a long moment, making the same calculations she had. It was possible that everyone thought he was dead, but if any of Lucifer's followers saw him on the street, he'd be dead for real.

Max sighed. "Fine. Just this one night. Only because I would kill for a shower right now. I'm not in the business of owing people favors. Besides, you owe me a ton of answers, Impossible Girl, starting with who the hell you are and how you keep surprising me."

Schuyler couldn't help but smirk. She found Aoife smirking too. Max might have lost his Blue Blood status, but he was still the same old Max deep down. "Yeah, yeah," she groaned. "I've got a lot of surprises up my sleeve. Come on, before it gets too light outside."

Schuyler said goodbye to Theo and Aoife and left for SoHo with Max, taking measures to keep a low profile. Aoife insisted he wrap himself in the moth-eaten blanket to hide, but as things stood

Max would remain shoeless, left to walk to Schuyler's house barefoot. If Max had been anyone other than Max, Schuyler might have offered him a piggyback ride, but she figured him walking on the dirty Manhattan streets might build some character. She was still a little sour about Max trying to kill Kingsley in the first place—and her, for that matter. Siccing a dozen hellhounds on a person was not easily forgiven.

It was still nighttime when they exited the Warehouse, but there was only an hour before morning. It was better than moving through the middle of the day, but they couldn't delay. This was the city that never slept, after all.

"I'll get your biggest question out of the way right now," Schuyler said, peering around for any lurking threats. If she had to fight anything, she would be on her own on top of having to protect Max. "I'm a vampire."

"Bullshit." She showed him the blue veins on her wrists as proof. "This day can't get any weirder. How can you exist? I know every Blue Blood ever and you're not one of them."

"How does it feel being wrong for once?"

Max grumbled something under his breath and Schuyler couldn't see his eyes, but she could tell he'd just rolled them. He looked like a Russian peasant in a babushka wrapped up in the blanket as he padded along next to her, his bare feet pale against the dark sidewalk. Schuyler had to admit he looked out of place at her side, so they needed to hurry before anyone saw them.

"There's a lot of stuff going on that I'm not sure even I can wrap my head around these days. I have memories of another world, including another you."

"Another me?" Max asked, surprised.

"Yes. In that world you were a girl named Mimi. I'm sure you'll be pleased to know that you were as much a pain in the ass in that other world as you are in this one. Sometimes I have flashes of memory of that world if the divide between it and our current world gets thin. Kingsley called it the Superimposition. He knew all about the multiverse."

"Kingsley. In this other world, was he my . . ."

"Yeah. He was your bondmate there too."

Max was very quiet for a moment, then he said, "When Aldrich used the machine on me, I saw images . . . Memories that weren't mine. You're saying they were memories of other worlds?"

"Yeah. Maybe Aldrich is using vampire power to build up enough energy to bring parallel worlds closer together, thinning the barriers between realms. It would explain why you saw what you did. I was seeing double for weeks when it first happened to me. It's the best theory we've got right now."

Max fell silent once more. She could tell he was deep in thought and wondered what he was thinking about, then continued, "It's not just our world that's at stake, but the other ones too. If Lucifer breaks the layers of the universe, he'll destroy all the worlds. I don't know how or why my consciousness merged when it did, but I know it was for a reason."

"Why are you telling me all this?"

Schuyler thought it was obvious. "We both want to find Jack, we both want you to get your power back so I can get the sword and stop Lucifer. Admit it, we need to work together."

"*If* I were to believe you, because *maybe* Kingsley and Aldrich had both said the same science-fiction nonsense . . . What makes you think I'd help you?"

"Because Kingsley and Jack did."

Max got quiet again.

They had a lot more to understand about each other, but Schuyler was prepared to give him the benefit of the doubt that he was on board for the long run when it came to fighting Lucifer. Max didn't say anything more as they took Schuyler's route back to her house and climbed the fire escape. Still not used to his human-level strength, Max needed a boost and Schuyler helped him up. Together, they sneaked through her window. The sun was already starting to rise, the day quickly approaching.

Max dropped the blanket as he looked around Schuyler's room, taking in the reality of the situation. Had he ever imagined he would be staying in his enemy's Broadway-themed bedroom, among her *Hamilton* posters and Nancy Drew books, while hiding from his adoptive father and all his silver-eyed minions? Schuyler didn't dare tease him about it. She never would have imagined he'd be here either. At one point they'd wanted to kill each other. Funny how fate played these tricks on people.

"My bed is yours," Schuyler said, keeping her voice low. "You need it more than I do right now."

Max looked confused. "Where are you going?"

"Duchesne. It's a school day."

"You've got to be kidding me. You can't leave me here alone!"

Schuyler shushed him. She was sure her parents were awake. If he raised his voice any louder, they would know something was up. "Listen, once they leave, my parents will be out of the house all day. You'll be able to shower, and sleep, and eat anything you want in the fridge until I come back."

"What, your parents don't know about your secret life doing . . . whatever it is that you do?"

"No, they don't. And I'd rather keep it that way. You have to stay out of sight."

Max huffed. "Fine. Being a fugitive really is inconvenient."

"I'll try to get you some of my dad's clean clothes from the dryer before I leave. As for food, you can get whatever from the kitchen after my parents go. Just don't eat the chocolate truffles. My dad bought the box for my mom for their anniversary."

Max rolled his eyes. "I'm not a complete monster. Relax."

A knock at the door made both of them whip around.

"Schuyler?" It was Aurora. "Are you okay?"

"Uh . . ." Schuyler stared wide-eyed at Max, who threw his arms wide, as if to say: *Well? Say something!* "Yeah! I'm okay! I'm fine! Don't come in here!"

"What's going on? I heard a noise."

"Oh? Yeah! It's, um . . ." She stared at Max, who gave her an incredulous look. "I was watching a video and my volume was up."

Max mouthed, incredulous: *Really?* Schuyler mouthed back: *Shut up!*

"Okay . . ." Aurora said, sounding less convinced by the second.

"I'm almost dressed! Be right out!"

She heard her mom linger at the door for a minute longer before she stepped away. The clatter of pots and pans coming from the kitchen was a sure sign that Schuyler's dad was getting ready for breakfast.

"This is a bad idea," Max whispered flatly.

"You're here now. Just stay put and stay quiet. You can go wherever you want later."

"Fine by me."

Schuyler moved to her closet to start getting ready for school, but she paused, her mouth open around half of a thought. "Max, I . . ." She wanted to talk about Kingsley and everything that had happened at city hall, but she wasn't sure what to say or how to say it. Her feelings were all mixed up inside her, and now that Max stood in her room wearing an absurd T-shirt and pants that smelled like the sewer, she couldn't help but feel like he looked more human than he had ever looked before.

Trusting him completely to roam freely in her house alone when any second he could change his mind and run back to Lucifer was a risk she had to be willing to take. For the sake of getting the sword, she had to believe in something good, and that something good had to be Max.

He watched her with a flash of something she couldn't quite name in his eye, and she wondered if he thought she was going to hit him. It would have felt nice in the moment, for everything that had happened, leading up to this point, but instead Schuyler said, "I'm glad you're alive."

Max pressed his lips together. Whatever he expected her to say, what she did say had caught him off guard. "Yeah. Me too."

"Turn around," she said. "I need to change out of these clothes. They stink of you."

"Rude." But Max did as he was told, busying himself by the window while she quickly pulled on a new skirt and sweater. Today was continuing to be one of the weirdest days of her life.

When she closed the door behind herself, Max was still standing at the window, his gaze lowered to his hands once more.

FOURTEEN

SCHUYLER

*S*chool that day was infinitely more tolerable now that Schuyler knew that Aoife hadn't enrolled at Duchesne specifically to hunt her down and kill her on Lucifer's orders.

As she entered the building, joining the rest of the students filing in, Schuyler couldn't help but wonder what Max was up to at that very moment. A small part of her worried that she had been too trusting of him, that she had granted one of her sworn enemies full access to her home because she believed he had switched sides, but it was too late now to go back and lock him in her closet. She could only hope that Max would do nothing worse than waste all of her favorite fruity shower gels, throw off her perfectly curated Netflix algorithm, and eat the giant bag of caramel popcorn she had forgotten to tell him she had been saving for a movie night with Oliver.

As Schuyler walked down the softly lit main hallway of Duchesne, blending in with the crowd, she pondered the fact that Max used to be the king of this school. While she was mostly invisible, an outsider in the eyes of the rest of the students, he was the exact opposite. He could part the sea of students with a single look, open his locker to a dozen love letters from adoring classmates, make teachers apologize to *him* for assigning homework. Everyone paid attention to what he was wearing and what he ate and what music he listened to. Now, though, he was no more than a refugee hiding in her bedroom. No one outside of herself or Aoife knew otherwise. Let the others keep thinking he was on holiday, jet-setting the way only rich kids could do. The fewer people who knew about Max, the more time they had to figure out what to do next.

Before shutting her phone off for the start of class, Schuyler noticed she'd missed a text from Oliver.

Not feeling hot. Sick in bed ☹

She texted back quickly before a teacher could see what she was doing and confiscate her phone: *Boo! I'll bring you some pho after school!*

In seconds, Oliver replied, *You're a lifesaver.*

Oliver was hardly ever absent from school. If he felt sick enough to stay home, whatever was ailing him must really be hitting him hard. At least if he was home, he couldn't be ambushed by some roaming monster on his way to school. Schuyler would miss him, but she had a new friend to keep her company.

She found Aoife at her locker before classes started. "Morning, Aoife," she said, around a yawn. She didn't mean to sound so tired, but she couldn't help it. So much had happened last night, she'd barely had time to *think* about sleep much less sleeping for real.

Aoife had evidently gone home before coming to school too, but she looked more awake than Schuyler felt. She was wearing her usual nineties grunge style, this time opting for cargo pants,

Doc Marten boots, and a jean jacket, and her eyes danced brightly behind her glasses.

"Good morning!" she said. "All good with . . . a certain someone?" Saying his name out loud was off-limits.

"He's fine. Spoiled as ever, but fine."

"How about you, though? How are you feeling?"

For a second, Schuyler wondered if she looked like she'd gotten dressed in the dark and glanced down at her own outfit. Thankfully, she was wearing everything that a Duchesne student would wear if she didn't want to be noticed: no sweater inside out, no skirt tucked into her belt. She was glad to observe she had at least managed to put on matching shoes.

"Don't worry, you look great," Aoife said with a laugh. "It's just that I know my life can be a little much to newbies."

"Not sure I'd call myself a newbie."

"When I first learned about Paladins, I don't think I slept for a whole week. I thought a monster was literally going to crawl out from under my bed and attack me."

Schuyler grew deadly serious. "That's not a real thing, is it?"

Aoife laughed again. "I think the monster under the bed is more afraid of you than you are of it."

Schuyler decided to drop the subject. "I thought I had enough to worry about with . . ." She glanced around, expecting eavesdroppers, but everyone was too focused on their own conversations to be listening in. Still, to be cautious, she silently mouthed, *Lucifer. Now there's monsters. It doesn't exactly make me feel all warm and fuzzy inside.*

Aoife's smile split wider. She looked like a kid in a candy store.

"I've brought something that might cheer you up. You're going to like this, I think." The bell rang, making them both snap to attention. "Meet me at lunch. We'll talk then."

"Behold. This is the *Liber Monstrorum*, literally translated as *The Book of Monsters*," Aoife explained as she and Schuyler sat together at the back of the dining room. Between their lunch trays sat a large hand-bound book with a soft leather cover imprinted with a stamp of a monster's mouth, full of fangs. It was definitely the book Schuyler had seen Aoife writing in before. "It's a field guide to all the creatures we've encountered as Paladins through history, copied by hand. This book has saved my butt too many times to count, especially now that some of these monsters are back. Memorizing it means the difference between life and death. Go on, take a look."

Schuyler flipped the book open and found parchment pages, sketchbook pages, lined pages. Some had ink-drawn images of creatures, others were cutouts from magazines pasted in, and a few were torn from other books with handwritten notes in the margins. It was like the Frankenstein's monster of monster books, stitched together from all different mythologies spanning the entire world. A missing person poster fell out from between the pages, police reports of strange animal sightings, printed blog posts about supernatural phenomena . . .

Everything a Paladin would need to fight monsters.

Next to each drawing or photo was a list of traits, known weaknesses, and any information that might be relevant to the fight.

KELPIE: *cursed water-horse*
ETYMOLOGY: *Scottish Gaelic for "colt"*
STRENGTHS: *water, hypnosis*
WEAKNESSES: *none*
WARNING: *Never touch a Kelpie. You will not be able to let go as it drags you to the nearest body of water. You will surely drown.*

The next entry read:

CHIMERA: *multi-animal quadruped hybrid*
ETYMOLOGY: *ancient Greek for "she-goat"*
STRENGTHS: *see warning*
WEAKNESSES: *silver weapons*
WARNING: *Different types of Chimera exist, some spit poison, others spit fire, some have wings. Combinations of any quadruped animals can produce different subgroups. Approach with caution. Mother chimerae protect their young to the death.*

Another read:

GOBLYN: *neutral imp*
ETYMOLOGY: *Germanic Kobold*
STRENGTHS: *hiding, misdirection, confined spaces*
WEAKNESSES: *puzzles and thinking games*
NOTE: *Many goblins have been found to nest in the sewers of large cities. Extremely territorial. Scavengers. Mostly keep to themselves.*

"So crazy," Schuyler whispered, flipping the page in amazement, trying not to think about the possibility that a horde of goblins might be fighting over territory below her feet. "Pretty sure if I knew half of what went on in this town, I'd never walk home alone at night again."

"But you're not alone. Not anymore."

Schuyler smiled at that. She was starting to see Aoife not just as an ally but as a friend. It was a new feeling. She couldn't remember the last time she'd made a friend. "When you're not at the Warehouse, where do you live?"

"With my aunt. She's got a place up by Columbia University. She teaches there. She's a Duchesne alum, actually."

"Does your aunt know what you are?"

"Yeah, Aunt Natalie is a rare exception to the general rule," Aoife said. "She figured me out pretty quick. I guess we can never really hide from our family, right? She was freaked out at first, mostly because she was afraid for my safety, but now she knows I'm helping people. I'm not sure what I'd do without her."

"Kind of sounds like Oliver."

"Oh, right, your friend the Conduit. What does that mean exactly?"

"A Conduit is a liaison between vampires and humans. But Oliver is also my Familiar. It's an unbreakable bond. When a vampire drinks directly from a Red Blood, it makes the vampire super strong and boosts their power, but it comes with a lot of emotional baggage."

"I thought you said you don't hurt people."

"I don't, I promise. What Oliver and I have is totally consensual. We've only done it once, though . . . It was an emergency. I was getting ready to fight Lucifer at city hall and needed the additional strength."

"I trust you, don't worry," Aoife said. "I've come around to accepting the whole vampire situation. It was scary at first, don't get me wrong. Most monsters try to kill me any chance they get, but you've helped change my mind about a lot of things. Can anyone be a Familiar?"

"Technically, whenever a vampire feeds directly from a vein, it opens the psychic connection, and the Familiar bond is formed. So yeah, but I wouldn't ask it of just anyone. It's a lot of responsibility and risk; I need to be super careful. It helps if your Familiar is someone you trust, someone you care about more than anything. That's why Oliver means so much to me. He was one of the first people I turned to when I changed. I don't think I'd be where I am today if it wasn't for him."

Aoife bobbed her head. "How do you think he'll react now that you've got an *unexpected guest*?"

Schuyler hadn't had time to think about that yet. She'd been so exhausted, she didn't stop to think about how Oliver would react to her news about Max, but thinking about it now seemed obvious. Oliver had seen Max captured and Kingsley killed, and he'd rushed right over to tell her. He'd been terrified. She still remembered the way he trembled under her hands when he described the fight. "He'd be shocked, of course. But . . . it might be for the best if I don't tell him."

Aoife's eyebrows shot up. "You don't trust him?"

"No, I do. With my life! But until we know you-know-who is safe, we can keep Oliver safe too. Plausible deniability in case the worst happens. The fewer people who know that Max is still alive, the better. I can tell him when the timing is right."

Aoife hummed in agreement. "I admit, when you offered him a place to stay, I was surprised. Even though we know the prophecy says he'll help us, he doesn't seem like the sweetest peach in the bushel."

Schuyler rolled her eyes. "Rotten to the pit."

Aoife's laugh made Schuyler smile. "Don't take this the wrong way," Aoife said, leaning in, "but if you could keep that I'm a Paladin under wraps . . ."

"Did you just make a mummy pun?"

Aoife blinked. "I guess I did, didn't I?" Then she snorted into her lunch.

"I get what you mean, though," Schuyler said, still smiling. "Definitely. My lips are sealed. It's not my place to go telling anyone who you are."

"Me too. I love Aunt Natalie, but once a secret is out there, it's harder to control."

Schuyler fiddled with the corners of the book. She couldn't remember the last time she'd had lunch with someone who wasn't Oliver. "It's nice knowing that I can talk to you about this stuff."

Aoife's eyes shone. "Same!"

After school, Schuyler followed through on her promise to bring Oliver some pho from their favorite Vietnamese restaurant on Madison Avenue, the Pho Place. It made the best broth in town and Schuyler knew a bowl would be just the thing to make Oliver feel better.

She knew Max would be waiting for her to come home after school but decided he could wait a little longer. Her Conduit needed her. He delivered blood to her, she could at least deliver pho to him. He met her at the elevator when it opened on his floor, but Schuyler's smile fell when she saw him.

"Ollie," she gasped. He looked like he'd been hit by a truck. His skin was pale and his eyes were sallow. His hair was pressed flat on one side and sweat glistened on his upper lip.

"That bad?" He smiled weakly at her.

She stepped out of the elevator as it dinged angrily at her before closing and descending again. "I should have brought you the whole restaurant." She held up the paper bag, the soup sloshing around in its plastic container. "How are you feeling?" she asked.

Oliver mussed his hair and squinted in the light. "Just got up from a nap."

The elevator doors dinged once more. Schuyler hadn't anticipated anyone else would be coming over. Oliver's parents had decided to stay in Europe, even after the threat of a vampiric virus had passed, so Oliver still had the whole top floors of the building to himself. When the elevator opened again, they saw it was occupied by Ruby from school. She was petite, smaller because she always hunched her shoulders, and her cheeks flushed when she realized Oliver wasn't alone.

"Uh. Hi, Oliver," she said, then, "Schuyler."

"Hey, Ruby." Schuyler grinned at Oliver, already primed to start teasing him. *Mister Popularity!*

Ruby tucked her hair behind her ear and bowed her head as she held out a plastic to-go container. "I heard you were sick, so I brought you something to make you feel better. Chicken soup. From my grandma's restaurant." She sounded breathless, like she was about to faint. Schuyler could tell she was nervous.

Schuyler couldn't stop smiling as Oliver accepted Ruby's gift and said, "Thanks, Ruby, um . . ." He trailed off. He was just as awkward as she was.

As if startled, Ruby quickly said, "Okay, I'm going to go now." She pressed the Close Door button a few times on the elevator before it finally did close.

Schuyler waited a few seconds before she let out a giggle.

"Don't," Oliver warned, though he was smiling too.

"What? It's cute, the two of you! You're very popular."

Oliver took her by the hand—his fingers clammy and cold—and led her to the kitchen, where he set out some bowls and chopsticks for the two of them. He left Ruby's soup on the counter and opened Schuyler's.

"You two must be working well together on the charity concert fundraiser. She seems nice," Schuyler said.

"She is." That seemed to be the end of the conversation. Schuyler knew Oliver well enough not to tease him too much about Ruby. His feelings for Schuyler weren't a secret anymore, but she hoped that he was starting to expand his horizons a bit. Ruby was quiet, but Schuyler could picture the two of them together.

"Chicken soup will help you too. You really don't look so good," she said as she took a seat at the island counter.

"I've been worse. It's just a nasty bug."

Schuyler watched him with a furrowed brow as he moved about the kitchen. He looked frail in his pajama pants and soft cotton T-shirt. He'd seemed fine yesterday, but whatever illness he'd caught made him look like he was dying. She wished she could do something for him, but when he opened the plastic tub of soup and breathed in the steam, he did look a little better.

"Sorry I couldn't be at school. I didn't miss anything big, did I?" he asked.

"Nothing too out of the ordinary," she said as Oliver poured them each a healthy serving. Schuyler took a moment to breathe in the steam; the beef, garlic, and ginger combination was enough to lift her spirits too. Oliver sat next to her while they ate, holding his head in one hand and using the spoon in the other. He looked exhausted.

"Do you want me to run to the store and get you some medicine?" she asked.

Oliver smiled softly when he glanced at her. "I'm fine. Really. I feel a thousand times better already, especially now that you're here. I promise, I'll be back on my feet in no time." He took her hand in his and squeezed. "You don't look great either. Didn't sleep last night?"

"No, I—"

"When was the last time you fed?"

Blood. She hadn't had any for too long. She had planned on drinking some when she got home from school, figuring she could wait, but the night had taken a lot out of her. The mere mention of blood reminded her how hungry she was. Her stomach was in knots and the back of her teeth hurt, making her feel like she'd had a mouthful of sour candy. It had only gotten worse since she picked up the soup at the restaurant; smelling the raw meat almost drove her crazy. But she could control herself. She wasn't a monster like some Paladins thought she was.

Oliver twisted his wrist around, baring the soft part of his flesh for her. "Go ahead," he said.

Schuyler leaned back. "Ollie, I can't. You're sick. You need to rest."

"I'm worried about you more than I'm worried about myself. Please. It's my job."

To say his offer wasn't tempting would be a lie. Schuyler's instincts were strong. She'd been around enough blood today, first Aoife and then Max. She wasn't sure she could decline a vein that was presented so freely to her. Slowly, she wrapped her fingers around Oliver's delicate wrist. She could feel his pulse beneath her fingers. All she had to do was bite down and everything would feel better. She closed her eyes and breathed. Oliver's pulse rabbited beneath her touch. Schuyler held her breath, then let it go. She kissed his knuckles then stood up and crossed the kitchen.

"I'm pouring you some more soup," she said. "Ruby's seems perfect."

FIFTEEN

SCHUYLER

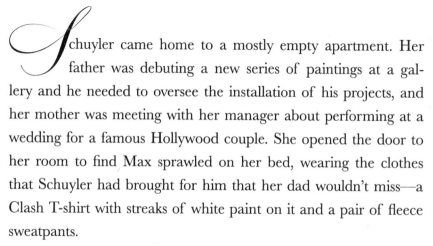

*S*chuyler came home to a mostly empty apartment. Her father was debuting a new series of paintings at a gallery and he needed to oversee the installation of his projects, and her mother was meeting with her manager about performing at a wedding for a famous Hollywood couple. She opened the door to her room to find Max sprawled on her bed, wearing the clothes that Schuyler had brought for him that her dad wouldn't miss—a Clash T-shirt with streaks of white paint on it and a pair of fleece sweatpants.

"Finally!" He groaned and snapped Schuyler's laptop closed when she walked in. Strangely enough, he looked more like himself to Schuyler now that he wasn't fighting against her. It was like he'd been wearing a mask this whole time and only now had he dropped it. His hair looked shinier, his cheeks fuller, and the dark circles under his eyes had faded. Working for Lucifer had been literally killing him. Now he looked refreshed and smelled of Schuyler's springtime shower gel. "Where have you been?"

"Out," said Schuyler. From beneath her bed, she pulled her

cooler packed with blood pouches out and opened one with her teeth.

Max watched her down the pouch in two huge gulps with a queasy look on his face.

She gasped with relief when she was finished and noticed him staring. "What?"

"Can you please not feed in front of me? It's disgusting."

Schuyler would have laughed, but she was too tired. One of the most notorious vampires of his age was getting squeamish over a little blood. Funny how turning mortal could do that. She went to her closet to get changed.

Meanwhile Max climbed off her bed and set her laptop down on the desk. "While you were taking your sweet time coming home, I've been working on tracking down my power." Schuyler twirled her finger, and Max turned around to give her some privacy. He went on: "Aldrich will probably be keeping it on him at all times. But we have the element of surprise on our side, so I say we charge into city hall and ambush Aldrich—"

"And how do you suppose we'll fight an entire Coven of Silvers that stands in our way?"

"Don't you still have the hellhound whistle?"

"Not anymore." Schuyler pulled Oliver's sweatshirt over her head. It still smelled like him. "Besides, all the hounds are dead. The Silvers killed them when we were providing you with a distraction."

"Fine, we'll be more stealthy this time. We can climb up the elevator shaft and break into his office. We'll kill anyone who stands in our way."

"You keep forgetting something."

"What?"

"You are human now. You can't do all the amazing things you used to."

Max's shoulders puffed up as he inhaled, like he wanted to explode. He'd been so used to being a Blue Blood, being anything else didn't feel like an option.

"You need to start thinking like a human," Schuyler told him. "Doesn't feel so good, does it, now that you're up against a whole army that's stronger than you?"

Max sneered. "At least I'm doing something. You're off at school, pretending like everything's normal, while I'm here trying to figure everything out by myself."

She threw herself onto her bed and covered her eyes with her forearm, blocking out the light from her desk lamp. Everything felt so heavy, including her eyelids. She wasn't in the mood to argue with him. "Max, please. I just need fifteen minutes. Let me rest my eyes for a little bit and then we'll work, I promise."

For once, Max didn't protest, but she could tell he wanted to. She heard him sit down in her desk chair with a heavy sigh.

Schuyler truly meant to rest for only fifteen minutes, but it was as if all she did was blink and the next thing she knew she was dreaming.

The dream felt too real, even as she flew through the night, carried along by the wind whipping through the streets of Manhattan.

She was invisible as she soared, her toes skimming the trees of Central Park, then turning down Fifth Avenue, coasting over cars like a leaf on the wind toward the Force mansion, as if drawn to it by some magical power. The building stood like a Gothic mausoleum in contrast to the other multimillion-dollar homes on Billionaire's Row—a testament to the endurance of power.

There was an open window on the third floor, and as she floated through it, she was greeted by the sound of demolition.

Silver Bloods had laid claim to the Force mansion, leaving destruction in their wake as they went from room to room, tearing into mattresses with long daggers, ripping Max's clothes from his closet and tossing them into the fireplace, smashing towering bookcases and ripping out the pages of Jack's books, breaking mirrors and porcelain vases in the bathrooms. No room was left undisturbed.

They cursed Max's and Jack's names, turning everything the twins had once owned into dust.

Schuyler floated through the mansion, carried deeper into the house by some unseen power, until she stopped in the main entrance with its plush red carpet, warm wood paneling, crimson curtains. It had yet to be destroyed by Silvers.

Aldrich Duncan stood in the middle of the foyer, his hands clasped behind his back as he looked at a giant oil painting on the wall. It depicted him and the Force twins, his hands on their shoulders. The Force boys looked more haunted than their home did.

What Aldrich saw in that painting, Schuyler didn't know. When he attempted to analyze it, he sounded like a tour guide at a museum might sound: distant, removed, and clinical.

The front door opened and a Silver entered. "Your hecatomb, my lord," he said.

A line of twelve mortals filed in and stood in a row behind Aldrich, their faces slack, emotionless. They were under compulsion. Schuyler knew if they had their wits about them, they would be running for their lives. Instead their eyes were totally blank. They looked to be people struggling with homelessness or drug addiction, their clothes shabby and their faces haggard.

Aldrich turned to see them, his eyes hungry. He walked up and down the row, looking into their faces, as if searching for imperfections.

"Your wrist," he said to one woman. She held out her arm, her wrist limp, and he clasped it tightly with long fingers. He pressed his nose to her skin and breathed, closing his eyes, as if savoring the aroma of his morning coffee. His fangs extended and he sank his teeth into the woman's flesh. She didn't react at all as he drank, her eyes fixed on nothing.

"Yes," he said. "They will suffice." The woman's bright red blood stained his lips.

A single tear slid down her cheek, and Aldrich reached up and brushed it away with his thumb.

"Do not cry," he said, his voice soft and gentle. He smiled. "I'm sparing you from what is to come. It's better this way. Be afraid for those who are not as lucky as you are. Rejoice, for you are saved."

The woman didn't react, though Schuyler knew that she was terrified, despite the compulsion. The woman understood what was happening, and she was powerless to do anything to stop it. Aldrich Duncan was unstoppable.

Aldrich grasped the woman by the shoulders and sank his fangs deep into her neck, draining her completely. Tears fell before she collapsed to the ground, and then she was dead. One by one, Aldrich moved down the row, consuming the life force of every single Red Blood, their bodies pale in death.

Schuyler couldn't do anything except watch. She wanted to scream, but she didn't have a voice, she didn't have a body. She was a ghost.

Wake up, please, wake up, she thought desperately. She didn't want to be here anymore. She was forced to watch as Aldrich murdered a dozen people in front of her eyes. How many more were to come?

Once the final mortal fell, Aldrich gasped, full and satisfied. Blood had coated his hands, and he wiped them with a handkerchief he removed from his jacket pocket.

"Get rid of the bodies," he commanded, frowning at a particularly stubborn spot under his nails.

More Silvers appeared out of the shadows, picked up the corpses, and dragged them out of sight.

Alone again, Aldrich pushed his hair back into place with both his hands, now clean, and his eyes went back to the oil painting. Something passed over his face, something hard and bitter, and he reached up and took the painting down. The frame was huge, and heavy, but he didn't seem bothered by its weight. He looked into the faces of the boys he'd raised, and he frowned.

Slowly, he brushed his fingers along Max's and Jack's painted faces, as if he missed them. Then his jaw hardened and he curled his fingers into claws.

He dragged his fingernails down the length of the canvas, as easily as slicing through paper, cutting through the young boys' faces with stoic determination until they were mauled and disfigured.

They were dead to him. And if he ever saw them again in person, he'd do so much worse than destroy a painted portrait. Schuyler didn't know how she knew, but she could feel it peeling off him, pure betrayal. It radiated like smoke and she choked on it.

He tossed the painting aside, trash like the rest, but at that moment something made him look up. Aldrich's eyes locked on the spot where Schuyler stood watching.

He shouldn't have been able to see her, but he did. Fear coursed through her. *Wake up, wake up.*

"Who's there?" he asked. Something passed over his face. "Is that . . . *you?*"

Schuyler couldn't breathe.

She felt another ghostly presence behind her. Someone else, someone invisible, was with her.

Aldrich stepped closer, his focus narrowing upon her. "No, you're not . . ."

He reached out, his fingers inches from Schuyler's eyes. She squeezed them shut.

And then she woke up.

Sunlight crept in through her bedroom window, chasing away the remnants of the dream. With a start, she thought Jack was in her room, but when her brain caught up to her eyes, she realized it was Max. He was sitting on her windowsill, his arms folded over his chest as he looked into the alley below, but his gaze was unfocused, his thoughts a million miles away. He barely moved to signal that he knew she was awake. He must have been up all night.

She was about to tell him about her dream, but she stopped herself. It wouldn't make Max feel any better knowing she'd dreamed of Aldrich. Besides, it was just a dream, wasn't it?

"What time is it?" she asked, sitting up.

"Time for you to go to school," he said bitterly.

That morning, Oliver was back at Duchesne. Like he'd said, he bounced back quickly from whatever bug he'd caught. He was Schuyler's same old Oliver, sitting with her through classes, snapping jokes and making her laugh, especially during lunch. Schuyler couldn't help but notice that Ruby kept glancing their way, smiling at Oliver's jokes too, as if she were sitting there with them. But Oliver didn't seem to notice. *He is such a boy, honestly,* Schuyler thought, amused, as Ruby bowed her head and got back to her food.

"I think Ruby likes you," Schuyler said.

"Who? Oh."

"Come on, she's nice," she said, nudging him.

Oliver smiled, though his cheeks pinked. "I'm . . ." But his gaze flicked toward Ruby, and he raked his fingers through his hair. "I don't know."

"Give her a chance. You two might really hit it off."

"I'm not sure about that. Besides, I've got a lot going on. . . ."

Schuyler knew he was just being bashful. "I just want you to be happy."

"I *am* happy, especially whenever I'm around you. But I've got a lot of plans, something I'm working toward, and I don't want to screw it up."

"Really? What?"

Oliver's bright brown eyes twinkled mischievously. "It's a secret."

"Tall, dark, and mysterious. Now I see why Ruby likes you."

Oliver smiled down at his food, then looked up at her again.

"Have you thought any more about coming to the concert with me? Since we'll all be there for Duchesne for Change anyway . . . Maybe we could make it a date?"

"Ah, Ollie." The concert had completely slipped her mind. The nightmare she'd had last night had wedged itself into the forefront of her thoughts instead. "I still need some more time to think about it. I've got a lot going on too. I'll let you know soon."

"Sure, babe," he said, still smiling.

Her heart melted. She loved it when he called her that. He was the best thing that had ever happened to her. But she remembered the nightmare, and Aldrich's ability to compel mortals to do anything he wanted, and she couldn't help but think about something like that compulsion happening to Oliver next. What if it wasn't just a dream? What if he was truly in danger?

Schuyler was about to tell Oliver about the dream, but at that exact moment Ruby appeared at their table. "Hey, Oliver," she said, hunched over but blushing bright red beneath her curtain of hair. "I was wondering if you had a second to talk about the concert. Snap and Pop?"

"Uh, sure," he said, slightly flabbergasted. Her nightmare could wait. Schuyler wiggled her eyebrows at him and he gave her a withering look, but he followed Ruby across the dining area. As Schuyler watched them go, she noticed Aoife framed beneath the doors to the room. Aoife spotted Schuyler and waved her over.

Schuyler gathered her books, tossed away her lunch, and went over. "Hey, Aoife, where have you been? Missed you during lunch."

"Sorry, bit of *business* on my radar." Schuyler's eyebrows shot up. "Anything I can do to help?"

"Yeah, actually. Just not here. We can talk later."

"Do you want to come over to my house after school? Maybe you-know-who can help."

Aoife's eyes sparkled. "Sure! Sounds fun."

As they walked together from school, Schuyler learned that she and Aoife had a lot more in common than she'd originally thought.

Aoife was also a fan of Broadway musicals, and she looked forward to seeing some shows now that she lived in the city, and she also enjoyed cheesy horror movies. They talked about some of their favorites all the way to SoHo, and Aoife even had recommendations for shows Schuyler had never seen before. She couldn't remember the last time she'd made a friend so easily and naturally. For so long it had just been her and Oliver, two outsiders at Duchesne, but now there were three. Not to mention someone new she could confide in. Oliver was great, but there was something special about connecting with another girl. Not only that, but Aoife knew what it felt like, living two lives and feeling like she needed to save everyone.

"I've been wondering," Schuyler asked as they turned down her street, "is Megan able to locate Azrael's power? Or find Jack? Can she use her power to home in on anything?"

"No, her sight isn't omniscient. Her gift is in prophecy and reading palms. Trust me, if she could do things like that, she would. She's a Paladin, she wants to do everything she can to make sure Lucifer is annihilated. I'm hopeful, though. It's an all-hands-on-deck sort of situation now. With Azrael's power in Lucifer's hands, we've called in Paladins from all over the world, pooling our gifts and resources. We expect to have a few hundred here by the end of the month."

"That's amazing. How do you communicate with each other?" Schuyler asked.

Aoife gave her a look, like Schuyler had just landed on Earth from another planet. "Um, texts?"

Schuyler laughed. "I'm sorry! I figured you all would have some secret network of communication figured out."

"You're making me jealous! Now I want to know if you vampires have any special tech!"

"There's this thing called the glom; it's sort of like telepathy. Words, feelings, sometimes images. We can reach out to one another there, but it's not perfect."

"So that's why you can't find Jack?"

Schuyler nodded. "Either he's shut himself off, or he's trapped somewhere and he can't reach out to me." She refused to believe he was dead. No one could simply kill Jack Force. "I just want him home . . . I need to know he's safe."

Aoife looked at her, sympathy in her eyes. "You're keeping Max safe though, so it's not nothing."

But when Schuyler and Aoife came home and Schuyler opened the door to her room, expecting to find Max impatiently waiting for her, he was nowhere to be found. Her desk and bed were empty.

"Max?" Schuyler called out. No answer. The bathroom was dark.

"He didn't leave, did he?" Aoife asked.

Schuyler doubted he was *that* stupid, but he was bullheaded enough that it could be possible.

From the window Aoife said, "Schuyler, over here." She pointed outside. Max was in the alley below. By then, she could hear glass shattering and Max's voice carrying on.

The girls confronted him in the alley together, Schuyler marching up to Max as he pitched bottles at the brick wall, where they exploded and rained glass down on a dumpster. The cacophony would draw anyone's attention, not to mention Max shouting, "No good! Weak! Stupid!"

"Max! What are you doing?" Schuyler asked through clenched teeth.

Max turned around, looking at her through lidded eyes. He wavered on his feet, an almost-empty bottle of bourbon in his clenched fist. She could smell the alcohol radiating off him.

"Never been drunk before," he said, slurring. "Being a vampire, never could. So this is what it feels like. Guess it's real. Guess I really am mortal. It's official." He downed the rest of the bottle and then smashed it on the ground. Glass scattered everywhere.

"Max . . ."

"What? Am I supposed to be doing something else? What else am I good for? I'm already a failure." He stooped down and picked up another empty bottle from a pile in the trash and lobbed it at the wall. Shards of glass sparkled like a waterfall. Max lost his balance and wobbled, falling hard on the dumpster. He pushed himself upright, but it was a miracle he was still capable of standing. He'd been drinking all day by the looks of it. Schuyler had told him not to touch her parents' chocolate truffles, but she hadn't thought about their liquor cabinet, which they opened only for special occasions.

"Come on," she said gently. "Let's get you back inside."

"To do what? I'm just a waste of space."

Schuyler was not in the mood for this. She sighed. Max's eyes wouldn't focus on anything. He was too far gone and deep in self-loathing. If he wanted to stay outside and throw empty glass bottles at a wall all day, maybe she should let him. But it was too dangerous. Anyone could hear.

"What's the point anymore? I lost my power, my sword. Look at me." Max threw his arms wide. His eyes were glassy, rimmed in red. Emotions shifted on his face like passing clouds, and his despair turned into rage. "Me!"

He spun around and punched the brick wall and cried out, clutching his hand. His knuckles had already started to bleed. But he was so angry, and so drunk, he reared back and punched the wall again, and again, crying out each time his fist made contact before Schuyler grabbed his wrist and whipped him around, pinning him to the wall with her forearm.

"Stop!" she said. "Just stop it. You're bleeding."

"So? Here, have some blood," he said. He reached his bloody fist toward her mouth and she slapped it away. His arm flopped like a fish.

There was no reasoning with him, not when he was this drunk. This close to him, the smell of bourbon was overwhelming, and it made her stomach churn. "You are the absolute last person in the world I would drink from."

The way Max laughed, it almost sounded like he was saying: *Me too.* Then his laugh turned into a sob. "Just kill me," he whispered. He closed his eyes, thudding the back of his head against the wall. "I've got nothing, no one . . . Just do it."

Schuyler might have disliked Max before, maybe even hated him, but she didn't want him dead. She glanced at Aoife, who watched, concerned. She'd never seen the Max who brutally killed Blue Bloods when they dared to stand between him and power, the way he smiled at the prospect of spilling blood, the joy of inflicting pain. Schuyler looked back at Max, and she couldn't stop her eyes from going to his throat, seeing his pulse flutter. It was in her nature to feed, but to kill was another story, even if it was someone she thought of as an enemy.

Max stared at her with heavy eyes, waiting, and his Adam's apple bobbed when he swallowed. Rock bottom was a new look on him, and it only made Schuyler's decision easier.

"I'm taking you home," she said.

They put Max in Schuyler's bed. He'd passed out sometime between the alley and the loft, forcing Aoife and Schuyler to carry him the rest of the way. They turned him on his side so he wouldn't hurt himself and pulled the covers up to his ears. He was already snoring.

"Well, that was fun," Aoife said, sitting heavily in Schuyler's desk chair.

Schuyler had taken up a spot on the floor, her back pressed up against her bed. Having Max sleeping above her made her feel a little more at ease. At least now she knew where he was.

"You're friends with this guy?" Aoife asked.

"Max has tried to kill me too many times for us to be friends."

"What?"

"I didn't mention it? Let's see: He chucked a lacrosse ball at my head once, tried to blow me up in the Repository of History, oh yeah, and he sent a pack of hellhounds to tear me to shreds. I'm probably missing a few. We don't exactly get along."

Aoife looked surprised. "And still you let him sleep in your bed?"

"I mean . . . Yeah. I have every reason to let him rot in the street, but I can't. It wouldn't be right."

"You think he'd do the same for you?"

Schuyler lifted one shoulder. "Doubtful. But that's all the more reason why I helped him. I don't think anyone is undeserving of kindness. When he broke in here the other night, barely conscious, he asked for help. I'm not even sure he remembers doing it . . . he was almost dead . . . But I helped him. Didn't even think about it."

Aoife smiled. "I see. You're a rebel, you know that? You're kind, even when it's easy not to be."

"I don't know if that makes me a rebel."

"In this world? It does."

Schuyler blushed. She'd never thought about it that way. "So, what Paladin business did you want to talk about?"

"Right! I almost forgot."

They left Max to sleep off his inevitable hangover in peace and went out into the living room. From her backpack, Aoife pulled out a stack of missing person posters.

Schuyler's heart sank at the sight of them. She took them from Aoife and flipped through them. They were all men, all with desperate pleas from their families trying to find them. She understood their plight entirely.

"All of these people have gone missing from the same area, the East River Park, all around the same time. The police don't have any leads. But they don't know what we know. I think it's a siren."

Schuyler's eyebrows shot up. "What makes you think that?"

"A body of water, missing men, a cluster of disappearances in a short amount of time. It's all in my book."

Schuyler looked at all their faces again, all of these victims. Could Jack be among them? It was a stretch, but at this point Schuyler could believe anything. "So what do we do?"

"To be honest, I've never faced a siren before. They've been thought to be extinct up to now."

"Before Lucifer, you mean," Schuyler finished, nodding.

"Would you help me get some more info? See if we can't hunt it down together? Maybe save some people?"

Schuyler's heart leaped. "Yes! Absolutely!"

Aoife's smile spread wide.

The rest of the day, they worked together, learning more about sirens from history and folklore, and before Schuyler knew it, her parents were home. They walked in together, chatting and smiling. Aoife and Schuyler squirreled away the missing person posters as quick as they could.

"Oh! Schuyler!" Stephen said. "Good, you're home. Who's this?"

Aoife stood up and held out her hand. Schuyler's parents shook it in turn. "Hi, I'm Aoife! I'm new."

"She's a friend from school," Schuyler explained. "She just enrolled."

Something passed in Aurora's eyes, a brightness that made her almost glow. "Very nice to meet you, Aoife! You're welcome to stay for dinner."

Stephen called from the kitchen, "Pizza! Homemade from

scratch." He held up a glass bowl of dough that had been sitting out on the counter.

Aoife truly looked disappointed. "I wish I could, but I've completely lost track of time. My aunt will be expecting me. Thanks for having me over, Sky." She surprised Schuyler by wrapping her in a tight hug. It was nice.

"Anytime."

Schuyler showed her to the door and Aoife said, keeping her voice low, "Thanks again, really. The siren doesn't stand a chance with us on the case. See you tomorrow?"

"Definitely. Get home safe."

Aoife hopped down the front steps and waved before she disappeared around the corner. Schuyler closed the door, still smiling.

She told her parents she was going to clean up before dinner and went back to her room. There she found Max sitting up in bed, clutching his head with his hands.

"Good. You're alive," she whispered flatly. "Are you hungry?"

Max squinted at her. She could almost see the headache pounding his skull. "For what?"

"Pizza. My dad makes a pretty mean Hawaiian pie."

"Pineapple? Ugh. I'm going to puke," he said.

"Take it or leave it. Your choice."

Before Max could answer, Aurora's voice came through the closed door. "Schuyler, can you come out here, please?"

She didn't sound happy. Schuyler looked at Max with round eyes and whispered, "Wait here. Don't make a sound." He nodded and Schuyler left her room, closing the door behind her. She found her parents standing at the dining room table instead of sitting like she expected. Was she in trouble? They looked at her with somber expressions.

"Is there something you want to tell us?" Aurora asked.

"No." Even Schuyler herself wasn't convinced by the way she said it.

"There is an extra toothbrush in the bathroom. It's not mine, it's not your father's, and it's not yours. Is there someone staying here?"

Schuyler's heart leaped into her throat. Her first instinct was to lie. Her primary goal was to keep her family safe, and the less they knew about the Forces and their ties to Lucifer, the safer they'd be, but she couldn't think of a word to say. She held her breath, waiting for a miracle.

At that moment, the door behind her opened and Max emerged. Her parents stared as he ambled forward, his eyes shifting as if he were ready to fight. If they'd expected to see a handsome blond boy wearing Stephen's old clothes, they didn't show it. The room went coldly still and silent.

No one spoke. The silence deafened.

Schuyler was so screwed.

Sixteen

MAX

Max knew this would happen.

He'd heard Schuyler's parents through the door and knew he'd messed up. Of course, he'd forgotten something as stupid and small as the toothbrush Schuyler had given him. He had a lot of other things on his mind, to be fair, but he was still responsible for the mistake. There was no use hiding anymore.

When he came out of her room, he felt everyone's eyes on him fire. It was obvious how it looked: a guy like him, emerging from their daughter's bedroom, guilty as sin. He'd never met her parents before, but something about her mom rang familiar even though he couldn't quite put his finger on it. He saw the family resemblances immediately—Schuyler had her mother's face and her father's eyes. The pair of them stared at Max, who was starting to feel like a wild animal trapped in a corner. He glanced at Schuyler and saw that her mouth was pressed into a thin, flat line, an expression reserved for the guilty. There was no more pretending.

"Schuyler, what's going on here?" her father asked, more concerned than angry. "Who is this?"

"I . . ." Schuyler looked at Max again. "This is Max. He's my friend."

Max looked at her, surprised. She'd never called him a friend before, and it made him feel off-kilter.

Schuyler kept going. "He needs help. A safe place to stay, so I told him he could stay here. I didn't want you two to freak out . . ."

Max was impressed. Clearly, Schuyler lied as easily as he did, readily blurring the line between truth and falsehood. Her parents looked at each other, a whole conversation happening between them through a single look, the kind of look only married couples could share after years of being together. He'd seen his own parents do it so many times when they were alive.

"Where have you been sleeping?" her mother asked him, bewildered.

Schuyler answered for him. "My bed." Then quickly, "Not like that . . . We take turns. No one can know he's here."

Her parents exchanged another look and both of their shoulders dropped.

"Are you in trouble, son?" Schuyler's father asked. His blue eyes were soft, and kind, and so unlike those of Aldrich Duncan. Hearing the word *son* come out of his mouth sounded different than how Aldrich said it too. Max needed a moment to process. Now was the time to answer truthfully; it's what Jack would do.

"Yes," he finally said. His head was pounding from the remnants of the bourbon. He was pretty sure he wouldn't be able to lie even if he wanted to. Thinking hurt too much. It was all he could do but be truthful.

Schuyler's mother's dark eyes took him in thoughtfully. With her mind made up, she nodded and said, "I think you'll need some more clothes, then. Toiletries too. I'll pick up some things for you at the store. I think we've got an inflatable bed somewhere in our storage unit in the Village, right, Stephen?"

"Definitely. Our old camping gear could finally come in handy. And I've got plenty of clothes you can borrow in the meantime, Max."

Max blinked. He wasn't sure he was hearing things correctly. Any other parent would have thrown him out by now. He'd already started mentally preparing for it. Now he didn't know how to react. "You really want me to stay?"

"Of course. Schuyler, go ahead and set another seat at the table for dinner." Schuyler was already hurrying into the kitchen to grab plates. "How many slices of pizza would you like?"

After dinner, Stephen invited Max to help him with some repairs on his car. Max had the impression that the request wasn't just about the car, but that Stephen wanted to talk. Even Schuyler nodded encouragingly at the idea. It would be foolish of Max to decline the invitation, so he went. He was starting to feel better, but his head was still throbbing from last night's indulgences. He swore he'd never drink again.

It was already dark outside, so Stephen handed Max a sturdy flashlight and led him through the narrow alley to a small garage on the ground floor between buildings. He pulled open the garage door and turned on a light. Inside was a classic red 1969 Ford Mustang, well polished and cared for. Max let out a low whistle.

"She's a beaut, isn't she?" Stephen said.

Max ran his hand over the hood. She truly was beautiful, even though he had no idea in the slightest about cars. He just knew what a good car looked like when he saw one. Though he had to admit, he never would have taken Stephen for a muscle-car kind of guy.

"I've poured my blood, sweat, and tears into this thing. Four-speed manual, Windsor V-8 engine, work of art." Stephen casually flipped a wrench he'd retrieved from the workbench end over end, catching it in his palm as he admired his car.

"I promised myself when I sold my first painting, I'd buy my dream car," he said. "Turns out owning it was a lot more hands-on than I thought. I found her at an old garage in Jersey. The mechanic who ran the shop said she needed more work than he was willing to put into her. She was just taking up space in his lot, abandoned by the previous owner, but I knew I needed her. I would have to start over from scratch with her, though. She was basically a skeleton, all gutted and broken down. She'd been in a bad crash, beat up and barely recognizable, but I fixed her up, bit by bit. All it took was a little love and attention, and now she's better than new."

Max had to appreciate the dedication it took to rebuild what anyone else might consider a piece of junk.

Stephen popped the hood and locked it open. He asked Max to hold the flashlight steady for him while he got to work checking the engine. Max had never been interested in cars. He'd had loftier dreams and goals, barely even considering the idea that he could do anything else besides what Aldrich wanted from him, expected of him.

Stephen must have sensed that Max was a novice when it came

to cars, and he showed him different sections of the engine, identifying parts and explaining what they did. Max actually found himself asking questions, appreciating that Stephen would bother teaching him. According to Stephen, maintaining the car was a frequent ritual. Schuyler used to be the one holding the flashlight, especially when she was little. But he figured Max could use the fresh air. It was a nice story, but Max still felt like an intruder.

"I'm sorry for hiding from you," he confessed while Stephen checked the oil level on the dipstick. "It wasn't Schuyler's fault. She was just trying to help."

"I know. My kid's got a good head on her shoulders. Obviously, we're doing something right," he said with a grin. "But there's no need to apologize. It's more than okay."

"I didn't have anywhere else to go and I know Schuyler and I should have said something, but I didn't want people finding out where I was. I can't trust anyone."

Stephen wiped his fingers clean on an oily rag. "Look, Max. You don't have to explain anything. We won't ask questions that you're not comfortable answering. We want you to come to us if you're comfortable, but it's none of our business. Our business is making sure you're okay. You're welcome to stay here with us as long as you need to, all right?"

"But . . ." Max couldn't help but ask, "why?"

Stephen laughed brightly.

Max bristled a bit, but tamped the feeling down. "I'm serious. I'm not useful, I'm not important. We're not family. Why help me?"

"Because it's what people do," Stephen explained. "We help each other. What more can any of us do but try?"

Max gripped the edge of the hood. It didn't make sense. His whole life, he'd been taught to do things and get something in return. He would be the shining example of the true power of Blue Bloods, the epitome of perfection, and in return he would be granted everything his heart desired. And it had all been a lie.

Once Max wasn't useful anymore, he had been discarded. For so long, he'd convinced himself that becoming Aldrich's heir was the life he wanted to lead, and he had been completely blind to the reality of his trauma. He'd ignored the fact that life could be lived any other way, on his own terms. And all it took was for him to lose everything to see that. He hated himself more than ever. He hated everything he'd done and everything he'd wanted to become. Why couldn't Stephen see that he didn't deserve any kindness? Maybe Max should prove to him that he really was a monster, make him regret believing Max deserved any compassion, and then it would prove Max right. He could sabotage his way to a self-fulfilling prophecy that would inevitably lead to the dark, bitter future he thought he deserved. It would mean he hadn't wasted his entire existence trying to be the thing Lucifer wanted him to be. But he didn't want to do it, couldn't do it. He didn't want to hurt Stephen, or Aurora, or Schuyler. So if he wasn't a monster, and he wasn't a vampire anymore, then what could he be?

A part of him wanted redemption, but an uglier part wanted his old life back. He wanted Aldrich to forgive him—the prodigal son returned. He wanted his title, his legacy, his power, but every time he listened to that part of himself, he heard it speaking to him in Aldrich's voice. None of it was real. He was trying to attain the unattainable, a fantasy, for someone who didn't truly love him. So then what was it all for?

Aldrich's love had been conditional, a contract, all business. Max had been a tool used as a means to an end, and when his time was up, he was tossed aside. All of his work, for nothing, no one. Not even himself.

Max found himself staring blankly, miles away in thought, and he needed to remind his lungs to breathe. Stephen had paused from his work on the car and was watching him closely.

"Does your family know where you are?" he asked.

Max shook his head. "My brother is missing. And if my father found out where either of us was, he'd kill both of us. He's already tried to kill me once. . . ."

"You're not exaggerating? Your father actually tried to kill you?" Stephen saw the look on Max's face, and mercifully, Stephen didn't press him about it. A deep sadness lined the crow's-feet of his eyes. It seemed that he too had suffered his fair share of pain in his life, but it hadn't hardened his heart. When Max used his pain as a shield, he thought it had made him strong. Now he saw how foolish he'd been.

Stephen lowered his voice meaningfully. "Family isn't about blood, it's about the choices we make."

How was that possible? What kind of family could Max choose for himself? Would anyone even want him? He'd already lost the one person he wanted to be with. And the only real family he had was still missing. Who else would ever love him? Max's heart felt like it was being squeezed with a cold fist of guilt.

"If you're going to live here, though, I have one condition," Stephen said. "Stay out of the liquor cabinet?" His eyes twinkled, amused. Of course Schuyler's dad had known. He was a dad. Dads always knew.

Heat flushed Max's face. "Yeah, okay." It was a promise.

Stephen held out a wrench for Max and gave him an encouraging smile. "Bit by bit," he said.

Max accepted the tool, feeling the weight of the metal in his hand, and got to work on the car.

SEVENTEEN

JACK

The siren fed on Jack's blood, and he was trapped in a dream.

His life in the forest cottage by the sea had become a cage.

No matter which way he ran, he always came back to the cottage. He'd take off into the woods, running as fast as he could, only to come to a sliding stop in front of the porch. Every time he ran, he always came back.

His dead father waited for him on one return and caught him with a firm hand on his arm.

"Jack, what's wrong?" he asked, concerned.

"I can't . . ." Jack shook his head. He couldn't remember. He knew he needed to escape, but how could he? Every muscle in his body was pleading for him to run, even though he didn't know which path was the way out. Jack struggled against the illusion of perfection. No matter how hard he fought, Harmony's hold on him was as complicated as a knot he couldn't unravel. This was magic he'd never experienced before.

"Come inside," his father said. "It's safe here."

"No," Jack said, and he pulled away from him. "You're not real."

"How could you say that? Of course I'm real."

Jack's head felt like it was about to burst. He stumbled back and ran, only to wind up at the porch once again. His house was looking more and more decayed, as if decades passed each time he returned, trapped in a time loop, doomed to repeat forever the same trajectory. Every time he found himself in front of his house, a different person would be waiting for him there. His mother. Max. Schuyler.

But it wasn't Schuyler. The smile on her lips wasn't her smile—it was the siren's: hungry and evil.

"We can start over, Jack," the siren made Schuyler say. "Let me try again. I can realize your heart's desire here. What are you missing? Is it this house? Is it this world? I can make it however you want it to be. I can give you everything. Don't leave me. You can't leave. I need you."

He didn't know anymore what was real and what was an illusion. The only real thing he could believe was his fear, as solid as a brick in his stomach. And the siren seemed to like it that way, liked him confused.

Jack opened his eyes again, in the darkness of the shack that smelled like rotting flesh and salt water, just as the siren leaned over his body, hissing with delight. He'd lost a lot of blood. Too much. How long had he been here? Where was here? He could barely keep his eyes open, he was so weak.

The only thing that Jack knew for certain, as real and as sharp as the siren's fangs digging into his neck, was that he was dying.

Eighteen

SCHUYLER

*S*chuyler had settled into a new rhythm with Max, Aoife, and the Paladins.

She could hardly believe that her parents had been so cool with Max staying with them. It made sense, though, in hindsight. Stephen and Aurora never would have thrown a kid in need out onto the street. That wasn't in their natures. They'd always been of the opinion that when a person needed help, you offered a hand, not a boot out the door.

Her parents outfitted Max with some of Stephen's old clothes and set him up with an inflatable bed that smelled like campfire smoke even after sitting in the back of a storage container for years. They turned a part of the living room into his own room, divided by a privacy screen so he could have a small space entirely to himself.

Schuyler felt safer knowing that Max's situation was under control, so she could focus more on helping the Paladins. And with more Paladins arriving in every day, she felt like they were making progress, even though it was slow. Max even joined in on the research to help find the siren.

"I'm so bored I'm clawing at the walls," he said one day when

Aoife came home with Schuyler. He had a stack of papers in hand, pages from the internet printed out and still warm off the press. "I got carried away."

"You're pretty good at this whole research thing," Aoife said, impressed.

"Yeah, well, half of my job working as Venator for Lucifer was research. I'm putting my skills to better use now."

Schuyler grabbed everyone some snacks and they gathered in the living room, going over the latest results of Max's research.

"Sirens make nests . . . of course!" Aoife said, looking over a page. "That's why people are all disappearing from one area. The siren needs to stay close to home. Maybe if we find the nest, we can catch the siren off guard. Good find, Max."

Schuyler looked at the entry for *sirens* in Aoife's *Liber Monstrorum*:

SIREN: *malevolent aquatic spirit*

ETYMOLOGY: *"to knot; to entangle"*

APPEARANCE: *Unspecified. Reports indicate that the siren can assume the form that would be most appealing to the perceiver to better lure its victims, appearing differently to different eyes. A siren feeds off its victims' blood and can sustain their victims for long periods of time, often using venom to slow blood flow. Multiple reports of half-fish, half-bird creatures, though evidence suggests they may be two separate genera (OR genuses). Sirens prefer to consume men of all ages and are still dangerous to all. Elusive creatures, highly dangerous. Hunt near bodies of water. Beware the song. Ear protection mandatory.*

STRENGTHS: *water, music, blood*

WEAKNESSES: *susceptible to iron, all silver, and fire*

Schuyler was ready for a fight. If monsters kept emerging through thin spots of the fabric between worlds, who knew how many more were out there? This was the closest she'd come to actually helping someone since being on her own, and she wanted to prove that she could help the Paladins.

"I don't have any weapons to fight the siren," Schuyler said.

"No worries," Aoife told her. We'll stop by the Warehouse on the way and find something for you. We don't need Michael's sword for this mission."

Schuyler stood up. "I'm ready to go, then."

"Me too," said Max, standing as well, but Aoife shook her head.

"You identify as male, right?" she asked.

"Yeah. Why?"

"It's not safe. Did you forget? Sirens *love* men and they are picky eaters. If you came with us, you'd be vulnerable to the monster's song, and she'd have you under her spell like that." She snapped her fingers.

Max rolled his eyes. "Like a siren is any match against the likes of me."

"Oh yeah?" Aoife kicked him in the back of his knee and he yelped. "Mortal," she said with a grin. Max gave her a stink face. "You really want to go risking your butt against a man-eating siren when there's a chance you could get your power back?" That seemed to shut up Max real quick.

"They actually eat men?" Schuyler asked Aoife.

"You know the legend. Sailors throwing themselves into the sea after hearing the sirens' song and all. Sirens definitely have a type."

"So what, I'm supposed to sit here and do nothing?" Max asked.

Schuyler could tell he was feeling sidelined, but they couldn't risk him getting caught out in the open, especially in his current state.

"Hopefully, it won't be for long," Aoife told him. "My spy has a theory about what Lucifer is planning to do with your power. Can't be sure yet, though. We need more info."

Max said, "You keep mentioning this spy. Who is it anyway?"

"Wouldn't you like to know?"

"Ha."

Aoife sensed that Max was on the edge of losing it and shifted her approach. "Your job is to figure out whatever you can about Project Montauk, see what records are out there on the dark web. Give my spy some info to work with. If we stop Lucifer, we won't have to worry about sirens anymore."

Max and Schuyler looked at each other. "Aoife has a point," she said. If Max couldn't safely fight a siren, he could still do more to help than he was now doing.

But Max stood up straighter and squared off against Aoife. "I don't take orders, I give them."

Schuyler gave Aoife an apologetic look.

"Is he always like this?" Aoife asked, amused.

"Try living with him."

"I appreciate your moxie," Aoife said to Max, "but you're more help to us here than you are chasing sirens. You want your power back? Prove it. Stay put."

Max ran his tongue over his teeth, seething, but he looked at Schuyler again. Whatever he saw in her face, he relented. "Fine.

Whatever. Just remember I'm letting you go only because I'm so nice."

Aoife stepped up beside Schuyler as she stared at the wall of weapons in the Warehouse. The display was lit up like a showroom at a mall. Schuyler felt like she was shopping with Aoife, a perfectly normal pastime for two teenage girls. Except instead of dresses and shoes, they were surveying a wide array of battle armor.

"What do you think would help us fight against a siren?" Schuyler asked.

Aoife listed off the various options, but Schuyler didn't know how to shoot a bow and arrow, and she felt like a hammer was a bit too brutish for her style. "How about a crossbow?" Aoife took a T-shaped crossbow from its shelf and hefted it. It wasn't the most subtle weapon in the world, but Aoife plucked her finger on the tip of an arrow already notched and ready to go. "Silver tipped," she said.

"I think it might be a little disturbing if I'm walking around town carrying that thing."

Aoife sighed. "Sometimes I forget you city folks don't know how to have a good time, honestly." She put the crossbow back on the shelf with a heavy *thunk*.

Schuyler laughed. Laughter seemed to come more easily when Aoife was around.

"All right, then, what are you used to? What do you like?"

"A blade will be fine." Schuyler allowed her eyes to skim over the section reserved for all manner of swords and daggers, looking for the right one.

"Classic," Aoife said. "I like your style."

Aoife flexed her fingers, stretching her bandages easily. Her whip would serve her well, and Schuyler had to go for something she could hide too. She chose a small iron dagger. Its blade was dull, solid, but it had a wicked tip. She traced her finger across the edge and nicked the skin on it, letting it blossom blue.

"Is this one magical?" Schuyler asked.

"No, it's not like my Banner. But it suits you nicely."

Schuyler and Aoife arrived at the East River Park just after sundown. People were walking along the riverside path: couples arm in arm, dog walkers maintaining a hold on ten pets at once, and spectators roaring at a club soccer game, illuminated by giant lamps overhead.

"So what are we looking for?" Schuyler asked, eyeing a vendor selling balloons. Anyone could be the siren in disguise. Aoife seemed a little more at ease with the situation, looking around casually.

"Just relax," she said. "If we look like we're looking for something, it draws attention." Schuyler forced herself to take a steadying breath. Aoife smiled at her. "I was like you on my first hunt too."

Schuyler returned the smile. "I'm just glad I'm not doing it alone."

Aoife nodded. Together they walked along the river, keeping a subtle lookout.

"The nest would be hidden," Aoife said. "Stay alert for anything out of the ordinary."

Schuyler scanned the area as surreptitiously as she could. The idea that they were walking straight into a monster's lair looking for a fight sent her stomach dropping into a cold pit. They passed by a bulletin board where notices, mostly advertisements, fluttered in the breeze cutting across the river. One of the notices, however, was a missing person poster. A man in his thirties. Another victim of the siren.

Just then, something different than the briny river smell cut across Schuyler's nose and it made her stop dead in her tracks.

"What is it?" Aoife asked.

Schuyler sniffed the air. "Do you smell that?"

"No."

Schuyler looked around for the source. "I smell blood."

Aoife looked impressed. "Cool. Gross, but cool."

Schuyler shrugged. "Perks of being a vampire." She followed her nose, leading Aoife down the river walk and through a small garden. By then, the smell was overwhelming; it made Schuyler's eyes water, and—even more—her mouth. Blood was somewhere nearby.

Beneath an overgrown bush, Schuyler found a pool of blood and a piece of torn athletic shorts in the dirt. There was enough of the liquid to make her think that regardless of what happened here, the victim couldn't have gotten away. The blood was dark, mostly congealed, and could have easily been mistaken for mud. If not for Schuyler, no one would have found it at all.

"We're close," Schuyler said.

She followed the scent of blood, finding small droplets winding through the garden and across the lawn. They dodged cyclists and sunset yoga classes, the smell getting stronger and stronger as they went, finally ending at an old fireboat house near the water on the south side of the park. The redbrick building was two stories tall with a large tower on top, a viewing station, most likely. But the fireboat house hadn't been used for ages. Better technologies had replaced it. It was now a relic of a time long gone. Wild grass and flowers grew behind a tall fence blocking most of the building from view, locked and cordoned off with a sign saying it was scheduled for demolition; its windows were shuttered and barred.

"Oh, weird," Aoife said.

Schuyler expected her to be looking up at the building, but instead she was staring at the ground. The flowers that were growing behind the fence spilled through the gaps in the chain links. Aoife traced her fingers over the bell-shaped white petals.

"What is it?" Schuyler asked.

"This type of snowdrop is only found in the Mediterranean."

"How do you know that?"

"My aunt—she teaches sustainability science at Columbia. I picked up a thing or two from her. This flower shouldn't be growing here."

"Well, the smell of blood is coming from in there," Schuyler said, pointing. Although the building looked long abandoned, the smell washed over her, overwhelming all her senses, and she needed a moment to pause and collect herself. She knew whatever they were going to find in this place wouldn't be good.

"Are you okay?" Aoife asked.

"I'm fine," Schuyler replied. "There's just a lot of . . . it."

Aoife clenched her fists, and the bandages creaked as she did. "We're in the right place, then. Come on." They put foam plugs into their ears. When all sound was muted, Aoife gave a thumbs-up.

No one saw them as they vaulted over the fence with ease and disappeared into the overgrown brush.

The smell of blood, tangy like copper on the back of Schuyler's tongue, was even stronger inside, mixed with something even worse. Decomposition. Aoife gagged, the smell overwhelming even for her. She put her hand over her mouth and took a moment to get used to it, even though she looked like she wanted to puke. With all other sound muffled, her heartbeat thudded in her head.

All around them were figures, bodies like mannequins, sprawled on the floor and in piles. Dead. Schuyler had never encountered anything like it before. The smell of death would haunt her dreams for years.

Slowly, and as quietly as they could, they made their way deeper into the building. Strips of light coming in through the boarded windows provided Aoife with enough brightness to see by, but Schuyler was used to searching in the dark. She and Schuyler kept close, back-to-back with their weapons out, scanning for any sign of movement.

When Schuyler turned a corner and peered deeper into the building, her heart almost dropped out of her chest.

"Jack!"

He was lying on a table, not moving, his head turned toward her. She rushed to him and put her hands on the sides of his face. He moaned, as if he was sleeping.

"Jack," she whispered, gently shaking him.

"Schuyler, be careful," Aoife said, clenching her fists and looking all around. "The siren can't be far. This could be a trap."

"Jack, please. Wake up! It's me! It's Schuyler! We have to get you out of here."

He was bleeding, his neck slick with his blue blood. His skin was pale, his lips paler.

Schuyler kissed him, but he didn't stir. She was running out of ideas. "Jack, come on!"

"I won't let him wake up."

The voice made both Schuyler and Aoife spin around. Standing behind them was a figure, keeping to the shadows. Schuyler's whole body felt icy cold. Aoife unleashed her Banner and the whip cracked with lightning. The entirety of the boathouse lit up. The siren couldn't hide in the shadows anymore. Her body was covered in purple scales; she was draped in seaweed, her hands were claws, but she had a pretty girl's face and white-blond hair. Any man might throw himself at her before realizing he had just made a deadly mistake.

The siren circled the table, catlike. "He's mine. He can't leave. I won't let him go." She kept her voice quiet and contained, like she was holding back. Like she was loading a weapon before she released it.

"What are you doing to him?" Schuyler cried.

"Making him forget. He saw my true face, so I put him back to sleep. He's a fighter, that one. I've never tasted anything like him before. He's lasted longer than the others . . . And," she added pointedly, "what is he?"

"We're taking him. Back off!" Aoife snapped her whip and the lightning cracked in the empty room. The electricity made every hair on Schuyler's body stand on end.

The siren laughed, but it sounded like air being let out of a tire. She smiled, showing off a row of sharp teeth. Her eyes landed on

Schuyler. "So you're the one he thinks about all the time. His soul mate, Schuyler. No wonder he was so hard to control knowing you were out there looking for him. It doesn't matter now. I can make him see anything I want him to see. *I'm* his soul mate now."

Schuyler's breath came out quick and short, pain spiking in her chest.

The siren smiled. "Soon he'll be under my total control. He's the most powerful creature I've ever encountered. But his mind . . . so delicate. I'll keep him forever. He won't ever want to leave me."

"I'm warning you one last time. Release him." Aoife was already ready for battle, fire blazing in her eyes.

Schuyler brandished her iron dagger. The siren sang and a pink haze drifted through the air, and surrounded Jack's head, entering his nose and mouth. His back arched above the table, his hands clenched into fists. He screamed with his eyes shut tight, trapped in a nightmare.

The siren laughed. "They always taste better when they're scared—"

Schuyler charged, swinging her dagger through the air, but the siren was quick. She let out a deafening scream. Even though they had ear protection, the air in front of Schuyler rammed right into her, as solid as a wall. She staggered, dazed. Aoife cracked the whip and the siren leaped back. Hastily, Aoife pulled her headphones out of her jacket pocket and put them over Jack's ears.

"He won't be able to hear her anymore!" She lifted Jack's upper body upright. He flopped forward onto her shoulder, moaning. He was starting to wake up. Her idea was working.

The siren appeared out of the darkness and swatted at Schuyler's head. Schuyler lashed out. No way was this beast going to touch Jack ever again. The iron nicked the siren in the arm and she howled in pain, her skin steaming where the blade touched. The siren elongated her claws and threw Schuyler across the room.

As Schuyler scrambled back to her feet she noticed that Aoife and Jack had almost reached the exit. Aoife looked over her shoulder, eyes widening as the siren leaped after them, claws out.

Schuyler pushed off the floor as fast as she could and stabbed the siren in the side, dragging the blade all the way down her scaly torso.

The siren's screams rocked the boathouse. Bricks started to fall from the ceiling.

The building was collapsing.

Schuyler screamed at Aoife to "Go! Go! Go!" Aoife did as she said, Schuyler close behind.

The siren's rage cracked the walls and bricks rained down on the two girls. They were almost out. Schuyler looked over her shoulder just as the siren reached out to grab her, but at that moment the ceiling came crashing down on the siren's head. Her scream died, but the damage was too much. Schuyler didn't stop running.

A brick clipped her shoulder just as Schuyler threw herself into the open air and the structure collapsed behind her with a tremendous *boom*.

She coughed in the dust, panting in the dirt. She was alive. The others lay sprawled on the ground ahead of her.

"Jack." Schuyler scrambled to him, still draped in Aoife's arms. His eyes fluttered open. Schuyler lifted his face to hers.

"Schuyler . . ." he whispered. "Are you real?"

She smiled through her tears. She was so relieved. "Yes. You're okay." He held her hand, his fingers weak against her palm, and she squeezed, reassuring him that what was happening was real and he was being rescued. He was safe now. She'd found him.

Nineteen

MAX

ax paced back and forth, clenching and unclenching his fists, waiting for Schuyler and Aoife to finally show up. With Jack. They'd found Jack.

After what felt like weeks of the entrance to the Warehouse remaining dark and empty, he threw his head back and groaned at the ceiling. "Ugh! What is taking them so long?" His insides were all twisted and warped and he couldn't wait for the girls any longer.

Schuyler had called him, telling him they'd found his brother, alive but hurt. That had been over an hour ago. He'd rushed all the way from SoHo to the Warehouse, and still, they were nowhere to be seen.

Theo hovered nearby, watching the entry too. "They'll be here," he told Max. "Just be patient."

"Patience has never been one of my strong suits." Max couldn't stay still. He needed to keep moving or he was certain he would explode. He heard a commotion at the entrance and Schuyler and Aoife suddenly appeared, in a frenzy, the two of them carrying Jack, his arms flung about their shoulders. He looked drugged. No—worse than drugged. He looked half-dead.

There were deep bite marks on both sides of his neck, and his blue blood coated the front of his T-shirt. Deep gouges from claws had shredded his chest too. His skin was smeared with dirt and grime, and he smelled like the docks. Max didn't have time to be scared for him.

He and Theo leaped into action, helping the girls carry Jack to Theo's worktable.

Whatever the siren had done to him, it had drained him almost completely. Blue liquid still flowed from open bite marks in his neck as Jack floated in and out of consciousness. His eyes drifted open and closed, and he mumbled something under his breath.

"It's been too long since he's last fed," Schuyler said.

"What does he need?" Theo asked.

Schuyler started to say, "He needs—"

But Max was already cutting open his hand, slicing with a pair of scissors he'd found on the table. He'd made a straight slice down his palm with a single cut. As the blood started to pool in his open palm, he winced. It burned, but he didn't care. He was beyond caring at this point. "Get me a bowl," he said.

He squeezed his fist, draining his blood into a bowl in Schuyler's hands. When there was enough, she tipped the bowl to Jack's lips. The floor seemed to shift and Max realized he'd given too much blood too fast. He should have known it would make him woozy. Theo grabbed him just before he fell and gripped his hand. The glow made the pain and the light-headedness go away in an instant.

Already some of the color was returning to Jack's face. Max would do it again in a heartbeat.

Jack's eyes opened wider and the wounds in his neck started to close. The blood was working.

"Schuyler . . ." he whispered. He touched his hand to her cheek as she leaned over him, whispering again and again that he was okay. Even Max had to admit it was a tender moment.

Max flexed his fingers, making sure everything was as it should be. Theo's help had been incredible. "Maybe a little heads-up next time before you decide to cut yourself open," said Theo. "I can't be everywhere at once."

"I did what I had to do. Whatever it takes."

It was no *Caerimonia Osculor*, but Max's blood would be enough. Becoming Jack's Familiar would make Max's mortality feel too real, as if he would remain human forever. At least his being human in that moment of need had saved Jack's life. It was the one good thing to come out of all the crap that had happened so far.

"Max." Jack's voice was stronger now. He was able to sit up on his own. All the gashes in his body were closed. He looked fully healed.

Schuyler stepped back as Max went to him and wrapped him in a tight hug. He didn't care that Jack smelled like death. He had never wanted to hug anyone so much in his life. Jack held him too tightly, as if he was afraid that Max would slip through his arms like smoke. Max didn't mind the pressure; he didn't need his spine intact anyway. "I'm so sorry," Jack mumbled into his shoulder. "I'm so, so sorry."

Max pulled away and said through a smile, "For once, you look terrible." And he thumped Jack hard on the biceps. His bravado couldn't mask the truth from his twin, though. Jack looked him straight in the eye and Max knew that he sensed what was wrong. Jack turned Max's bare wrists over and he became very still as the puzzle pieces all came together in his mind.

"What happened to you?" Jack asked.

"Yeah." Max cleared his throat. "Funny story . . ."

"That machine, Jack, it was . . . nothing like I've ever seen or experienced before," Max said. He sat next to Jack on the table, his arms folded firmly across his chest. Schuyler and the Paladins had left them to talk in private. He caught Jack up on everything. "I felt like I was dying. I *wanted* to die. It made me see impossible things. They tortured me, would have tortured you too, but . . . They got what they wanted in the end. I couldn't stop it. Aldrich took everything from me. If they catch you, they'll do the same to you. I can't let that happen."

Of all things to ask, Jack had chosen the one question he was sure would surprise Max the most: "Are you okay?"

"*You're* the one who almost died ten minutes ago. How'd you get caught by a siren anyway?"

"When you didn't contact me after getting Kingsley out of Duncan's trap, I had to find you. I thought I'd tracked you down at the East River Park, but it was a trap. The siren had me before I even knew what was happening. I've been stuck in a nightmare ever since."

Max felt like he'd failed on more than one front. He'd let Kingsley down; now he was doing the same to Jack. . . . "That's

Aldrich's fault too, by the way," Max said. "All those monsters? The siren? Every time he uses that machine, he thins the gap between worlds. You can thank him in person."

Jack ran his fingers through his hair. He lifted his gaze to the ceiling and took a deep breath. "What have we done?"

Of course Jack would blame himself. He and Max had worked for Aldrich for so long, they were equally responsible for all the criminal acts he'd performed. They had both been ensnared by Aldrich's promises, his assurances that following him was the only way. But of course, if they'd stood up to him earlier, they'd be dead already.

Max said, "We can't change the past. All we can try to do is fix things, best we can. I mean, the best *you* can. I'm useless. If it wasn't for Schuyler and Aoife—"

Jack interrupted. "You're not useless. You almost died and it's my fault."

"Blaming yourself is stupid, you idiot. I do it enough for both of us."

Jack actually smiled. "Maybe we're both bad at saving each other."

"Don't make a habit out of it."

"I won't." Jack's eyes sparkled as he grinned.

Max let himself smile too. When was the last time he'd sat with Jack like this and talked? He couldn't remember. He couldn't remember the last time he'd smiled with him either, a real smile, not a hungry or ambitious smile, but one that felt good. Under Aldrich's care, there wasn't a lot of reason to. Maybe under better circumstances, they could make talking a more common thing.

"So," Max said. "Were you ever going to mention *your* plan to betray Aldrich, or were you just going to let me have all the fun?"

Jack braced himself on the table, staring at the floor. A muscle in his jaw throbbed. It had always been a nervous tic of his, a reflection of his true urge to say what was on his mind. "I was trying to save you from doing something you'd regret. Betraying Aldrich was an inevitable outcome."

"And you teamed up with Schuyler." Max's eyes flicked to the alley she had disappeared down with Aoife. "What is it about her anyway? She's good-looking enough, I guess."

Jack's ears turned red. Max had never seen his brother blush before. "I, uh . . . She's special. I feel it, deeper than anything I've ever known." Max waited, knowing Jack wanted to say more, and eventually he did. "She's my bondmate."

Max's heart thudded painfully in his chest. He'd never have a future with his own bondmate. "So you know what she is?"

"I do. I also know she's killed Lucifer before, but I died. In another world. We have to protect her if she's going to kill him again. It's the only way we can make things right."

"Well, you're not dead here. That's all I care about. This world is the one that matters to me. Ugh, this multiverse thing is giving me a headache," Max said. He rubbed his temples for emphasis. "How is she possible? No new Blue Bloods can be created."

"And we used to think no Blue Bloods could become human. And had no idea that Paladins existed." Jack glanced at his brother out of the corner of his eye. "Things have changed."

Max hated change. As far as he was concerned, it did nothing but make his life worse. His power had been stripped from him, his control taken away. Before, he'd felt like he was the architect of his own fate. Now he was as helpless as a paper boat in a hurricane, subject to the whims of destiny and prophecy. He needed to do something.

"I need my power back," he said. "Now that you're safe, it's the only thing I can think about. Every time Aldrich used the machine, monsters broke through and the worlds were that much closer to colliding. It's only a matter of time before Aldrich uses my power to collapse all the worlds and I lose my power forever."

Jack added, "Also, everyone will die."

They shared a look. Max could try to make a joke, a default defense mechanism, but he didn't have the energy. Both he and Jack went steely quiet for a moment.

"This crystal you mentioned . . ." Jack said, breaking the silence. "What did it look like?"

"Clear quartz, with a gold sheen."

"You're sure?"

"Yeah, why? Do you know what it is?"

Jack nodded, but he didn't look happy about it. "I think it's a charm stone. I've read about them in our library at home."

"What's it do?" Max couldn't help himself from sounding hopeful.

"If I remember correctly, there's old vampire lore about how the sangre azul could be stored inside stones to grant special healing powers. Mortals who drank from one of the stones could be cured of disease or injury. But there was a risk. The drinker's blood would boil if they weren't pure of heart, and they would die. If they were pure of heart, though, after drinking enough of it they would absorb its power, and their blood would turn blue too. But everyone thought the stones were lost to time."

A bolt of adrenaline jumped down Max's spine. "That's it, it has to be!" He leaped to his feet, unable to sit still any longer. "So, you're saying whoever drinks the blood—*Azrael's* blood—from the charm stone, they'll get Azrael's power? And everything with it?"

"In theory."

A wide, hungry smile spread across Max's lips. "Aldrich said he needs a celestial sword to shatter the barriers between dimensions, but the only way to get it is to give Azrael's blood to someone who can summon it for him."

"I fail to see how this is a good thing."

"Don't you get it? It means there's still a chance," Max said. His cheeks were starting to hurt from smiling. He wasn't used to it. "Once I get my hands on the charm stone, I can become a Blue Blood again. I can be me again. I won't be stuck like this forever."

Jack looked like he was going to be sick, but Max was too pumped up to care.

"We can get everything we want. I can get my power back, I can get the sword, Schuyler can use it to fulfill the prophecy with her Blade of Flame, all that jazz. Everything will be right again."

Jack sighed and shifted in his seat. "Max, I—"

"There's still time; all I need to do is figure out where it is and take it—"

"Max," Jack said sternly.

"What?" He was practically buzzing with excitement.

Jack leveled his gaze on him. "Until then, Aldrich will keep trying to make more vampires, and he'll kill a lot of Red Bloods to do it."

Back at Schuyler's apartment, Max splashed water on his face at the bathroom sink. The cold snapped some sense into him, even if Jack's words still clanged around in his head.

Jack had stayed behind at the Warehouse while Max went back to Schuyler's to gather his things. Now that Jack was safe, he'd decided the best place to be was at the Warehouse with the Paladins, so that meant Max would stay with him too. While the generosity of the Cervantes-Chase family was noble, Max couldn't hide in their house forever. He wanted to be with Jack. Schuyler said he could take her family's camping gear to make living at the Warehouse a little more comfortable and she got to work packing up a go-bag for Jack. Who knew how long they would need to stay in hiding?

The twins could never go home. The Force boys were considered worse than dead—exiled. Their existence would be erased.

At one time Max had had the entire world at his feet, and now he had nothing. Except Jack. At least, he reasoned, they had each other. And Jack still had power, which was something. Max would sooner die than let Aldrich get his hands on Jack.

The water dripped down the length of Max's nose, and he watched it disappear down the drain.

Making more vampires? Really? Then again, was it out of the realm of possibility? With himself as Regent and Coven leader, Aldrich Duncan had pushed vampires beyond their limits. Would making more vampires truly be that impossible?

The very idea scared Max. Vampire power was strong enough to thin the veils between worlds temporarily, but the machine needed souls in order to work. If he was burning through the number of available ones, he'd run out before long. Aldrich needed more souls to keep going. And why was it taking him so long to break open the barriers between worlds with Azrael's sword? Why hadn't he used it yet? Had he not yet found a person who was pure of heart enough to wield it?

Another startling thought was troubling Max. *Was this how Schuyler had been created?* What if she'd been given blue blood to drink and that had turned her into a vampire? Max splashed some more water on his face. No, he sensed there was something else at play. Schuyler's mother, Aurora, still intrigued him. Why did he have the feeling that he knew her somehow? The Superimposed memories had played with his brain and he was still sorting through the mess.

Max glared at himself in the bathroom mirror. Why did he have to be so useless?

The lights flickered and the bathroom momentarily fell into darkness. The ground shook slightly as if a truck had rumbled through the building, and Max braced himself against the counter. His heart thrummed in his ears, but the earthquake passed quickly. Max stood rigid, waiting for the aftershock. The city rarely experienced earthquakes, so he knew this wasn't a natural phenomenon. It was Aldrich. He was using the machine again. He was using more vampire power to thin the veil between worlds. More monsters were coming through.

The lights flickered back on and Max allowed himself to breathe. He was sure that when Aldrich finally got what he wanted, when he finally used the sword, the lights wouldn't come back on ever again.

But now, when the light did come on again, a girl in the mirror was looking back at him.

He jerked back with a yelp. The girl in the mirror did the same.

At first, Max had a thought to bolt for the door, but instead of acting on the impulse, he stood frozen. His heart thumped hard in his throat. The girl also looked shocked. She was thin, with creamy-white skin, flowing golden hair, and emerald-green eyes. *His* eyes. Like Max, she was standing in a bathroom, her makeup having just been finished. She was, to say the least, beautiful.

All at once his mind was flooded with a vision, like drinking water from a fire hose. The Superimposition layered memories over his own.

He was the girl, seeing through her eyes, and she had Kingsley. The two of them had been bondmates in another world. Their love for each other vibrated through the fabric of the universe. And in that world, he died too. The girl's grief and fury were his own. He watched her travel into the deepest level of hell to get Kingsley back. She had the power to do it and no one could stop her.

"Mimi."

She stared back at him, her lips pursed. When she spoke, her words were muffled, as if she were speaking from behind a closed door. "Jack? Is that you?"

Of course she would think he was Jack. They had the same face. But after a moment, she realized she was wrong and her brow furrowed. "Who are you?"

He didn't know what to say. With tentative fingers, he reached out to the mirror and touched the cool glass. The mirror fogged around his fingertips. The girl moved in sync with him, reaching out curiously. But the moment their fingertips touched, the lights flickered again, and when the power came back on, she was gone. Max's vision of another world passed.

He needed his power back. Or the girl in the mirror would be dead too.

TWENTY

JACK

Jack dusted his hands clean as he stood back and admired the work he'd done clearing out a section of the Warehouse Aoife had generously offered to him and Max to use as a temporary living space. All it needed was a quick cleaning, a sweep of a broom, and it was ready. It was a far cry from his room at home, but it was safe, and that's what mattered. Their sanctuary was surrounded on three sides by towers of boxes, and Jack could feel them all humming with magical energy, but it was calming, like a weighted blanket. He and Max would take anything they could get.

The fact that Max didn't have Azrael's power anymore was still a revelation to grapple with. Regret churned in Jack's gut, knowing as he did that Max had been tortured all the time he himself had been sleeping. And now that Max didn't have his power, Jack felt like he needed to protect him even more. Especially if Lucifer was planning on making more vampires and collapsing universes onto one another. He hoped this theory was wrong, but he knew better than to hope.

Their whole lives Jack had been watching out for Max, making sure he didn't get in over his head, but Jack had always hated Abbadon's power. To know that Max didn't have Azrael's power anymore made Jack a little jealous and wish for it himself, but at the same time, he knew he had to use the power he had to protect his brother. To protect everyone. He would not let Lucifer win.

Aoife came from around the bend, carrying a lamp for them to see by. "Sorry it's not as swanky as the storage containers we have for the Paladins who live here permanently, but we're working on it."

"This is great, thank you. Really. All we need is a place to lay our heads."

"You are so unlike your brother, it's crazy," she said, grinning. "I'm not sure the words *thank you* are in his vocabulary."

"Max is an acquired taste. I apologize on his behalf."

Aoife chuckled and her eyes dropped to someone standing behind Jack. He turned around to see a little girl with dark hair and a toy princess tiara staring at him.

"Say hi, Megan," Aoife said.

The girl just looked at Jack with wide eyes.

"Hi there," he said, smiling.

Then the little girl's eyes widened even more and she disappeared around the corner.

"I hope she's not afraid of me," Jack said to Aoife.

"She's just shy. She'll warm up to you in no time."

"She's the seer, right? The one who saw the prophecy about Schuyler?"

Aoife nodded. "I think maybe seeing figures from her visions in real life is a little overwhelming."

"I don't blame her. I'm still getting used to the idea."

"If you need anything, just holler," Aoife said.

Just then, Schuyler appeared, carrying a duffel bag in one hand and a backpack in the other. Her round blue eyes brightened when she saw Jack.

"Hey," she said.

"All good? No trouble?" Aoife asked.

"No trouble. Not counting Max. He's in a mood. He'll be here with the sleeping bags soon. He's just taking his own sweet time."

"I'll see if he needs any help," Aoife said, leaving Schuyler and Jack alone.

Schuyler set down the duffel bag and backpack and tucked her hair behind her ears. "It's not much, but I brought you some clothes and snacks. Oh, and some books too. I know you like to read."

Jack's heart grew warm. He was touched to learn that she remembered. One of his favorite places was the library at the Force mansion. Now that he could never go back there, it felt like a part of him had been removed. But the fact that Schuyler knew about his love of reading made him blush, and he couldn't stop smiling.

She continued: "I didn't know what you liked, though, so I brought you a bunch of stuff. Manga, mystery, one of my dad's books about boats, a musician's biography from my mom's shelf, plus . . ." She pulled out an old book with strange markings on it, chaos sigils. "I borrowed this from the Repository of History before it was destroyed. Kingsley was going to teach me some sigils. I've only flipped through it, it's not exactly a page-turner. But it's still kind of cool. Figured it might pique your interest. I can get you more if these are too boring."

Jack took the book into his hands. "It's perfect, thank you so much."

Schuyler tapped her thighs with her hands awkwardly. Jack had been asleep for two months, two months he could have spent with her, and the two of them felt like strangers again. He'd been trapped in an illusion for so long, hearing her voice again was like seeing the blue sky after years of rain.

He flipped open the chaos book and traced his hand on the thin pages. The text was so small, and the pages so wide, he would have a lot of reading to do. He noticed that Kingsley Martin had made notes in the margins.

"I heard about Kingsley," Jack said softly. "Max told me."

Schuyler looked down at the threads in her hands. "Kingsley was like a brother to me . . . I miss him. But it's not your fault."

Jack closed the book and sat down on the cot. "I just wish I had been able to make everything better. I don't want to leave you again."

Schuyler took a seat beside him and he could feel the warmth of her closeness. His whole body buzzed; her presence was enough to make him dizzy. She smelled like springtime, just like always.

"How are you feeling?" she asked.

"Better, thanks. Especially now." He saw Schuyler's cheeks pinken and she lowered her head bashfully. "I'm sorry I left. I didn't mean to be gone for so long."

"I know," she said. "You told me not to come looking for you, but you had to know I wouldn't listen." She pulled out his letter from her coat. It was as smooth as cloth from being handled so much.

Jack smiled softly. "I'm glad you didn't listen to me, for the record."

They sat in comfortable silence, both of them looking at their own hands, before Schuyler whispered, "I never stopped looking for you."

Her gaze made his insides turn to mush. All Jack wanted to do was kiss her, lose himself and all sense of time in her touch.

He remembered that night when he'd come to her room after he first tried and failed to break Kingsley out of confinement. She looked at him through her window with surprise and a little bit of fear, and she had every reason not to let him inside, but she did anyway. She had held him then, and pressed her forehead to his, and he could finally breathe again.

That felt like a lifetime ago. His gaze fell to her lips, but he felt like he couldn't kiss her now. He wasn't sure he deserved to look at her with so much longing, not after what the siren had made him see. Schuyler leaned in, but he cleared his throat and turned his head away.

Schuyler's breath hitched and she bit her lip. "I'm sorry," she said. "I know, we still barely know each other . . ."

"It's not that. It's . . ."

"What?"

"The siren was powerful," he said. "I didn't know what was happening until it was too late."

"What did she do to you?"

Jack thought about it for a breath. He wasn't sure he wanted to tell Max, but he trusted Schuyler. When he looked into her eyes again, he never felt safer.

"The siren . . . her name was Harmony. She sang me songs that hypnotized me. I would have done anything for her. I would have killed for her. She tried to keep me in a world she thought I would never want to leave. It was supposed to be perfect. But she forgot one thing."

"What?"

"You weren't there."

Schuyler flushed deeply and tucked a curl behind her ear. He loved it when she did that.

Jack continued. "She tried to convince me that I was happy there, that I could finally be free from the burden of my past, but it never felt right. She tried so hard to keep me caged, and the scary part is that it almost worked. Once she knew how to manipulate me, she tried to use you against me."

"What do you mean?" Schuyler must have noticed the pain dart across his face because she quickly added, "You don't have to tell me. It's okay."

"No, it's all right. I would want to know if I were you." Jack took another deep breath. "When I tried to fight against her, tried to escape, she showed me visions that were so real, I could have sworn they were really happening. My worst nightmares, come to life. She showed me visions of my life outside the dream, what would happen if I left her; she desperately tried to prove that my existence would only bring more suffering. She showed me what would happen to you. My curse, Abbadon's curse, destroying everything I cared about. Destroying you." He looked at Schuyler, hoping to find no judgment in her eyes, and when he didn't see any, he said, "I found you, dying, because of me. I held you in my arms, and you looked at me . . . You asked me why, and I couldn't say. I saw the light go out in your eyes, Schuyler. I held you as you died."

Her hand found its ways into his. Her skin was warm and soft. That simple gesture made him feel a thousand times better. Panic had bubbled up inside him when he thought about the illusions of the siren, but it vanished when her hand touched his.

"So when you woke me up," he said, "I heard your voice, saw your face, but thought I was still stuck in that nightmare. I thought it was just another trick. It had been so real."

Jack swallowed thickly. Saying it out loud was putting his worst fears out into the universe. For years, he had convinced himself that he had killed his parents. There was no evidence, no tangible proof of his suspicions, but he was sure his curse had destroyed their airplane, sent them plummeting to their deaths, even though he had been nowhere near them when the accident occurred. Accidents, no matter the distance, happened frequently around the one who was burdened with Abbadon's spirit.

Generations of Blue Bloods before him had fallen in tragedy. Plane crashes, house fires, assassinations, freak accidents, and he'd carried that guilt for them in each of his incarnations. His destiny as Abbadon had haunted his every step, reminding him that his only purpose in this life was to cause ruin and rot to all of creation. He would never create anything. He was only good for one thing and it was to turn the world to ashes. Harmony used that against him, made him believe his worst fears about himself.

"It's not going to happen," she said. She squeezed his hand, assuring him. "I'm not going anywhere. I know you won't hurt me."

He wanted to believe her, but a part of him knew that the universe operated in ways beyond even his control.

Schuyler fished around in her coat pocket. "Here," she said. "This is for you."

She held out a red cord, a bracelet. It was made of soft embroidery thread knotted and wound into a tight-laced chevron pattern in bright red. She chewed off the last bit of thread with her front teeth and Jack held out his arm. The cord was long enough; she wrapped it around his wrist several times, and when she tied it securely in a knot, it fit him perfectly. He traced his finger over it. It was still warm from being in her pocket. "You made this?"

Schuyler nodded and blushed. "Aoife mentioned once how objects created by hand can have a certain power. I thought about you when I was making this. I kept thinking, when I found you, I'd never let you feel like you were alone again. That you'd always have me right there with you, no matter what."

"Thank you," he said, smiling. His gaze drifted to her lips again. He wanted to taste her, feel the nip of her front teeth on his lower lip, breathe her in.

Schuyler shifted even closer to him, her eyes drifting to his lips as his eyes were drifting to hers. When she looked him in the eyes again, his heart wanted to fly. All his thoughts scrambled into one malfunctioning mess and it was glorious. Touching her was like touching a live wire. She was absolutely incredible.

Jack wanted her so badly, his whole body ached. All she had to do was say the word, and he would be hers. Being with her wasn't the same as being under Harmony's spell. He'd never felt this alive.

"Jack," she whispered. Her breath tickled his face; they were so close. He only had to close the last distance. "Please kiss me."

Before he could, a voice made them both jump.

"Hate to break up this little love session . . ." Max stood there, his arms folded across his chest, and Schuyler and Jack pulled away from each other. Max had a smug little smile on his face and Jack huffed. Typical. Max just couldn't resist being himself. Annoying.

Schuyler gave Jack an amused smile before saying, "Can we help you with something?"

Max stepped forward and tossed the rolled-up sleeping bags to the floor. "In case you two forgot, my power is out there somewhere and Lucifer could be using it to break open the universe any minute. If he really is trying to make new vampires, we have to end it now."

"Wait, what?" Schuyler looked horrified. "New vampires?"

Jack explained the old vampire myth and added, "I don't know for certain, but I think Aldrich needs to find a host who's capable of consuming Azrael's blood so they can use Michael's sword to break open dimensions. But I don't have any proof."

"Did you tell Aoife?"

Max nodded. "Just now. Any way this goes, I need my power back. It's the only way for sure we can get the sword before he can find someone who will break open the dimensions for him."

Schuyler blinked a few times, processing the new information, before she rose to her feet. "If we get Azrael's blood back, we get the key. We can stop all of this. But we need a better plan. We can't just waltz in and take it. We need the Paladins . . . maybe Aoife can talk to her spy."

Max said, "I want to help. It's what Kingsley would do." Jack admired his determination. It was something he'd always admired about his brother; the guy never knew when to quit, even when it was bad for his health.

"You need to be careful," Jack said. "You can't rush into things like you used to."

"Screw that. Kingsley would have had a plan by now. If I could walk into Purgatory myself, I'd pull Kingsley out with my bare hands and he'd tell you himself."

Schuyler gasped. Her eyes widened as an idea sparked in her mind. Her gaze went from Jack to Max and back. She was as bright as the sun and Jack couldn't look away. In that moment, he truly knew how much he loved her. She wasn't some illusion to toy with his heart or his head. She was real.

"I have an idea," she said.

TWENTY-ONE

MAX

*S*chuyler pointed to a huge tome in Jack's hands. "Kingsley's book," she said.

Max recognized the symbol on the leather binding. It was a chaos sigil. He'd seen the same kind of markings when he'd been hunting Kingsley, back when he intended to kill him. He ran his hand over the cover, feeling the impression of the chaos sigil beneath his fingers. The book hummed with latent power.

"A book is going to get my power back?" he asked Schuyler.

"No. Give it to me." Jack handed the tome to her, and she flipped it open, pacing back and forth as she pushed through the pages.

"Care to fill us in, or do you just want us to sit here like morons?" Max asked. Jack elbowed him and Max added, "Please." Which prompted Jack's satisfied little smile. Schuyler didn't seem to notice, though. She was focused on finding something in the book.

"I have no idea if it's even possible," she said under her breath, more like she was talking to herself than to others. "But Kingsley proved to me that anything is on the table so long as you set the right intention. The universe was born out of chaos, so it wants to go back to its natural state. You just need to know how to get it there."

"Right," Max said. "How much did he teach you?"

Schuyler shrugged. "Enough."

"More than enough. She's good at it too," Jack said. "She created smoke out of nothing so we could escape city hall."

"I'm nowhere near as good at Kingsley was, but thanks." She blushed. Max rolled his eyes. These two could not get enough of each other, and it was starting to turn from sweet to sickening.

"Come on, my patience is thin," Max said. "Once Schuyler finally tells us what she's doing, you two can start reciting poetry to each other again or whatever."

Jack gave him a back-off look.

"That's what you want, isn't it?" asked Max.

Schuyler was too focused on her work to care. She scoured through the pages, her eyes moving quickly over the text. The pages were so thin they were almost transparent. "One second, hold on. This book isn't exactly light reading. I barely know if it's real or not, but I recall—yes, I found it." She put her finger down on a page about halfway through the book, her eyes bright with excitement.

Jack read the header aloud. "'Resurrection Sigils.'"

Max's heart leaped. He pulled the book closer and scanned it over. The text on the page was small, and he had to lean in close to get a better look. It was packed with information, but immediately, with the first word, he knew this was everything he'd been looking for. He read from the book: "'Resurrection of an eternal soul is possible so long as balance is maintained. A soul can be returned to the physical realm if another soul takes its place in stasis. Equilibrium in the void. Balance in nothingness.'"

"A soul for a soul," Jack said softly, lost in his thoughts.

Max remembered the vision he'd had of Mimi journeying to hell to get Kingsley back. She had to give up a part of her soul in exchange for his return. That otherwise selfish girl forfeited a part of herself to save the love of her life. It's what was required to bring about something so monumental: ultimate sacrifice.

What could Max give up to save Kingsley now?

He was mortal. Mimi had been at the height of her power. Would it even be possible for Max to journey to Purgatory now that he had no power at all?

"I'll do it," he said. "I'll switch places with Kingsley."

"Like hell you will," Jack said, his eyes sharp. "Because if you do, then I'll have to go in after you."

"Oh, stop, both of you. We are not starting an endless cycle of self-sacrifice," Schuyler said. She gestured to the page. "You are missing the point. Don't you see?"

Max waited. He exchanged glances with Jack, who looked equally expectant, and Max threw out his arms. "How about you clue us in?"

The look in Schuyler's eyes was something akin to a bolt of lightning, beautiful but scary.

"What if," she said, "we trade Kingsley's soul for Aldrich Duncan's?"

TWENTY-TWO

SCHUYLER

*S*chuyler was practically vibrating with excitement when she told them her idea. The boys looked at each other, mirroring their shocked expressions back to each other. Schuyler could barely keep it together. Her mind was rushing so quickly through all the possibilities, even the small chance that she could somehow save Kingsley was enough to send her stomach into somersaults.

Max turned back to her. "I admit, it's not the worst idea."

Schuyler had to smile. "That's halfway to a compliment."

"Don't get used to it."

"Is chaos capable of doing something like that?" Jack asked. He looked at the book too, his emerald eyes dancing as he read the page.

"I don't see why not. Chaos makes up everything. We just need to know how to harness it. It would seal Lucifer in Purgatory and get Kingsley out in the process. If we stop Lucifer, we can stop the universes from collapsing onto one another. We can stop the monsters from coming through and you can get your power back," Schuyler said, the last part to Max. "We can finally end this."

No more Superimposition. No more memories of another world, she thought. In a way, she felt like she'd be losing contact with a part of herself, but she had to do it. It was the only way to make sure all the worlds were safe.

Max started pacing. He pinched the bridge of his nose tightly with his thumb and forefinger, something Schuyler noticed he did whenever his mind started racing.

Jack had read enough from the book and he nodded. "It's crazy, and dangerous . . . but it could work. But to bring Kingsley back, it would require an insane amount of energy. The spell would have to be strong enough to move mountains."

"Where do we even get energy like that?" Max asked. "The power of Abbadon and Azrael combined might have had a shot, but just you alone? I don't know."

"Aldrich is using energy in a similar way, right?" Schuyler said. "He's using vampire power to weaken the barriers between worlds."

"But how would we do it? I'm not letting Jack get strapped to any machine."

Schuyler definitely didn't want that either, but just then she remembered something. "Kingsley mentioned once how chaos sigils can be used for different purposes. Some of them can be super small, but some can be enormous, as large as a city. Cities built thousands of years ago by ancient civilizations used to have roads that would loop and wind around in shapes as protection against spirits, giant sigils charged by people using them every day."

"Well, do you know of any ancient civilization that used chaos magic in its city planning?" Max asked.

That was the tricky part. Schuyler had no idea. She didn't think they had time to go out into the middle of the desert and draw a sigil as large as a state to bring Kingsley back. It would take years, maybe a decade to create something that big. She stared at the sigil, trying to find an answer in the intersecting lines and circles.

"It's a good idea," Max said, "but unless you figure something out, it'll stay just that: an idea. Do we have another plan?"

While the boys talked, debating the best course of action, Schuyler tapped the tip of her thumb against her front teeth. Something had to be there. The sigil . . . She felt like she was missing something, that it was right in front of her nose, but she wasn't able to see it. The sigil somehow looked oddly familiar.

"Wait." She held out her hands, frozen in thought. The twins stared at her.

"What now?" Max asked.

Schuyler didn't reply. Instead she tore the page out of the book. "Aoife!" she yelled.

"Hey! We might need that!" Max cried. She ignored him. If she was right, this would change everything. She rushed out of the alcove and deeper into the Warehouse.

Jack asked, "Schuyler, what is it?" But she was too far down the aisle to respond.

She found Aoife and Megan sitting in the weapons cache at the ammo table, and Aoife looked up curiously when she flew in. "What's up?"

Breathless, Schuyler asked, "Do you have any maps?"

"Tons," Aoife said, standing. "Follow me."

She took Schuyler to a large crate filled with hundreds of rolled-up maps, all of which looked ancient. Jack and Max caught up then, eyeing each other curiously. "Anything in particular you're looking for?" Aoife asked.

"New York."

Aoife flipped through the documents, past drawings of mythical creatures and odd markings on aging parchment. "Here we go." The map was a few decades old, but it would do.

"Jack, I need a light. Max, you and Aoife hold this up."

Jack brought her a lamp from the corner of the room, and Aoife and Max held the map between them. It took a moment to adjust everyone, moving back and forth until the arrangement was just right. Then Schuyler held the page of the book up to the light. The paper was thin and translucent enough that the lines of the sigil appeared as shadows on the map; she turned the page slightly and it all came together.

Max swore under his breath, Jack's eyes widened, and Schuyler's heart leaped.

The streets of Manhattan lined up with the lines of the resurrection sigil. Perfect match.

TWENTY-THREE

SCHUYLER

"The streets of Manhattan form a resurrection sigil," Schuyler explained. "We can trap Lucifer in Purgatory and bring Kingsley back from the dead." Saying her idea out loud, she felt like her whole body was vibrating. Her hands shook as she smoothed out the map Aoife and Max had laid out on the table. She'd explained everything to Aoife, and thankfully her friend was able to keep up. Max and Jack had chimed in whenever she needed them to fill in the gaps. Megan was too little to understand what was going on, so she watched quietly from atop a crate as Schuyler traced the lines of the sigil along the lines of the map with a marker. Most of the lines moved through the city like arteries in a human body. The whole island was primed for magical workings. This entire time, the answer had literally been at their feet.

Jack held up the book. "According to this, the sigil lines themselves are dormant unless these four points of the circle are activated with their own sigils. Once that happens, the chaos sigil is complete and primed to go," he said. Schuyler handed him a marker, and he highlighted each point with an X. Each lined up with various landmarks across the island, most of them historical sites.

"Grand Central Terminal, the Brooklyn Bridge, the Apollo Theater, and Rockefeller Center," said Schuyler, pointing to each site in turn. She knew the island so well, she could navigate around it with her eyes closed. "Do you think Paladins designed the city, anticipating the prophecy? Knowing it'd be useful one day?"

Aoife tugged at her lower lip thoughtfully as she watched the plan unfold. "It's not out of the realm of possibility," she said. "Honestly, this is the first I'm hearing about chaos magic, though, so you're going to have to take it slow. One more time. How does it work?"

Before Schuyler could answer, Max interrupted, "The sigils act as a sort of tuning signal to the chaos that makes up the universe. The right sigil with the right intention can make anything happen."

Schuyler looked at him, impressed.

Max shrugged. "What? Hunting Kingsley before took some work. I had to figure out what he was doing to sabotage my plans when I was working for Aldrich, so I did some reading of my own. Chaos magic isn't just exclusively a you thing."

Schuyler couldn't help but smile.

Jack continued: "But timing is key. We need to draw sigils with something, like chalk or paint, at the same time. If the activation sigil is broken or incomplete, the whole thing won't have enough power and we'll miss our chance."

"Graffiti, trespassing, slight misdemeanors—sounds like my kind of Friday-night fun," Aoife said. "Okay, so then we split up into teams. We tackle this head-on. I think we need to go in teams of two, at least. Preferably more."

"Do you have any Paladins to spare?" Schuyler asked.

"We do, but . . . What about Lucifer? How does the sigil know to exchange him for Kingsley? What's to stop it from taking any other person standing in the magic circle? No offense, but I don't want to go to Purgatory for this Kingsley guy."

"Remember, the sigil is all about intention," Max said. "It's like drawing a bow and arrow, it won't know where to strike unless you aim it. And that's where Schuyler comes in. Your chosen one."

Jack read through the book. "It says here that the exchanged soul will be marked. But it's vague. I'm not sure what that means. Like, does it mean you point to him, or curse his name, or draw on him with a sigil?"

Max rolled his eyes. "Of course a cryptic old book of magic spells isn't going to make everything so easy."

Schuyler nodded. "We'll have to figure it out before we do anything. Aoife's right, we can't risk sending an innocent person to Purgatory." She glanced at Jack, knowing that this time she wouldn't lose him to do it. How exactly she was going to "mark" Lucifer, though, she didn't know. It was the one unknown variable. Improvising would not be an option, not for this.

Max seemed to have one other thing on his mind. "What about my sword? Michael's sword, I mean. I need my power back. I can't keep going on like this forever." He gestured to himself.

"If we remove Aldrich from the equation, it'll be easier to get the sword," Jack said. "We can figure it out from there. Trapping Lucifer in Purgatory clears the board."

Max sighed and pressed his lips shut. He didn't seem entirely satisfied, but he kept his thoughts to himself.

"When do we do this?" Aoife asked. "It might take us a bit to coordinate our teams."

Just then Theo burst into the room. "The concert!" he gasped, breathless, brandishing a piece of paper above his head. Before anyone could ask what he was talking about, he slapped the paper on top of the map. "The charity concert." It was a flyer for the event, a one-night-only extravaganza. Schuyler had seen those flyers posted all over the city. "The concert. That's when Lucifer will end the world."

"How do you know?" Schuyler asked.

"I just got word from our spy on the inside, someone working close with the event." Theo swallowed thickly and put his hands on his hips, still winded from rushing to deliver the news. "I bet a million people will be there. Easy."

An eerie silence fell on the room. Schuyler saw Aldrich's plan unfolding in front of her as everything started to make sense. "He wants an audience for the end of the universe," Schuyler said, suppressing the chill snaking down her spine.

Max nodded. "That's exactly what he wants. A show. And we can give it to him. With this." He jabbed his finger down on the map of the resurrection sigil.

"At least it gives us a few days," added Jack. "We just have to make sure we're quick and work as a team to see it through."

Months ago, Schuyler never would have believed that she would be collaborating with Lucifer's heirs and a group of mortal Paladins to stop Lucifer from collapsing the universe. But she wouldn't trust anyone else with what they were about to do. This was the best team for the job, and she was glad they were all there with her. To do it alone would have been impossible.

She met Jack's gaze and nodded confidently. She was ready for this.

Jack gave her the smallest smile before he looked at the map, like a chess player analyzing a board. "I'll help Aoife and the Paladins coordinate. Plan our strategy. If we're going into battle, we need to be prepared."

"Good idea," Aoife said.

They had two of Lucifer's top agents on their side now; it was a rare opportunity to take advantage of knowing the enemy. Jack and Max had exclusive insight that they couldn't leave on the table. They needed every trick in their pockets to pull this off.

Schuyler still had other things on her mind. "As long as we're settled here, I think I should go home. I'm worried about my parents."

Jack looked worried. "Is something wrong?"

"No, no," she said. "I want to put up some protective sigils around the house. It's the least I can do to make sure that they're safe. I can't stay away from them for long."

"I can help you," Max said. "I know my way around a sigil or two. You can thank me later."

She was grateful for his confidence. The two of them bade the others good night, then Schuyler and Max were off.

Manhattan at night was never quiet, so Schuyler and Max merged into the flow of people walking on the sidewalks. Schuyler always felt something like whiplash when she rejoined the mass of normal people who had no idea what was really going on in the world. Ignorance was bliss.

Max walked in step alongside her and sighed. "Listen, I know you're the prophesied chosen one who will defeat Lucifer, and that's great and all, but you understand that this plan can go wrong in fifty million different ways, right?"

"You have a better idea?"

"No. I'm just saying. This isn't going to be easy."

"In my experience, anything worth doing is never easy. We're getting Kingsley back and putting Lucifer someplace where he can't hurt anyone ever again."

"I want Kingsley back just as much as you do. Probably more than you do. I'm just worried. If anything goes wrong and we miss our shot . . ."

"Are you afraid?"

Max made a face. "Me? Afraid? Yeah, right."

He was an awful liar. "Are you afraid that Kingsley might come back different? If Purgatory changed him in some way? What if it drove him mad? Would it be a worse fate to bring him back to Earth when his soul has already crossed into a plane of ethereal nothingness?"

"Shut up," he growled.

"Well, that's what *I'm* afraid of. All of that and more. So if you think you're the only one who gets to worry, you're wrong. I have to believe this is the only way to save him and everyone. I'm responsible for Kingsley's death too, and I need to make it right. Even if I'm scared."

When she looked at Max, his gaze was firmly on the ground. They didn't say anything even as they turned the corner onto Schuyler's street.

"Want to know something else?" she asked.

"What?"

"I'm scared that I'll never succeed . . . even if we win here. What if, like in that other world, I defeat Lucifer, then I wake up in some new world? Everything I've done, every person I've met, every relationship I've had, back to square one *again* and I'm destined to defeat Lucifer again and again, forever? When will it be over?"

Max didn't speak. What could he even say?

She admitted, "I haven't said this to anyone yet, not even Jack. We haven't had time to really talk. So, congratulations. You're the first to know about some of my deepest insecurities. I can't wait for you to hold that over my head forever." It felt good getting the words off her chest, but she regretted spilling her guts out to Max Force of all people. If it were Mimi, Schuyler expected the girl would have laughed in her face. But Max just watched the traffic speed by as they waited for the light to change at a crosswalk together.

"Yeah," Max finally said. "I'm afraid too."

That, surprisingly enough, made Schuyler feel a tiny bit better. It didn't fix everything, but it at least made her burden a little lighter.

They made it back to Schuyler's loft and found it empty. At least her parents wouldn't be tempted to ask her why she was drawing cryptic markings above the doorways and on the windowsills. She and Max used the book to find some of the simplest sigils for home protection and Schuyler borrowed some of her father's blue paint.

Max held the book open for her so she could copy the sigils while standing on a dining room chair, gently tracing the lines as carefully and with as much intention as possible. After the first sigil, she could already feel the invisible wall cascading across the frame like a curtain. Any supernatural monster intending to hurt anyone inside was going to have to break the sigil to get through. They moved to every possible entrance in the house, finally ending in Schuyler's bedroom, protecting her window. She put the finishing touches on the final line in the sigil and admired her work.

"I should do this over at Oliver's," Schuyler said.

Out of the corner of her eye, she sensed Max grow very still. She looked at him, taking in the shadow that had passed over his face, a mix of anger and surprise.

"Of course . . ." he said. He put his hand to his head and squeezed his eyes shut.

"What's wrong?"

"My memories were all scrambled from the Superimposition. It's clearer now, like everything snapped into focus when you said his name. Shit, I remember. When I brought Kingsley out and Leviathan caught us, he was with someone."

"Max, come on. What?"

Max snapped the book shut with a thud and tossed it onto her bed. He leveled his gaze at her and that was enough to chill her to the bone. "How much can you really trust your friend?"

"What are you talking about?"

"Oliver Golding-Chang. He led Leviathan to us. He's working for Lucifer."

Twenty-Four

SCHUYLER

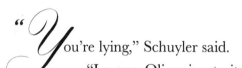

"You're lying," Schuyler said.

"I swear. Oliver is a traitor."

"That doesn't make any sense."

"The Superimposition messed with my head, but I remember it now, clear as day. The look in his eyes when he caught us. Schuyler, you have to believe me."

She couldn't. Max was a liar. He might have changed for the better over the course of these past few days, but would it really be beyond him to mess with her like this now? Max took a step toward her.

"Kingsley and I almost made it, but Oliver had been spying on us. He told Leviathan where we were and got us captured, said something about a reward too. It's Oliver's fault that Kingsley died. He betrayed you, Schuyler. He's been working for Aldrich Duncan this whole time, right under your nose."

"No! You're wrong! Oliver is a good person. My best friend! He would never—"

"Schuyler, think about it. I'm begging you."

Schuyler's ears rang and her face burned. "You don't know him!"

"It doesn't matter! Tell me what he said."

"He said he saw it happen, saw you and Kingsley get ambushed, but he was hiding, and he ran away—"

"Exactly. How exactly did he manage that when the whole place was crawling with Silvers? You really think a monster like Leviathan would let any Red Blood in a five-block radius escape?"

She desperately tried to fight the sinking feeling in her gut. "He's careful. He's not like the others. He's my Conduit."

Max sneered. "Oh, I bet it was real easy for him to get you blood in those pouches under your bed, wasn't it?"

"Stop."

"Lucifer has had all the Conduits systematically wiped out, yet you're telling me that Oliver got away. Lucky, is he?"

"Stop talking."

"And all this time you haven't questioned any of it? Oliver used you. Who knows what for, but it's obvious. It's the perfect cover."

"Why? How do you know?"

Max's eyes flashed. "Because it's what I would have done."

Schuyler's vision was swimming, and she clenched her hands into fists. A part of her knew that what Max was saying made sense, but her heart felt like it was shattering, and the other part of her, the part that desperately wanted to cling to years of memories with Oliver, didn't want to listen to a word that Max had to say.

She struggled to keep her voice even. "If he really is working for Lucifer, why hasn't he turned me over already? He could have lured me somewhere at any time. Why didn't he, then? None of it makes any sense. He wouldn't betray me!"

Max looked about ready to punch his fist through the wall. When he started pacing, he pinched the bridge of his nose so hard it looked painful. He squeezed his eyes shut and groaned, "Don't be so naive."

"I know Oliver's heart. I know he wouldn't do anything to hurt me. You must not be remembering right. The Superimposition could be making you confused. You're sure you saw him?"

Max had stopped pacing all of a sudden and looked at her. "Wait. How do you 'know his heart'?" She didn't need to say the words in order for him to figure it out. "You— What did you *do*?"

Schuyler's mouth worked as she tried to find the words. She could only tell the truth. "He's my Familiar."

The Sacred Kiss was a deeply personal and private affair between a vampire and their chosen Familiar, and once it was sealed, there was no going back. That night at the Mercer Hotel had been the closest she'd ever gotten to another person in this world. When she fed from Oliver's neck, she tapped into his feelings for her. It all poured into her body, the depth of his love for her filling her up to the point of overflowing. She remembered how sweet he tasted, how she almost couldn't stop drinking from him, until she made herself stop out of guilt. She couldn't reciprocate his feelings. She loved Jack, and Oliver had gotten so angry with her when he learned of it, like she'd led him on. She understood his heartbreak, but their bond had been sealed with blood.

Max collapsed into her desk chair, holding his head in his hands.

"Of course you'd do something like that. Of course you would perform the Sacred Kiss with the enemy."

Schuyler's anger emerged hot and loud. "Don't you dare say that! I needed to prepare to fight Lucifer. It was the only way I could get strong enough."

"Don't you see? This was all a part of his plan from the beginning."

"What do you mean?"

"Oliver wanted to perform the *Caerimonia Osculor* with you, become your Familiar, because he knew what makes it so special. It's not just a kiss, it's a contract. Now that your souls are tied together, you can't harm him without harming yourself. The bond you created is permanent. He can do anything Aldrich wants him to do and you can't stop him."

Schuyler felt like she'd been hit by a car. Tears burned her eyes. "There has to be something we're missing. . . ."

"There's nothing else to it!" Max shouted. "He used you!"

Schuyler stopped breathing. It was like her lungs had forgotten how to work. She hated Max's tone as much as she hated her own blindness to the truth. The way Max was looking at her made her feel like she was a foolish girl who had been duped, and she hated it.

"You're wrong." Schuyler shook her head. She didn't want to listen.

"Don't believe me all you want; it's true."

She couldn't do it. Max had given her every reason not to trust him. *He* was the one she should be wary of. He was the one who had tried to kill her, tried to kill Kingsley, and she was going to take his word about Oliver?

No. No! Ollie cannot be an agent of Lucifer.

"Where are you going?" Max asked. Schuyler had moved to her bedroom door.

She glared at him over her shoulder, pausing with her hand on the doorknob. "I'm going to talk to Oliver. I have to hear him say it, figure out the truth for myself."

But as soon as she opened the door, she stopped dead in her tracks. Standing in her living room with a small lunch cooler and a gentle smile was none other than Oliver Golding-Chang himself. Schuyler's heartbeat pounded in her ears as her throat got very tight.

"Truth about what?" Oliver asked.

TWENTY-FIVE

SCHUYLER

*S*chuyler closed the bedroom door behind her, shutting Max off from Oliver's view. Despite everything she'd just said to Max, she couldn't help the doubt wriggling in the back of her mind. Was it possible that Oliver had been working for Lucifer this whole time? Finding him standing in her living room after hearing Max's claims against him had put a small piton of fear in her spine.

"How did you get in here?" she asked.

Oliver put down the cooler on the dining room table. "I let myself in. Hope you don't mind. It's a habit now, I guess."

Schuyler tried not to make any sudden movements. Of course, she'd only set the intention of the sigil to keep out any supernatural monster. Oliver was free to come and go. She tried to act natural, but her body felt stiff and awkward. Oliver had brought her some fresh blood that had been donated to a nearby bank, fulfilling his Conduit duties as usual, and nothing seemed out of the ordinary. She needed to ignore the hot desire for fresh red blood. Her heart pounded painfully in her chest. She had to ask him if he was working for Aldrich—it was the only thing she could think about.

Perhaps he'd been blackmailed into it, or he had been given no other choice. Maybe his parents were being held hostage. There had to be an explanation as to why he was at city hall when Max tried to rescue Kingsley, why Max believed that Oliver had betrayed them to Leviathan, and gotten Kingsley killed in the process.

Oliver sorted through the blood pouches. "Are you hungry?" he asked. "Let's see. I got you some extra AB blood, I know how much you like it. Threw in a few O-negatives for good measure." Schuyler watched him without saying a word. She wanted to see if there was some clue on his face that would reveal his true intentions, some evidence she'd missed because she'd been blinded by their friendship. His loyalty toward her, his unwavering generosity, his devotion . . . Could it all have been a mask?

Oliver noticed she was staring at him, and he smiled. It was his classic, boyish grin that melted hearts in seconds. But in that moment, it was like a spell had worn off. Schuyler's heart had turned to stone.

"Are you working for Aldrich Duncan?" she asked.

Her question hung in the air for a moment, as if she were waiting for something, anything to happen.

Oliver's smile dropped and his expression turned into one of confusion. "What? Sky . . . What are you talking about?"

Schuyler just stared at him, peered into his eyes, searching for the truth. It made Oliver uncomfortable. He shook his head. "Why would you say something like that? How could you think that?" He came to her and took both her hands in his. She had to fight the urge to retreat. "Are you okay? Do you feel sick? Maybe you need something a little fresher."

She dropped his hands. "No, Ollie. No more blood. Answer my question. Are you working for Lucifer or aren't you?"

Oliver's eyes were swimming with hurt. "What has gotten into you? No! Of course I'm not! I'm with you!"

She backed away, but Oliver closed the gap. "Why are you asking me all these questions? Accusing me? I'm your Conduit. Why would I work for Lucifer?"

Guilt wormed into her gut. She was risking everything. She could very well lose her best friend because she was taking Max at his word. Her paranoia was tearing apart the only solid foundation of trust she had left. He had been her oldest, closest friend and she was putting it all on the line. But she sensed Ollie was lying. It was subtle, the way the skin around his eyes tightened and the corner of his mouth twitched. She clenched her jaw.

Oliver's face broke. The tears welled up, threatening to overflow. "You think I would do that to you? After everything we've been through together?" He started to cry, gentle tears falling down his cheeks. But Schuyler stood firm.

"Oliver."

And, just like that, he stopped. The facade dropped away. He let out an exasperated sigh.

"Fine," he said flatly. His entire demeanor changed. His shoulders dropped and he leaned back, wiping the tears from his cheeks like they were an inconvenient prop. "You got me."

Schuyler stood, horrified, rooted to the floor. It was as if her brain failed to fire up. Years of friendship . . . over. Just like that.

"You really spoiled it. I had the tears going and everything." He smiled at her, but it wasn't the usual boyish grin anymore. It was sharp and wicked, warped as if in a fun-house mirror. He traced his fingers lazily over the blood pouches. "After all these years together . . ."

"Oliver, what have you done?"

"What I needed to do, to get what I want. How did you figure it out? Who told you?"

At that moment, Schuyler's bedroom door opened and Max emerged. He glared at Oliver, his fists clenched at his sides.

Max, you prideful idiot! Schuyler thought. Everyone who had thought Max was dead would know he was alive now. One of their best-kept secrets was out in the open, glaring at Lucifer's secret agent.

Oliver's smile split wider. He looked surprised at first and then thoroughly entertained. "Max Force? Him? Really? Oh, this is *rich*. Disappointing son back from the dead!" He clapped, threw back his head, and laughed, and Schuyler spotted a silver chain around his neck. A small quartz crystal glowed beneath his shirt. It was filled with a blue liquid and swirled with a silver mist, moving as if it were an animal trapped in a cage.

Max saw it too, and his whole body stiffened. "Is that . . ."

Oliver noticed what they were looking at and pulled the charm stone out from his collar. "Oh, this? Just a little gift for my loyalty. It's the blood of Azrael. Aldrich gave it to me. Pretty, isn't it?"

"Ollie, what are you doing with that?"

Max looked downright murderous as he growled, "That belongs to me!"

Oliver's eyes narrowed. "What makes you so deserving of anything?"

"Thousands of years of undying devotion and labor."

Oliver smiled. "Only to throw it all away in the end."

The light from Oliver's pendant cast a shadow upon his face from below, turning it into a warped version of the Oliver Schuyler had once known. What had happened to the friend who had given her half of his sandwich when she'd forgotten hers in elementary school? What had happened to the inside jokes? And the movie nights? And talking about college? Had it all been a lie? Schuyler could barely comprehend any of it.

Oliver smirked at Max. "Look at you now: powerless, weak, and slow."

"Give it back, mortal."

"Mortal? Look who's talking."

Max seethed. "You have no idea what you're toying with."

"Don't I? Aldrich has been preparing me, testing me. He knows I'm strong enough, stronger than you. Once we transfer Azrael's power to me at last during the concert, I'll have everything I've ever wanted. And I won't waste my gifts like you did." Schuyler remembered how sick Oliver had been and how he'd bounced back so quickly. Lucifer had been experimenting on him the whole time. Oliver would give Lucifer what he wanted.

It had been the plan all along. Oliver would be the one to wield Michael's sword to break the universe.

"Max . . ." Schuyler warned. She sensed what was about to happen. The way Max clenched and unclenched his fists was as subtle as a fireworks show on the Fourth of July. "There's still time. He doesn't have the power yet."

"I want what is *mine*," Max growled at Oliver through bared teeth.

Oliver looked amused. "What are you going to do about it?"

Max lunged and Oliver sidestepped. Max took a wild swing, reaching for Oliver's necklace, but Oliver was faster. It was a fair match now, mortal against mortal. Oliver ducked and countered with a hit of his own, connecting his fist with the side of Max's head, and Max crashed into the dining room table, sending the blood pouches flying and Stephen's paintings falling to the floor. Max groaned in pain.

"Oliver!" Schuyler cried, and moved in. Fangs out, she reached forward, but as if by some spell, she was held back by invisible hands. No matter how hard she pushed, or which way she moved toward him, her arms would spring back uselessly. She was pushing against invisible bonds, and still, nothing she did broke through. She moved like she did in her nightmares, as if she were swimming through molasses, her limbs made of rubber. She couldn't harm Oliver, even to stop him. This was the result of their Sacred Kiss.

Oliver grabbed Max by the front of his shirt and punched him again. Max wheezed in pain and tried to fight back, but Oliver wasn't done. He yanked Max off the table and hit him one last time, and Max's head whipped to the side. He went down to the floor hard, and there he stayed. He wasn't used to fighting like an ordinary mortal.

"You may be mortal now, but I've been mortal for longer. I've had more practice," Oliver spat, looking down on Max's prone body.

"Oliver, stop!" Schuyler cried. She tried pushing through to help Max, but it was useless. Oliver was going to kill him. And she was going to have to stand there and watch. Oliver just smiled at her. She'd never seen this side of him before, and it terrified her.

"Aldrich is using you, Oliver! Just like he used Max! Please, don't do this." Schuyler struggled against the invisible barrier, but her strength was waning. Her bond with Ollie was too strong.

"You'll understand once I become a Blue Blood like you. You'll see. I'm doing this for us." When he looked at her, his eyes were full of conviction. He truly believed in his cause. He wanted to become a vampire in order to be with her.

Max started to get up, but Oliver stepped on his back, pressing him to the floor. "You're nothing," he said. "Know your place. I'll let you live so you can learn that." Then he fled through the door, disappearing into the night.

Schuyler hurried to Max's side and helped him to his feet. His lip was bleeding and he looked dazed, but he glared after Oliver. He put the back of his wrist to his lips and frowned at the red blood on his skin. Schuyler held his face steady, getting a better look at his injuries, but a sound at the door made her whip around.

She expected Oliver had come back to finish the job, but instead her parents stood framed in the doorway, looking winded and flustered as they took everything in in an instant.

"Mom! Dad!" Schuyler gasped.

Max fell hard on the couch, no doubt concussed. Stephen rushed forward to check on him and Aurora held Schuyler tightly, brushing her curls away from her face, checking to see if she was hurt. Schuyler insisted she was okay, and Aurora looked around at the mess in the house, taking in the aftermath of the fight. Her eyes went to the pouches of blood and the sigils above the door and Schuyler's whole body went cold.

"I can explain, I . . ." Schuyler had no idea where to start. She hadn't expected it to happen like this and words were hard to formulate. But her mother didn't look confused, or shocked, or angry. She just looked sad.

"So it's time . . ." Aurora said. "Come sit. We need to talk."

PART THREE
DON'T LOOK BACK

TWENTY-SIX

SCHUYLER

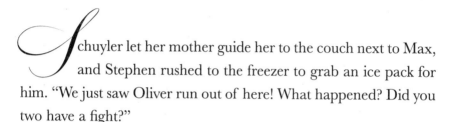

*S*chuyler let her mother guide her to the couch next to Max, and Stephen rushed to the freezer to grab an ice pack for him. "We just saw Oliver run out of here! What happened? Did you two have a fight?"

Aurora held her high heels in her hands, but she gently placed them on the dining room floor to pick up one of Stephen's paintings. It had been ruined in the fight. Her parents had just gotten back from Stephen's gallery opening, turning it into a date night. Schuyler was sure this was not how they'd expected their evening to end.

"Oliver attacked Max because . . ." Schuyler glanced at Max, who shook his head. Already the side of his face was starting to swell and bruise. This was all her fault. She should have stopped Oliver. Now that he had Azrael's power, ready to consume it for himself, he was the most dangerous mortal on the planet. They were running out of time.

"Attacked Max? Why would Oliver do such a thing?" Stephen asked.

"It's okay, Stephen," Aurora said. "It's time we tell Schuyler everything."

Stephen looked somber, but he nodded.

"What are you talking about?" Schuyler asked. Stephen handed the ice to Max as Aurora took her place on the love seat nearby. She sat with her back straight, her head high, and Stephen stood behind her, placing comforting hands on her shoulders. With a deep breath, she looked at Schuyler.

"We know you're a Blue Blood," Schuyler's mother said.

Shock knocked Schuyler halfway to Tuesday. Her whole body rang with her mother's words. She couldn't quite believe what she was hearing.

"How? How do you even know about Blue Bloods?" she asked. She tugged on her sleeves, self-consciously hiding her blue veins, even though there was little reason to do so anymore.

Aurora said, "Because I'm a vampire too."

Both Schuyler and Max went very still. Schuyler's vision shrank to a pinpoint as the truth came out. All this time, she'd thought her mother had been mortal. She managed to ask, "But . . . how?"

"I'm the archangel Gabrielle."

The room got so quiet, Schuyler swore she could hear the blood rushing through her skull. Kingsley had told her the archangels were dead, killed at Lucifer's command. How could he have been wrong?

Max shifted in his seat. "That's, no—it's impossible," he said.

Aurora just smiled. "And yet here I am."

Schuyler spoke quietly, afraid that her voice would break. "I don't understand. What's going on? Why didn't you tell me?"

"It was the only way to protect you. We needed to keep you out of harm's way until it was time," said Aurora. She grasped Stephen's hand and squeezed. He continued to rub her shoulders. "We had to wait for your consciousness to merge memories."

"So . . ." Schuyler's mouth felt very dry. She inched forward on the couch, too nervous to sit still. "You know about the life on another world? About another me?"

"Yes. I too have memories of another world, of my life spent in a coma. It was there in that world that Gabrielle reached out to warn me. She was able to contact me through the barrier separating our universes and showed me what was coming. I was still too weak to do anything, so she was the one who had allowed your consciousness to awaken, like hers. She was the one who opened your mind to other realities."

Schuyler swallowed thickly as she was reminded of another life sitting at her mother's hospital bed, holding her lifeless hand in the dark. Gabrielle had known that Schuyler, when she was in another world, would need memories of many Schuylers in order to beat Lucifer again.

"Will I have to go back? Once I beat Lucifer here?" Schuyler asked. "Back to that other world?" Without Jack, without Aoife, without the family she had found here?

"No. Your consciousness may have overlapped once, but you'll remain here. The other Schuyler you know still lives in her world, much like you live in your own. That's why it was imperative that we wait for you to settle into your memories on your own. We didn't want to shock you."

No kidding, Schuyler thought. She had so many questions, but she settled on one. "You mentioned that you were too weak. Why? What happened? Everyone thinks you're dead."

Aurora took another deep breath. "When Lucifer fell, my brother Michael and I were tasked with destroying him. But we failed. Lucifer killed Michael and then he offered me a place at his side in exchange for my life. I refused. Before he could deal the final blow, I used the last of my power to flee from my mortal body. It was my only chance at escape. The fight took almost everything out of me, so I remained in hiding for a millennium, being reborn into new bodies. It took Aldrich some time to recover his strength too, but he had had plans to dominate the world from the start. He found new ways of renewing his power faster than I could."

"Does he think you're dead?" Schuyler asked.

"No. He knows I live, but he also knows my power is not what it once was. Power is all that matters to him in the end."

"What did you do next?" Schuyler asked.

"I chose to stay, chose to fight, in my own way. Even though I can't do much else than communicate through dreams, I knew I had to hide and wait. Only recently, when I was reborn into this life, was I able to pass on my power to you. I could still shield you from Lucifer's eye and protect you, protect this family. But it would seem that our time has run out."

"So you're mortal? I really am a half-vampire?" Schuyler asked her father.

"We knew you'd be special, we just didn't know how special." His eyes sparkled with pride.

Schuyler held her own face, her fingers cold against her hot cheeks. It was a lot to take in.

"Were you able to rescue Abbadon?" Aurora asked.

Schuyler shouldn't have been surprised that her mother knew about him. "Yes."

"That's good. I tried to awaken him while he dreamed, but the spell he was under was strong. He'd been fighting for so long, but he needed you."

The ice in his ziplock bag shifted as Max lowered it from his face. His eyes shone as he asked quietly, "So then . . . do you know who I am?" He swallowed thickly, but Aurora smiled.

"Yes, Azrael."

Those two words seemed to break Max. He let out a shudder of a gasp like he'd been holding his breath, and he lowered his head in shame. "I'd been deceived by Lucifer's promises. I was so weak. Please, forgive me." It had been Azrael and Abbadon who had killed Michael and Gabrielle under Lucifer's orders. He'd failed on that front as well. But Gabrielle still lived. Whether he felt guilty or relieved, maybe both at the same time, Schuyler couldn't tell.

Aurora took Max's chin in her hand and gently raised his head. She made him look at her, but her gaze was soft. "I've been watching you for a while now. Though you might not have Azrael's power at this moment, you're not a failure. Your past is not what makes your future. You have a long road ahead of you."

Max lowered his head once more. Schuyler could tell he was crying silently.

She could hardly believe what she was hearing. Her head felt like it had been dunked in an ice bath. She licked her lips as words spilled out of her at lightning speed. "Monsters are breaking through dimensions because of Lucifer. He's opening rifts to other worlds, using vampire power. We think he'll use an archangel's sword to shatter the multiverse."

Gravely, Aurora glanced at Stephen and sighed. "Unfortunately, we know all too much about his plans. He's becoming stronger every day. And I fear that Oliver is at the center of it all. . . . Does he have it?"

It. Azrael's power. Max buried his head in his hands. He slumped into the couch like the weight of several worlds was resting upon his head.

"Yes," Schuyler said. "Is it even possible to pass the power on to a mortal?"

"It involves enacting a long-forgotten ritual, but it's possible. That boy . . ." Aurora let out a long breath and shook her head. "I sensed such envy in him. I didn't know exactly what he was planning or how deeply he'd truly fallen into Lucifer's clutches, but yes, Lucifer will use him to get what he wants. I tried to reach out to Oliver in his dreams, but I failed to get through to him."

Schuyler asked, "Do you think Oliver knows who you are?"

Aurora thought about it for a moment. It was a valid question, but she said, "Oliver would have no way of knowing who I am. As a mortal, he can't sense what a vampire can."

"But he knows I'm a vampire."

"He does, but he doesn't know your origin. Lucifer may be a master manipulator, but his focus can be narrow. It's his fatal flaw. He couldn't possibly predict that you could exist. He may think that you're like the monsters that have come through dimensions. But my power cannot shield you from his sight any longer."

"There's nothing else you can do?" Schuyler was starting to feel desperate. "Aldrich Duncan seems unstoppable. He's killing people, growing stronger. I had a vision . . . I thought it was just a dream, but now I don't know anymore."

Aurora smiled. "Ah, that must have been my doing as well. It's called remote viewing. My consciousness can leave my body, and I can watch events unfold from miles away. It's how I've been able to keep an eye on Aldrich all this time. You must have tapped into my session somehow."

Schuyler's heart leaped. "Can you show me Oliver right now?"

"I could try, but . . ."

"Show me. Please. Oliver mentioned consuming Azrael's power at the concert. There's still time to stop him. I need to see him."

Aurora nodded once and held out her hands. "Place your hands on top of mine," she said. Schuyler did as she was told. Her mother's hands were warm and soft as she gently closed them around Schuyler's. "Don't let go."

TWENTY-SEVEN

SCHUYLER

*S*chuyler had never done anything like remote viewing before. She didn't know what to expect, but she trusted her mother with her whole heart.

"Ready?" Aurora asked.

Schuyler swallowed and nodded, finding security in her mother's warm, dark eyes. Aurora gave her a small smile and swept her away.

It was just like her dream. One minute she was sitting in her living room; the next she was catapulted into the night sky, soaring across the city, the wind whipping through her hair. She was nothing more than a ghost, a whisper, but she felt her mother by her side, even though she couldn't see her. Schuyler had to remember she wasn't really flying, that she was still at home, but the sensation thrilled her.

She flew over the city, cutting across rooftops in SoHo, heading for Midtown. Everything looked so small from up high. Oliver's building loomed in her vision, and she hurtled up past story after story until she reached his apartment. It stood out like a lighthouse in the dark.

Like water through a sieve, she melted through the glass-window walls and entered Oliver's home. Being back here now, after everything she knew, felt like she'd stepped into another world. She'd lost track of how many times she'd stayed over, how many times she'd felt safe here. It was like a second refuge. She knew where all the snacks in the cabinets were kept, how to open the door to the bathroom in the hall so it wouldn't get stuck, she even had her own mug she used whenever she came over. How many nights had she spent here? How many days after school? Talking with Oliver, laughing, sharing secrets . . .

Had any of it been real?

The elevator door opened and Oliver stepped out, worrying at the charm stone around his neck. He looked troubled and thoughtful, his knuckles still red from his fight with Max. At first, he didn't notice a handful of Silvers lingering in the shadows. Then one Silver stepped forward, and Oliver took half a step back, startled.

"You can't hurt me. You need me," he said, clutching the pendant in one hand and holding out his other.

The Silver sneered at him, but a voice came from the living room. "At ease," it said.

It was Aldrich Duncan. He sat on the couch, his arms stretched out casually, a mug of tea—Schuyler's mug—steaming in front of him on the coffee table. "Good evening, Oliver."

Swallowing his fear, the boy steadied his nerves and strode toward Aldrich. "My lord."

"Where were you?" Aldrich asked coolly.

Oliver dropped to one knee and bowed his head. "I was . . . I don't have an excuse."

"You should be preparing for your ascension."

"I'm ready."

"Not quite. We've only just begun."

"I won't disappoint you. I have news." Oliver took a breath. "Max Force is alive."

Aldrich went as still as a statue. Slowly, he looked at Oliver, his eyes fierce. "How do you know this?"

"I saw him."

Aldrich stood. "Where?"

"Outside the Repository of History. He fled, though. He'll be long gone by now."

Oliver was lying. Why? And to Lucifer of all people.

"What of Jack?" Aldrich asked.

"I don't know where he is. He may be dead."

"Was Max with anyone else?"

"No one."

It didn't make any sense. Why was Oliver lying? Unless . . . He was trying to protect Schuyler. The most amazing part was that Aldrich seemed to believe him.

Aldrich snapped his fingers, and a Silver rushed forward. Aldrich said something, too quiet to hear, and the Silver nodded, signaled to the others, and half of them left the apartment. No doubt they were off to find Max. Aldrich went to the window, looking out across the city, his hands clasped behind his back.

"I should have let Leviathan kill him when he had the chance," Aldrich whispered to himself. "He may be hiding with that girl from city hall who interrupted my plans."

Oliver's Adam's apple bobbed as he swallowed. He knew

Aldrich was talking about Schuyler, yet he didn't say anything. Aldrich didn't notice, though; he was too busy staring out the window, his eyes hard in his reflection. What kind of game was Oliver playing? Did he think he could outmaneuver the devil?

Aldrich's eyes flashed dangerously as a thought occurred to him, but it passed like a cloud across the moon. He went to Oliver and helped him to his feet. The way Oliver looked at him was pure devotion, and Schuyler wanted to shake him, but all she could do was watch. Aldrich squeezed Oliver on the shoulder and patted him firmly. "You're the only one I can trust. You're the only one capable of seeing my vision. You are more worthy of being my son than Max ever was."

Oliver stood proud.

Slowly, Aldrich removed the pendant from Oliver's neck and twisted a small cork, opening the charm stone. The blue blood inside swirled on its own power, as if eager to be free.

Pinpricks of light glowed in Oliver's eyes as he watched it with growing hunger.

"But Max will stop at nothing to get this power back," Aldrich said. "He must not succeed. You won't let him, will you?"

"I want this. I need this," Oliver said. "I'll do anything you wish."

Aldrich smiled. "Then you must be ready. You must get stronger." He held up the stone. "More."

Oliver's breath quickened. Fear flashed in his eyes. He wanted this, but at the same time, he was afraid. Silvers yanked him onto the couch and held him down.

A Silver held his mouth open, another held his arms down, and Aldrich stood over him. Oliver's chest rose and fell, his eyes wide and afraid, but his fists were clenched in determination.

"There is no greatness without pain," Aldrich said, then he tipped the stone. He let a single drop of Azrael's blue blood fall onto Oliver's tongue.

Oliver writhed and cried and finally screamed.

When the vision ended, Schuyler blinked, and suddenly she found herself back in her body.

Aurora let go of Schuyler's hands and sank back into the chair, exhausted. Stephen rushed to her, but Schuyler reassured him with a calming hand and said, "I'm okay."

Schuyler's cheeks were slick with tears. She'd been crying. Furiously, she wiped the tears away, the echoes of Oliver's scream still in her head. Max watched her as he pressed the ice against his face. "What did you see?"

"Aldrich was with Oliver. He's torturing him." To her mother, she said, "Take me back there, I need to make sure he's okay."

Aurora's grasp on Stephen's hand tightened, and she rubbed her thumb on his knuckles. "I'm afraid I've reached my limit. I'm not as strong as I once was."

Frustration formed a bubble in Schuyler's throat.

Aurora continued: "Lucifer knows how to get others on his side. He promises things that appeal to the basest desires: power, money, love . . . Even the strongest of us aren't immune. You must be careful. He will show you everything you didn't know you desired and the temptation will be great."

"That's why I have to save Oliver. If I can get to him, I can stop the universe from collapsing. I can send Lucifer to Purgatory. We are going to use a resurrection sigil."

Aurora and Stephen exchanged surprised glances. "Where did you learn such a thing?"

"A Silver Blood called Kingsley Martin. He died and we plan to bring him back, exchanging his soul for Lucifer's. We can stop him once and for all. Max and I and a handful of Paladins are going to do it."

Aurora looked surprised. "Paladins! Here? I haven't heard that word used in a long time. To know that they've returned is truly comforting."

"You've met some?"

"In passing," Aurora said, smiling at a distant memory. "So then this means you know of the prophecy."

Schuyler's heart leaped. "You know about it too?"

Aurora nodded. "'Child of blood and bless'd,' of course. Though this plan of yours concerns me. You can charge the resurrection sigil, but without an angelic weapon, you won't be able to open the barrier long enough for souls to exchange."

Max sat up just as Schuyler jolted. They both had the same thought. "Of course!" Schuyler gasped. "We're tearing open a door to another dimension, like Lucifer did. If he needs an angelic weapon to make worlds collide, so do we. I have to *mark* Lucifer with an angelic sword."

"And we have one," Max said, eyes wide.

Schuyler and Max stared at each other as they said the word at the same time: "Gabrielle's."

Aurora smiled knowingly. They'd found the last missing piece of their puzzle. Schuyler could hardly contain her excitement. She could save Oliver, save Kingsley, save the worlds. Her team had everything they needed to get started.

"Jack still has it," Max said to Aurora. "It's yours to claim again."

"I don't have the power to wield it. It is not mine anymore." Her smile was sad, but hopeful at the same time. She leveled her gaze solidly with Schuyler's. "Aldrich will do everything he can to stop you. He knows a battle is coming. His army grows. This will not be for the faint of heart. We'll do what we can to help you defeat Lucifer, mi cielo. But ultimately, it's your destiny to finish what I couldn't."

TWENTY-EIGHT

SCHUYLER

At the Warehouse, Schuyler and Max found Theo, who saw to Max's injuries like a seasoned doctor on the front lines of battle. Theo had been busy these past couple of days, healing up Paladins left and right, seemingly without any rest in between.

Theo plopped Max down on the table. "Honestly, bro," he said, inspecting the split in his lip. "You have a habit of getting your butt kicked, don't you?"

Max winced. "It's one of the few things I'm really good at."

"Where are Jack and Aoife?" Schuyler asked.

Theo tipped his head toward the west wing of the building while continuing to scold Max for being really bad at being a mortal. Schuyler left them to it.

Sure enough, she found Jack and Aoife at the hand-drawn map of the sigil. Aoife had used some of Megan's dolls as stand-in figures for battle strategies, moving them around the map like generals in a war. Schuyler might have laughed at the absurdity of it if she hadn't felt like collapsing into a puddle of exhaustion. Both Jack and Aoife looked up when she rushed into the room.

Jack's face was bright, but when he saw the look on Schuyler's face, his smile fell. He went to her, immediately taking her hand in his, and asked, "What happened? Is everything okay?"

"It's Oliver," Schuyler said. "Oliver has Azrael's power. He's going to use Michael's sword to break the universe for Lucifer." She told Jack and Aoife everything that had happened, her vision, and Jack cupped her face, concern all over his. She loved how warm and soft his hands felt on her skin. The only thing she wanted in that moment was to be held by him, to breathe him in, to bury herself in his arms. Oliver's betrayal had left her feeling like her skin was raw and burned to a crisp, his deception as painful as a slap.

"Is Max hurt?" Jack asked.

"He's beat up, but Theo is healing him. Our element of surprise is gone. They know he's alive."

A muscle in Jack's jaw throbbed, despite the fact that he looked relieved about his brother. "I should have been there. I let both of you down."

"It's better this way. They still don't know where you are. If they capture you and take your power too, we're doomed."

Jack let out a long breath and closed his eyes. He and Schuyler pressed their foreheads together and stayed that way for a long while before Aoife spoke. Schuyler had almost forgotten that she was there.

"You didn't tell Oliver about us, right? About Paladins or the Warehouse?" Her dark eyes were intense, even behind her glasses. Schuyler had to admit that she was glad Aoife was on her side. The girl was scary when she was angry.

"No," Schuyler said. "Who knows what he could have done to

us if I'd told him? I can't believe all this time I thought I could trust him."

Aoife folded her arms over her chest. "No one will blame you for having faith in a friend. What matters now is how we stop him."

"Is the Warehouse in danger?" Jack asked.

Aoife shook her head. "We'll be fine here. But when we're out there, it's a different story." To Jack, she said, "You and Max should hide here, stay behind with the young ones."

"No," said Jack. "I'm done hiding. Whatever you need from me, I'm here to help. I'll just . . . have to be careful. Disguise myself somehow."

"All right, then, pretty boy. How good are you with a sword?"

Schuyler answered for him. "The best."

Jack summoned Gabrielle's sword to his hand, the weapon appearing seemingly out of nowhere.

"Ooh!" Aoife breathed.

The blade gleamed like moonlight, letting off a buttery, silver glow that filled the room. It was beautiful, to say the least, and in Jack's hands it looked like a piece of art.

"We're lucky to have Jack on our side," Schuyler said.

His face flushed. Could the great Jack Force really be blushing?

"Great," Aoife said. "We've no time to lose."

Schuyler's heart swelled. At least she wasn't alone in this fight. She had a circle of friends, friends in unlikely places, that were here to stand with her.

So that was it, then. They were up against the clock. And Schuyler needed to stop her best friend from doing something he didn't even fully understand. Why Oliver wanted to be a Blue

Blood so badly, she didn't know. Was it because he was jealous of her strength? Her power? Did he really think she didn't love him because he was mortal? Schuyler hated not knowing. She wanted to ask him why, talk some sense into him, but how could she reach him in time?

Aoife rushed off, calling for other Paladins to meet with her, leaving Jack and Schuyler alone at the map. Schuyler stared at the lines, the plan all laid out in full detail. If they could do this, if they could pull it off, maybe they could save more than one soul, not just Kingsley's.

"Jack, there's something else you should know," Schuyler said. "My mother . . . She told me the truth about who she is. She's Gabrielle."

Jack's jaw dropped, the color rushing from his face. His mouth worked, searching for words. "Gabri— I saw her in my dream with the siren, but I thought it was a trick. . . . How?"

"I know. She's been hiding this whole time. It's why I'm a vampire. This happened for a reason: the prophecy, my memories of another world, us, all of it. Lucifer thought he could win, but he doesn't know everything. My mother said we need an angelic weapon to open the portal to Purgatory, to bring Kingsley back." She looked at the sword in his fist.

Jack palmed the back of his neck, staring at the sword. She could tell what he was thinking.

"She forgives you. And Max," Schuyler said softly.

"I don't forgive myself."

Schuyler's chest ached. She watched him for a breath as his guilt and innocence waged war across his face. The muscle in his jaw worked, thumping in time with his heartbeat, and then he looked at her, holding the sword out to Schuyler. "Here," he said. "You should have it. I don't deserve it."

"I can't take it," she said.

"Why?"

"The prophecy. If I really am the one they think I am—'Blade of flame thy brand'—I need Michael's flaming sword." Gabrielle's sword was made of soft moonlight, the opposite of fire. "But a celestial blade will send him to Purgatory. If you have Gabrielle's sword, it's one more weapon in our arsenal. If I can't get Michael's sword in time, if something happens to me, you need to use Gabrielle's sword to open the dimension to Purgatory instead. It's our last resort."

Jack's emerald eyes flicked back and forth, peering deeply into hers. With another twist of his wrist, the sword dissolved into the ether, disappearing into thin air once more. "If they still think I'm dead, with no victor to claim it, they'll believe that Gabrielle's sword is lost forever. It'll be safe with me. But say the word and it's yours."

Schuyler nodded. "I just have to focus on Michael's sword, on Oliver." A chill raked down her spine and she shivered. She wondered what Oliver was doing at that very moment. His screams had stayed with her long after the vision faded, and it made her sick. Schuyler said softly, "I saw Oliver with Aldrich. They're experimenting on him, preparing his body. He wants to be a Blue Blood so badly, he'll do anything. That first night, after I found Max, Oliver was really sick right after . . . I should have known."

"It's not your fault."

Schuyler tried to smile. Jack was trying to make her feel better, but it still hurt. "What happens if it doesn't work? What happens if Ollie can't handle Azrael's power?"

Jack looked at her gravely. "His body might not survive the transformation."

She shook her head. "No. No one else has to die. There has to be another way we can stop Duncan."

Jack's eyes sparkled when he looked at her. "Do you love Oliver?"

"Not like that. He's my best friend. Of course I love him. That's why it's so hard to let him go. If I didn't, it would be so much easier to do what we need to do. Maybe Oliver is being brainwashed by Lucifer. Maybe there's a way to snap him out of it, like what happened to Max. There has to be a way I can save him. It's not too late."

Jack sighed. "The problem is, Max wasn't being brainwashed. Neither was I. We were committed to the cause because . . . well, because we chose it. We thought we'd been on a one-way street. Max wanted power, I wanted to protect him. Lucifer may have made us forget some things, but he didn't make us do anything. He can control minds, but he didn't control ours. And I'm still not ready to forgive myself for it. You didn't change me. I had to change myself."

Schuyler understood what he meant. No one else but Oliver could save him. Jack leveled his gaze, steady and strong, with her own.

"If you really believe that Oliver can be redeemed," Jack said, "I will help you. Otherwise, if he tries to hurt you . . . I *will* kill him."

Even though she knew Jack's heart was kind and honest, she also knew he would be true to his word. He was still the angel of destruction, Abbadon. Ancient civilizations worshipped him as natural disasters, unstoppable forces of nature, cataclysmic events of myth. If he was pushed, she could see him easily fall back into those depths of pure instinct. Darkness was like a second nature to him. Even though he looked like her Jack, he was still more powerful than she would ever know.

But Schuyler wouldn't back down. If Jack could change, so could Oliver.

She stood by her convictions—she was stubborn that way. She'd had a similar argument with Kingsley when she first saw Jack and Max working for Lucifer and Kingsley was convinced they were far past redemption. . . . And here they were, Jack and Max on her side now. She had to believe there was still good in Oliver's heart too. Both Jack and Max were proof that Aldrich Duncan wasn't a puppet master. Maybe Oliver was still like them.

Schuyler took Jack's hands in hers. Her fingers were still cold, but his were so warm. She didn't want those hands marked by regret. "Aoife said it herself: 'It's not fate until it happens.' Even up to the last second, there's still a chance to change destiny and make a choice. Until Oliver proves me wrong, I'm not giving up. The sooner we trap Lucifer in Purgatory, the sooner we can break Oliver free from his control."

Jack kissed her fingers and nodded, assured by her determination, then his face broke into a sad smile. "It's so strange. I used to fantasize about my powers being taken away. I was only a child when I was told who I would become. I used to think it was a curse.

I wondered what kind of life I could lead if I didn't have to be this way. Before they died, my parents told me what to expect, prepared me for my destiny, but they never told me what it would cost. They knew what would happen when I came into my abilities. I didn't want it, but I couldn't stop it. To think someone would want this life, volunteer their body for it . . ."

"Who would you want to be if you didn't have to bear the burden?" she asked.

"Anything that gives me a chance to be with you."

Then Schuyler kissed him. It took him by surprise, but he relaxed against her lips. When she sighed into his touch, he pulled her closer. She'd been waiting for this moment, just the two of them. She'd desperately wanted to kiss him for so long. She missed him, the ache reaching all the way down to her bones, and having him back was the best feeling in the world, even if they were facing an oncoming storm.

She kissed him deeply, holding the back of his head, her fingers wrapped in his short hair. His breath tickled her cheek and Schuyler thought of all the lost time that had marked their relationship. Months had passed since that night after city hall, but Schuyler felt like nothing had changed between them since then. In fact, her feelings had only grown stronger. Unlike Oliver, Jack gave himself to her, asking for nothing in return.

He always smelled clean, like soap, and something else, something earthy and entirely him, and she laughed a little as she felt his lips against her mouth. Her whole body felt alive, reinvigorated, as she pressed up against him.

Jack lifted her up and set her down on the table, their lips still locked. Schuyler needed to be closer to him, her whole body warm and wanting. Jack broke their kiss to move his lips across her jaw and down her neck, his gentle touch welcome against the soft skin of her neck, his lips smooth and his breath hot. Pleasure rolled down her back. Jack's hands were so steady and solid on her waist, and she could feel his muscles through the thin fabric of his shirt. He met her mouth once again, and he sighed with desire.

She wanted more. She'd never been more certain about anything in her entire life.

She and Jack could have this one moment together, even if it was the last thing at the end of the world. Being with him made time stand still.

Twenty-Nine

JACK

The first thing Jack saw when he woke up was Schuyler, still sleeping beside him. In the night, they'd moved to his bed, inside a tent, which shielded them from the light so they could rest. But now some light from the Warehouse was creeping through the tent fabric, casting the curve of Schuyler's cheek in a soft glow. Jack's heart raced when he looked at her. He liked the way her lips pouted as she breathed slowly and steadily, the curl of her fingers against the pillow as if she were holding an invisible hand, the way her brown curls fell over her forehead. He held back every instinct to tuck her hair behind her ear, not wanting to wake her. She deserved rest—she'd already done so much for everyone—so he let her sleep a little while longer. Despite his best efforts, though, she stirred in her sleep and her eyes fluttered open. She blinked a few times and Jack smiled. Her face lit up when she saw him.

He wanted to wake up beside her like this forever.

"Morning," she whispered.

Jack kissed her. When their lips met, his mind never felt so calm. Every doubt or worry he had been feeling faded into white noise, and he finally knew that he was right about one thing: He loved Schuyler, more than he could ever say.

"I could get used to this," Schuyler said.

"Me too."

"What time is it?"

"No idea."

She sat up, checked her phone, and sighed. "Time to get to work." She rubbed the sleep from her eyes and Jack leaned against her, savoring the warmth of her body for a microsecond longer. Normally kids like them would be spending the weekend lounging around or hanging out with their friends. Jack and Schuyler had bigger plans.

Jack got out of bed first. They'd slept in their clothes, ready to spring into action at a moment's notice. He sorted through the shirts and jeans Schuyler had brought him. "Aoife asked me to do some reconnaissance for her today. I can get the layout of the charity concert, find our best line of attack."

Schuyler furrowed her brow. "You're leaving?"

Jack pulled down his baseball cap. "I promise I'll be back. I'm not getting captured by any more monsters." That was a promise he meant to keep. "I'm not letting my new friends down."

Schuyler smiled and he took her hand, kissing her knuckles. He liked the way she blushed.

"I promise," he repeated.

Jack watched city hall from a food cart across the street, pretending to be just another face in the crowd of tourists, enjoying a bagel and coffee while peering through a pair of dark sunglasses. Silvers entered and exited the building, no one ever looking his way. He recognized those faces, but none recognized him back. He was a ghost.

Jack had learned from the best how to hide his true nature from the world; now he intended to use that talent against Aldrich. Lucifer had taught him to mask his feelings, to never wear his emotions on his sleeve. Aldrich expected him to be the stoic, strong leader he needed him to be. Secrecy was strength, emotion was weakness, and there was no room for weakness in the Coven. So Jack locked his heart in a steel box behind his sternum. He needed to hide it, or else it would end up being only one more thing of his that Aldrich would take away and destroy.

If his hunch was correct, Aldrich had taught this same technique to Oliver, who, like Max, was desperate for power and eager to please. Jack understood that it wasn't just himself and Max who Aldrich had foster-cared for over the years. He'd been using his influence to convert others. Oliver had been raised by Lucifer as much as the Force twins had.

Jack had learned to shut himself off from the glom, hide his power, project strength on the outside while he was screaming on the inside. He'd hidden the most vulnerable parts of himself, giving Aldrich only what he needed in order to survive and keep Max safe. Everyone who met him saw what they wanted to see: Aldrich saw a dutiful son; classmates at Duchesne saw a popular athlete and student; even Max saw a perfect golden child. But Jack felt as if no one truly saw him for who he was—until Schuyler came into his life. She'd seen that he was all of those things.

And when he was with her, he didn't need to be anything else. He only needed to be himself.

It was Jack's turn to put his practice to better use.

His disguise was simple enough—a standard hoodie, a well-worn jacket courtesy of Stephen, and a baseball cap, as well as Aoife's headphones. He looked like any other teenager on the street with his head down, walking to the beat of the music in the bright sunlight of the morning. He'd done this kind of thing dozens of times before when he needed a break from being the Jack Force that everyone noticed, like a celebrity expertly avoiding the paparazzi. No one would pay any attention to him now, and that was exactly the way he wanted it to be. He didn't need mutatio to become invisible. He shut himself off from the glom, muting his power like he was holding it underwater. To any keen eye, he would seem mortal. Under Lucifer's reign, vampires thought themselves superior to mortal Red Bloods. So who would bother paying attention to one?

A larger group of Silver Bloods—Jack counted eight total—piled into a series of black SUVs, and he followed, on foot or flying as needed. Another benefit to city living was the fact that people hardly looked skyward. This allowed him to move across the skyline of lower Manhattan, heading northbound, tracking the convoy all the way to Central Park, where a section of the Great Lawn had been fenced off. A giant stage had been erected on the grass, and huge lights were hanging from metal scaffolding; a truck unloaded a monstrous metal machine with Enochian symbols on its side. It looked exactly like the one Max had described.

There was no sign of Oliver, though. No doubt Duncan was hiding him until it was time for him to appear.

Innocent citizens nearby were enjoying Central Park as they would any other day, playing with their dogs or taking walks or feeding the birds, oblivious to the sinister activity going on around them.

To think, only a few months ago he and Max had been practicing lacrosse on this very lawn, still stuck in their old lives. He'd been so unhappy then and he didn't even know it.

Shaking off his gloomy thoughts, Jack took pictures with his phone to bring back to the Paladins.

Before he returned to the Warehouse, Jack needed to make one last stop. But when he came upon his parents' graves, he found that he wasn't alone.

Already standing there, head lowered, his hands folded across his chest, was Max. He didn't move as Jack approached, no doubt hearing him come but choosing to stay still, even as Jack stepped up beside him. It was a private cemetery in a quiet part of the Upper East Side, nestled on a small piece of land designated as a historical landmark for the most influential of New York's families. Dozens of Blue Bloods that came before Jack and Max's parents, spanning all the way to the founding of the city, had been laid to rest here. The sounds from the street were mostly dulled, muffled by the brick wall surrounding the property, and shade from a spindly weeping willow tree cut across the headstones. It was peaceful.

Normally, Max wore designer clothes, with his hair perfectly styled, but now he stood in front of their parents' grave with the hood of his denim jacket up and his shoulders slumped, almost unrecognizable.

Finally, Max asked, "Are you sure it's safe for you to be here?"

"I could say the exact same thing to you, and yet here we both are."

Jack knelt and brushed the headstone clean with his hand, feeling the smooth, cold granite beneath his fingers as he read the names.

MAXIMILIAN REGUS FORCE JR.

MIRANDA FORCE

VITAM AETERNAM

Max had already placed a bouquet of fresh lilies in front of the headstone, and Jack noticed it with a smile. Traditions were hard to shake. The lily was the flower emblazoned on the Force family coat of arms.

Jack wiped away the dirt that had collected in the grooves of his parents' names. He cared for their headstone, much like he would a beloved treasure. He'd spent hours in the cemetery, meticulously weeding the edge of the graves and cleaning up trash that had gathered in the Manhattan breeze. It was his duty to sustain his parents' memory.

"What are you doing here?" Jack asked.

"I figured I'd stop by. It's been a while since I've visited. Hasn't changed much. Don't have particularly fond memories of this place."

"Pretty sure no one has fond memories of any cemetery," said Jack.

Max let out a puff of breath by way of a laugh.

The brothers stood in silence for a long moment. Jack didn't mind the cold now that Max was with him. He couldn't blame his brother for not wanting to visit this place often. There hadn't been anything left of their parents to bury anyway, but funerals were always for the living anyway. Burying their remains had been a way to close a chapter of their life and start a new one, a life with Aldrich. Jack remembered the way Max's face looked simultaneously young and ancient all at once as they lowered the empty caskets into the ground at sunset. Jack had held his brother's hand so tightly because his own felt so cold, and just like that, they were alone together. Alone with Aldrich.

Jack gazed at the headstone. Seeing his parents again, even if it was just a siren's illusion, had been too good to be true. The siren had seemed to pluck them right out of his memories . . . the way his father's green eyes sparkled, and the way his mother smiled. The tombstone grounded him back into reality. They were gone forever. There was no Sangre Azul to recover, no way to recycle their angelic spirits back into the cosmos. All that was left of their legacy was in the two boys they left behind.

The night they died, Jack and Max had been waiting at home . . . waiting, waiting, waiting. Jack had been looking forward to telling them about getting the lead role in the school play. And then an hour of waiting became two, and then three, and silently Jack pleaded for them to walk through the front door as dread seeped into his gut. He'd known something terrible had happened, but he had been too afraid to acknowledge it. And when the door opened, it had been Aldrich Duncan standing there to break the news.

And here Jack was once more, on the brink of uncertainty, looking at the names carved on the headstone. He was that ten-year-old kid again, standing with his brother, unsure about his future. Jack scrunched his shoulders up to his ears. The cold had started biting at his neck.

"Do you think . . ." Max started to ask, but he stopped, his breath hitching. After a second, he continued: "Do you think, if Dad were alive, he'd be ashamed of me?"

Jack screwed up his face, shocked. "Why would you think something like that?"

"With Azrael's spirit taken from me, I'm not . . ." Max shrugged. "I shouldn't have his name, or his legacy. I'm not a Blue Blood. I'm not his son anymore, not in the way that's always mattered to our family."

It was true that every single person in the Force bloodline, all the way back to the beginning of time, had been a Blue Blood. No one in the family had ever been anything else. Now Max thought of himself as defective somehow, or unworthy of love, and Jack's anger felt like an icicle through his heart.

"There's nothing wrong with you," Jack said.

"We've been preparing our whole lives to come into our power, and now that mine is gone I feel like I've . . . failed. Aldrich told us, over and over, how we were superior, meant to rule the earth, that we were better than everyone else. And I believed it because a part of me felt like I really wasn't anything special without that. I know Aldrich lies, but it's so hard to shake it. I'd put so much of myself into my identity, convinced myself that it was what defined me, and now I feel like I've got to start over. As someone else. Someone different."

"It's not so bad, starting over. Starting over means you can try again. You've got another chance. You're lucky that way."

Max laughed. "Lucky? Me? Far from it."

"I never told you this, but I sometimes imagined what it would be like if I wasn't a Blue Blood," Jack said. "I used to think what my life would be like if I didn't have this weight bearing down on my head, heavy as a crown. I saw that my power could help people, but it could also hurt people. And I didn't want to do that. Who we are, what we are, was a lot to handle. But now I see what I'm supposed to do. I can be the person I want to be, not the one anyone else wants me to be."

"At least you can make that choice. My choice was stolen from me."

Jack couldn't imagine what his brother had been through. What did it feel like to have his power ripped from a body? "What would you do if you got it back?"

Max's eyes blazed. "Burn everything Aldrich built—all of it—to the ground."

After a moment's silence, Jack said, "I used to imagine being free of our destiny. But I couldn't stand the idea of you being alone."

"Is that what this is? Freedom?"

"You can make it whatever you want it to be."

Max let out a long breath, the steam of it clouding in front of him. He tucked his hands into the pockets of his jacket. "I lied to you before. I didn't come here on a whim. I came here because . . . I'm not sure I'll ever see this world again. Being mortal has really put things into perspective for me. If something happens to me, I'm done. I'm dead for real."

Jack couldn't help the rush of fury he felt at the mere thought of losing Max. "Nothing is going to happen to you. I won't let it."

His heart raced with panic. He tried to calm down. But he couldn't help but imagine himself standing over Max's casket. He forced the thought from his mind with a clench of his jaw. The weeping willow seemed to tremble, and if Jack wasn't careful, he could split it in two.

"But if something does happen to me . . ." Max's eyes were soft. It startled Jack to see just how much his brother had changed. "I want you to know it's not your fault. I know I haven't been a good brother to you for a long time. And I'm sorry."

Hearing Max apologize was a new experience, one that Jack appreciated. He sounded genuine, and Jack had never seen him so humble before. Max had always been the prouder twin, the one who wanted to prove something to everyone. In front of Aldrich, he was always the strong one. Jack envied him for that.

They'd been out of sync for so long, walking on two separate paths ever since Aldrich Duncan came into their lives. They used to do everything together, and now, for once, it felt like Jack had his brother back after a long trip abroad.

Max gestured to the headstone. "I'd like you to bury me here, with them. Don't frown, I'm being serious. Just let me know I'll be laid to rest here if our plan to take down Aldrich goes south. I want to rest in this place. It's not so bad." He scuffed his sneaker on the grass. "Do you think that's allowed? Or is this cemetery off-limits to me now?"

"No matter what happened, we're still brothers. Nothing will ever change that."

Max's eyes danced in the sunlight, and before the thin silver tears could overflow, he looked away. Jack was polite enough to let him wipe his eyes in peace. If that's what Max wanted, Jack would respect his wishes, even if he'd be the only mortal Red Blood buried here. Damn the tradition to hell. But Jack swore in that moment that he wouldn't let anything happen to Max. No one was going to die. He'd make sure of it.

Max sniffed and coughed, swiping at his nose. His eyes were rimmed in red. "Thanks," he said. "Maybe we can start over now, start better."

Jack smiled. "I'd like that."

THIRTY

SCHUYLER

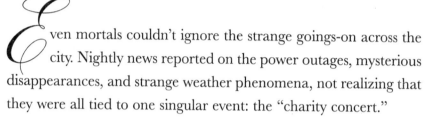

*E*ven mortals couldn't ignore the strange goings-on across the city. Nightly news reported on the power outages, mysterious disappearances, and strange weather phenomena, not realizing that they were all tied to one singular event: the "charity concert."

The day of the show was quickly approaching. Schuyler saw more advertisements plastered all over the city, urging people to attend. At school, students buzzed with excitement about it. She overheard Julie Bradford going on about how she had gotten front-row tickets to the concert and that she would try to get an autograph from Snap and Pop. Schuyler had every instinct to warn her not to go, but Julie wouldn't believe her even if she tried. Schuyler had to sit in class, listening to Julie excitedly tell her friends, while Schuyler bit her tongue. With everyone itching to get back to normal, the concert was the perfect cover for Lucifer's ultimate display.

A display during which Oliver was going to kill himself in order to become like Schuyler.

Today he was absent at school. No one knew where he'd gone.

Schuyler had expected as much, but she still hoped that maybe he would show—and that if he did, she'd be able to reason with him.

Yes, Oliver had lied to protect her, but Schuyler knew that would change and wondered when this would happen. Knowing as she did that Lucifer's Silvers were hunting her down at that very moment was almost worse than actually fighting them. She couldn't use her mother's remote viewing to find out more. She had no idea what they were planning next.

Aoife went to school with her each day, in case she needed backup, but Duchesne was woefully normal. Aoife sat at Schuyler's side during every class, her fists clenching her bandages tightly, keeping an eye out for anything suspicious. Schuyler too was on edge. Any minute she expected a group of Silvers to burst through the classroom door and attack. But they didn't do that, and Schuyler couldn't stand the anticipation. Aoife had become a kind of bodyguard for her, knowing full well that Schuyler was a prime target. In a way, Aoife had taken Conduit duties upon herself, filling in for Oliver, when Schuyler hadn't even asked her to. It was a comfort to have Aoife at her side.

At lunch, Schuyler wasn't hungry. She'd lost her appetite since that night with Oliver. Nothing seemed to sit right in her stomach. Aoife encouraged her to eat, waving french fries under her nose.

Schuyler blinked and snapped out of her ruminations.

"Come on," she said. "You need to eat, get your strength up."

"Thanks." Schuyler munched halfheartedly on a single fry.

"Tomorrow will be fine. Lucifer will be too busy with the concert to notice what we're doing. Everything is in place. We can do this."

The concert. It had come so quickly. Schuyler knew she was

ready, but the waiting was killing her. She felt like she was back again in the time when she didn't know where Jack had gone and she could only wait, and pray that he would return. She wished she knew if Oliver was okay.

"I'm worried about Oliver. I have to talk to him, but his phone is shut off, and obviously, I can't just go storming into his house." Schuyler sighed and rapped her knuckles on the table. "I have to get to him somehow and talk him out of his obsession with becoming a vampire. Does your spy know where he is?"

Aoife's smile was clever and knowing. "Why don't you tell Schuyler yourself, Ruby?"

Schuyler was surprised to hear the name and looked around to see Ruby, the shy, quiet girl who had a crush on Oliver, smiling down at them, her arms folded across her chest. Normally, she hid behind a curtain of hair and slumped her shoulders, but now she stood taller, her hair swept back from her face. She looked so altered, Schuyler almost thought she was a different person.

"Ruby?" Schuyler asked, aghast. "*You're* the spy?"

Ruby took a seat with Schuyler and Aoife. "Spy? Scout? Tracker? Semantics," she said. "Doesn't really matter. I was sent to watch out for any unusual activity. And boy, did I find it."

All this time, Schuyler realized, another Paladin had been going to school with her, and she hadn't even noticed. "You knew about Oliver this whole time?" she asked Ruby.

"I had my eye on a few people, but yeah, I've been keeping a watch on him for a while. He was a hard one to figure out."

"Who's your patron?" Schuyler asked, still dumbfounded.

"Ah," Ruby said, with a twinkle in her eye, "I'm a spy, remember? Gotta keep my secrets close."

Aoife tipped her head. "Ruby here is the one who found me when I first became a Paladin. I owe her everything."

"Yeah, yeah." She took one of Aoife's fries as a reward. "But to answer your question, Schuyler, even I don't know where Oliver is. They could be keeping him contained somewhere, probably under lock and key. He's too important to lose if he really is one of the few who can accept Azrael's power. Unless you can turn into a bat or something, we're in the dark on this one."

"You can't do that, can you?" Aoife asked, a little hopefully.

Schuyler shook her head as her heart sank. They were just going to have to stop Aldrich Duncan before he turned Oliver. She hoped it wouldn't get that far.

Ruby wasn't finished, though. "In even more terrible news, I also have it on good authority that Aldrich Duncan knows about the resurrection sigil."

"What?" Aoife hissed.

"It's not exactly a secret, what the founders did when designing these streets, but Aldrich doesn't know how or when we might strike. He knows Max is involved somehow, but I don't think he knows he's joined up with us Paladins. Aldrich has sent his Silvers to the activation points, scouring every bit of this island looking for Max, and that means they'll be looking for you. He needs to make sure nothing gets in the way of the concert."

Schuyler had hoped they still had the element of surprise on their side, but it seemed that Aldrich was proving to be far more in control than she had feared. "What about the machine?" she asked. "Max said it needed souls to power it."

"Still working on that part," Ruby said. "He might be storing some souls somehow, or he might not need them anymore if he's got Azrael's power. For now, we need to focus on stopping him from breaking the universe."

Even though Schuyler felt comforted by the fact that she had yet another ally on her side, the clock was ticking.

After school, Schuyler and Aoife headed right for the Warehouse. Ruby didn't join them, mentioning that she still had work to do before the concert, so Aoife and Schuyler made for Max and Jack's area, only to find Jack and Megan laughing. Megan watched in awe as Jack did some sleight-of-hand tricks with a coin. His eyes were bright and his smile warm as he pretended to pull coins from behind her ear. She looked even smaller outside her tent, surrounded by mountains of storage crates, but she looked happy.

Schuyler leaned on one of the crates, watching from afar, her arms folded comfortably over her chest. She smiled as Megan clapped and giggled.

"Don't you clean your ears?" Jack teased. He reached his hand behind Megan's head and flicked his wrist, and a coin appeared between his fingers. He feigned a look of shock as he showed her the coin.

Megan snorted into her hand. "How are you doing that?"

"Doing what?" He flicked his fingers once more and the coin disappeared.

Megan took his hand in her own and turned it over, searching for the coin, but it was gone. Her eyes danced with intrigue. "Bring it back!"

Jack flicked the fingers of his other hand and the coin reappeared. Schuyler knew what he was doing wasn't really magic, but the fact that Megan thought it was made her stomach feel like it was full of butterflies. Sometimes kids believing in magic was the real magic.

Jack noticed Schuyler and his smile grew wider.

"Show me! Show me!" Megan clapped her hands, and Jack placed the coin in her palm. He tried to teach her, but a sudden wave of exhaustion washed over the little girl's face. Her eyes drooped and she swayed. It was another one of her visions. They were occurring more and more often the closer they got to the concert. Aldrich was tearing open the universe again. More monsters were no doubt coming through somewhere in the city.

Jack put a protective hand on Megan's back as she dropped. Her head lolled back and she fell into a deep sleep.

Aoife rushed forward. "It's okay," she said gently. "It'll pass in a bit."

"Is she all right?" Jack asked.

"She'll be fine. She just needs to sleep. The fold in realities is opening to her again."

"Maybe you should take her to her bed," Jack suggested.

"Good idea. It's okay, Meggie." Aoife hoisted the child into her arms. Megan curled up against Aoife and started mumbling in her sleep, no doubt channeling another prophecy. "I've got her. You two could use some alone time anyway." She tipped her chin in Schuyler's direction and Jack smiled.

Aoife made soft hushing sounds to Megan as Jack went over to Schuyler, still smiling.

"Where'd you learn to do that coin trick?" Schuyler asked, twirling her fingers to illustrate.

Jack tucked his hands casually in the front pockets of his jeans and shrugged. "I grew up in an empty house with a huge library. Learned a thing or two to pass the time or else I'd have gone crazy."

Schuyler's smile fell a little. No wonder he had been drawn to Megan. Like her, he had been orphaned at a young age. Living in that giant mansion on Fifth Avenue with only himself and Max must have been terribly lonely. Schuyler's heart ached for him. There was nothing she could do to fix his past.

Schuyler reached out and touched the warm strip of exposed skin on his wrist above the bracelet she'd made and he looked at her, his eyes shining. She knew it was impossible to change what had happened to him, but with a touch, she wanted to remind him that she was there. He took a hand out of his pocket and held hers. His hand was soft, and she squeezed his fingers.

"Here," she said. From her coat, she pulled out a packet of blood. It had been one of the pouches Oliver had delivered, but Schuyler figured it was still good. "Are you hungry?"

Jack's smile widened and he gratefully took the pouch.

The two of them sat atop one of the towers of wooden boxes while they drank. From their position, they watched as Paladins moved below, preparing for the battle ahead. Aoife was right—the

Warehouse had become crowded. Two hundred Paladins all in one place made the air hum. In a way, Schuyler and Jack imbibing some quality red blood was a preparation as well. She couldn't ask any of the Paladins if they were willing to become another one of her Familiars. Even in the other world, she'd never had more than one at a time before. Besides, she'd already entrusted that task to Oliver, and he'd betrayed her. Her heart wasn't ready for another blow like that. She also knew that if she and Jack drank a Paladin's blood, it would weaken the Paladins, and Schuyler didn't want to risk that. All the Paladins were hard at work, sharpening magical weapons and making armor to hide under their clothes during the concert.

Jack sighed with relief as he finished his blood. Color flushed his cheeks, and his eyes were bright. "I needed that," he said. "Thanks."

"No problem." Schuyler took her time drinking her packet. She was hungry, but her stomach churned with anticipation. She doubted she'd ever get used to the tension of a night before a battle.

She and Jack watched the Paladins for a while in companionable silence. Paladins came from all over the world, but their language barriers didn't hold anyone back from embracing one another like family. Laughter carried through the air, despite the anxiety sizzling between them. No one wanted to talk about specifics, but they all knew that some people might not make it back here at the end of the fight.

Just then, Max appeared down below, chatting with Theo and helping move boxes of red spray paint they were going to be using to create the sigils. Max laughed at something Theo said, throwing his head back with his eyes closed.

"He looks like he fits in here," Schuyler said.

"Yeah, I know," Jack agreed. "It's nice for him to be around people again. Max was always the more sociable one. Extroverted. But we never had visitors at home."

"How come?"

"Aldrich didn't want us mingling with those he saw as inferior. He wanted us to be with our own kind, to surround ourselves with other Blue Bloods, because it would make us stronger. Unfortunately, the social pool was small. He believed that Blue Bloods were the superior beings, that Red Bloods were too weak, meant to be ruled, dirty. There was a natural hierarchy to the world. 'Why would gods want to mingle with ants?' he'd say." Jack sighed and frowned. It seemed that even saying it out loud, even though they were Aldrich's words, made him feel boorish. But when he glanced at Schuyler, he smiled. "It feels good to remember he's wrong."

Jack slipped his hand into Schuyler's, and they fell into silence again as they turned their attention back to the Paladins. Paladins sparred and practiced with each other, warming up their muscles and activating their powers. Everyone here was unified in a single cause to help protect innocent people, and that itself was worth fighting for.

But Theo and Max were obviously up to something as they cleared out the space, moving Theo's table to the side and pushing carts of boxes out of the way.

"I think I'd like a family someday," Jack said, breaking the silence. His fingers traced over the red bracelet Schuyler had made for him, still tied around his wrist. A promise. "I'd want to be a dad. I know my nature as Abbadon is to destroy, but it would be nice to create something for once. To make a life, make it good. I know, I'm young. It's still a long ways off, but . . . I'm just thinking about the future a lot lately. It's nice to look forward to something instead of always looking back."

Heat rushed to Schuyler's cheeks. The idea of starting a family was still so far beyond her, but she knew what he meant. She nodded; that was all she could manage to do. She was very aware of Jack's touch on her hand. She'd be lying if she said she hadn't thought about someday starting a family, and what that might look like. Memories of the other world still lingered in the outskirts of her heart. She knew that those versions of themselves had been happy once, dreamed of starting lives together there too. She and Jack had years to grow together. She could remember what it felt like being with him, standing with him in Florence, exchanging vows. And when she woke up with memories of that life, she felt like she was starting over, remembering a life that didn't belong to her. What she had here with Jack now was all she could ever have hoped for, and she wanted to fight for it. But what would that future look like if she failed to kill Lucifer? What if she succeeded? What about the monsters that might remain? Would she want her family to grow up fighting creatures at night? Learn that they were never going to be like the other children in their school? Exist in a world that was home to evil and darkness and danger?

Jack continued: "I don't want to be like Aldrich. I don't want to close myself off from the world. I want to do more. I want to make the kind of home I didn't have. I want to try to give my children the things I would have wanted; I want to care for them, and protect them, but I also want to make the world a better place for them and to let them be free."

"You will," Schuyler said. "And I can't wait to see it."

Jack's cheeks flushed and he smiled at her. They kissed, taking a moment to appreciate being together, and Schuyler's heart felt full.

Music began to blare through the Warehouse. Theo had brought out a large speaker and started playing electronic dance music. The rhythm of the beat bounced against the high ceilings. Some Paladins cheered and jumped into the space that had now become a dance floor. They danced to defy the future. Others clapped and sang along with the music, and their voices lifted through the air.

At the bottom of their tower, Max called up to Schuyler and Jack. "Are you just going to stay up there all day? Get down here— live a little."

Jack and Schuyler glanced at each other, thinking the same thing, both smiling because things were so easy when they were close.

Along with Max and Theo and Aoife, Schuyler and Jack danced, letting themselves be kids for just a few minutes longer.

THIRTY-ONE

SCHUYLER

"How about this one?" Aoife handed Schuyler a straight-edged steel sword with an emerald jewel in the hilt. It was time for battle, and Schuyler needed to choose her weapon. Doing so helped her focus on the task at hand, made her feel like she was ready to fight. The sword had recently been polished, and it hummed with power in Schuyler's grip.

Schuyler tested the weight of it, swinging the blade in figure eights. It whistled through the air as it went. "Where is this from?"

"This one was pulled from a lake in England a few hundred years ago, but its blade never dulled."

Schuyler paused. "Pulled from a lake as in . . . Excalibur . . . King Arthur's sword?"

"Just the same! Fun fact . . . it's actually Guinevere's. Huge misconception. We have some of her handwritten notes in a box around here somewhere. Her whole story was almost lost to time. She was quite the Paladin in her day, but early scribes scrubbed that from history. She killed many monsters back then. Maybe her sword can help you do the same now."

Schuyler admired the hilt and smiled. "Hopefully not too many monsters," she added.

Aoife said, "Let's plan on smiting Lucifer before he can even think about letting any more in. This will do until you get your hands on Michael's sword."

"Do you think the Paladins will be ready for what's to come?"

"They'll have to be."

Just then Max and Jack appeared. They had been coordinating with Theo all morning, putting together last-minute contingency plans before everyone was to head out to their mission. Jack immediately went to Schuyler, and she showed him the sword. He tested the weight expertly, admiring the length of the blade, and gave it back to her with a wink. "This will do nicely," he said.

Max, meanwhile, grumbled, "Without my sword, I feel naked. It's not exactly comforting to know that we'll be up against a variety of otherworldly monsters and I don't have anything to protect myself."

"You're helping us?" Schuyler asked. She had imagined that since he was without his power, it was safer for him to seek shelter in the Warehouse and wait out the storm. He would be exposed, more than anyone, and therefore more of a target for the Coven.

"Yeah, duh. I'm not sitting around while you save my boyfriend from Purgatory. This is too important to me."

Schuyler's mouth twisted into a smile. Boyfriend. Max and Kingsley, together soon. Hopefully. She liked the sound of the word *boyfriend* coming from Max's mouth. It softened his harder edges.

Aoife seemingly always had a solution to every problem. She

went straight for a shelf in the weapons cache and took down the shield she had liberated from the museum. Its dragon face and gem eyes glinted in the light. "Here," she said, holding it out to Max. "It'll give you some extra protection. No offense, but you'll need all the help you can get."

"What is this?" Max asked.

"It's an old Paladin's shield. We thought it was lost, but Schuyler here helped steal it back."

Schuyler immediately felt defensive as all eyes went to her. "Hey! No! I only smashed a glass display case to set off a booby trap for a mummy. I didn't intend to steal it."

Max rolled his eyes, and Jack shook his head with a smile.

"It feels good, actually," Max said. He strapped the shield to his arm with the leather bindings. "I think this will come in handy if Oliver ever tries to punch me in the face again."

"I think it'll be more useful than that," Jack said. "That's an impressive emblem. Is it magical?"

"The Paladin who wielded this killed a dragon," Aoife said. "It should give you extra protection since you don't have the ability to fight like you used to. No offense again."

"None taken, but you don't have to keep repeating it," Max said. He hefted the shield onto his arm, testing its weight. He tightened the leather straps and flexed his fingers. "I do need all the help I can get."

"You seem like you're adjusting to life on the mortal side," Aoife said.

"I've come to terms with it. It's not so bad. I make mortal look good." Max held up the shield, and the dragon's eyes glowed on the face of the metal. Schuyler could feel the air hum with the magic that surrounded it. Max seemed satisfied. "I've never used a shield before. I was always more inclined toward stabbing things. I'm not even sure how to use it."

"You're smart," Jack teased. "You'll figure it out."

Schuyler folded her arms across her chest confidently. "Am I seeing things or did becoming human actually make you . . . well, more human?"

It actually felt like she and Max were becoming friends. They still had a long way to go, but he was warming up to her, and she was warming up to him.

Max threw her a withering look. "Don't get used to it." But the admonition didn't have the heat that it might have had only a couple months ago. "Though I do admit, it's a nice change of pace."

Everyone smiled at that.

Holding up a finger as if she'd just remembered something, Aoife hurried to a crate that had been moved out from the others. From within the crate, she produced a small wooden box. Inside were dozens of gemstones, sparkling in the light. Some of them, though, gleamed entirely on their own. These were magical.

Max, who Schuyler had always known to be drawn to all things fancy, ogled them with wide eyes.

"We need a little extra boost for when we face Lucifer," Aoife said. "If Silvers are lurking all over the island, like Ruby said, we need to be ready. These should help us keep a low profile."

"What do they do?" Max asked, plucking out a blue crystal with a hole through its middle. He held it up to the light and closed one eye to peer through the hole.

"It shields you from detection. Any mortal who might look at you would just glance right over and forget they even saw you in the first place. It'll do wonders for moving quickly through the city in front of regular people. It's how Paladins operate most of the time in the field."

Max smiled wide. Schuyler noticed the fire burning in his eyes. "And we can make some chaos without interruption."

"But it doesn't really make you invisible. Just harder to notice, unless you cause a scene. You still have to stay out of sight, Max. Don't draw too much attention."

Schuyler chose one of the talismans and palmed the gemstone. Without the Paladins' help, she would have been up against an unbeatable army. But now her forces actually stood a chance. She pocketed the gemstone. Jack and Max chose one each as well.

"Well," Schuyler said. She looked around at this group of unlikely teammates. A fallen angel, a vampire turned human, a mortal blessed by a knight, and herself—a half-vampire destined to fight the devil. They were up against impossible odds, but seeing everyone gathered before her gave her a renewed spirit that she wouldn't have felt if she had been alone. They were going to bring Kingsley back and save every world in the process. "Are we ready?"

They looked around at each other, as if sensing the same thing. A silent resolve settled over the group and they all nodded.

"We're ready," Jack said.

THIRTY-TWO

MAX

*M*ax was about to follow Schuyler and Jack to meet with the other teams when Aoife said, "Max, wait. This one's for you too."

He held out his hand and she dropped a metal coin into his palm. The Paladin mark had been carved into both of its smooth faces. It weighed a lot more than he expected. "Pure silver. It'll protect you from the evil eye. If a vampire tries to compel you, it shouldn't work, so long as you have this on you at all times."

"You mortals are so industrious," Max said, already feeling the shroud of protection surrounding him. He slipped the coin into his back pocket.

Aoife grinned. "Takes one to know one." Then she hurried off to join the others, leaving Max to gather his wits for a moment. Even though the time had come for confrontation, he still couldn't believe it was really happening.

Max used to think that he was strong. Now that he was going to face the devil himself and finally bring him down, it felt like an impossible task. His knees shook, his palms were slick with sweat, and his heart was racing painfully in his chest. But no one needed to know that.

The only thing he'd ever known in his life was how to be what Aldrich wanted him to be. He didn't know how to be himself. And yet, when he stood with his new friends in the Warehouse, he felt like that was enough. He didn't need to be anything else other than what he was right then in that moment. With his shield humming on his arm and the coin in his pocket, he could wear his walls on the outside, use them to defend rather than to contain. Getting Kingsley back felt so close, he could almost swear that he was in the room with them. If Max could right one wrong in this world, it would be to bring Kingsley back to the land of the living. He wanted to apologize to the one true love of his life for failing him in the worst ways possible. He wanted to be better for Kingsley's sake, maybe even a little for himself, and now that he had a sliver of a chance of making this hope come to fruition, he couldn't wait to get started.

It was time to go.

Max pulled back his shoulders, held his head up high, and joined the others. The whole Warehouse was already active with Paladins readying themselves for a fight. The youngest, like Megan the seer, were going to hunker down in the Warehouse with some of the older ones until it was safe. In Max's opinion, the Warehouse was one of the safest places to be on the entire island. As long as he still had breath in his lungs, he would fight to defend this place. The Paladins had given him shelter. This was as much his home now as his old one had been.

Aoife and Jack stood at the table with the map of New York

spread across it. The rest of the Paladins hovered nearby or stood atop Warehouse boxes to get a better look. Everyone knew the plan, but it helped that they were running through it one more time.

Aoife was speaking when Max rejoined the group. "Theo will lead the Alpha team to the Apollo while Ruby will lead the Bravo team to Rockefeller Center. Jack and Schuyler are going to Grand Central, and Max and I are going to the Brooklyn Bridge."

She looked at Jack, who now took over for her. "Our intel says that Lucifer is planning to start the collapse at seven tonight. That gives us three hours to complete our work. We'll meet the rest of you at the concert once we're done. Try to get as many people to safety as you can. Lucifer won't go down without a fight."

"What if they're all vampires?" someone asked from the back.

Paladins murmured to one another. They quieted when Aoife held up her hands.

"Then we do what Paladins do best," she said. She turned to Schuyler, who stood next to her. "Destiny is on our side."

Max almost laughed. There was a time when he didn't think anyone's destiny could be changed—when he didn't know he was destined to love. How wrong he'd been. Max couldn't wait to hold Kingsley in his arms, breathe him in again, and never let him go. Every time he smelled coffee, or caught a whiff of leather, he immediately thought of Kingsley. The darkness of the club, the heat of Kingsley's breath in his ear as he told him to remember . . . It had taken him too long to wake up.

Even if Kingsley didn't love him anymore, he still wanted him back. Kingsley deserved to live. His whole life, Max had done nothing but selfish things, and returning Kingsley from Purgatory could be the one good thing he would do for someone else. Even if it was the last thing he'd do.

"Schuyler?" Aoife asked. "Anything to add?"

Schuyler thought for a long moment as everyone watched and waited. Max found himself holding his breath. Eventually, she declared, her voice strong and sure, "Happy hunting."

The Paladins cheered and everyone split off to join their designated teams.

Jack went to Schuyler's side. Instinctively, Max wanted to be the one to go with Jack to Grand Central Terminal, but he knew Jack wanted to stick with Schuyler. She was too important to lose and needed to be protected. And Jack was the best bet to get the job done. He'd always been the best, and he would do right by her. Besides, they'd been separated too long. They had earned this time together.

Aoife wove her way through the crowd to join Max. "Let's go," she said.

Max nodded. He wasn't sure he'd be able to speak anyway. Worry had become a lump in his throat.

They needed to leave now to make good time. Before they got going, he spotted Jack across the way. Jack caught his eye and weaved through the crowd, Schuyler holding on to his hand the whole way.

The boys stopped in front of one another, mirror images. Max wanted to say something profound, but he knew it would sound stupid. Instead he settled for simple.

"See you soon," he said, holding out his hand to Jack. It was oddly reminiscent of their meeting in the underbelly of city hall. Doing it then had been awkward, and too formal, but neither of them was quite sure how to act toward the other at the time. It had been too long since they'd felt like brothers, and anything remotely close to showing some sort of kinship now felt to Max like he somehow still hadn't earned it. Jack sensed this and decided to change it. He ignored Max's outstretched hand, wrapped his arm around Max's neck, and pulled him in close for a tight hug. Max stiffened at first but relaxed when he realized it was the one thing he needed right then, even though he hadn't known it.

They held each other for a long moment.

"You will meet us on time, right?" Jack asked.

"I'll be fine," Max said. "You take care of Schuyler, okay?"

Schuyler watched them from afar, smiling gently. Max took that as a cue to cut the hug off before he looked too clingy. He hoped, though, that this wouldn't be the last time he'd ever see his brother.

Schuyler gave him a reassuring nod and both she and Jack took off together toward Grand Central Terminal. Aoife tightened the bandages around her wrists and leveled a look at Max.

"Ready?"

"More than ever." He returned her easy smile. Never would he have thought he'd be teaming up with the likes of her. The Max who had worked for Lucifer all this time would have balked at the very idea. But being a mortal had taught the new Max a thing or two.

He situated the shield on his back, strapping it on like a rucksack. It was now or never. If he couldn't journey to hell for the love of his life, he was going to do everything in his power to get him back.

He made a single promise to the universe, speaking under his breath so it felt real.

"I'm coming for you, Kingsley Martin."

THIRTY-THREE

SCHUYLER

To be back with Jack was one of the greatest gifts Schuyler could ever ask for. Granted, she would have preferred spending their time together with him curled up next to her on the couch watching a bad movie and buried under a pile of blankets.

She and Jack did their best to act like everyone else around them acted as they emerged from the Warehouse first, keeping an eye on anything out of the ordinary. The coast was clear. The day was dimming, and growing cool, and already Schuyler could smell a storm coming. Thanks to Aoife's amulet, she was able to walk down the street carrying Guinevere's sword without arousing too much notice. By the time they arrived at the train station, dusk had already settled.

Grand Central Terminal was exactly as she remembered it, bustling and brimming with activity. The statue of Mercury sat atop the stone building looking down upon them, smiling with his winged helmet and hand extended outward. The tall windows glowed in the ever-encroaching darkness.

She and Jack weren't totally invisible, but people who didn't know what to look for wouldn't really see them. People moved about their day, rushing to catch their trains, shouting for taxis, or checking maps. To the side were a couple of "living statues," people who painted themselves gray and white to look like marble, surrounded by tourists and various business folks staring at their phones as they walked briskly with their rolling luggage.

Most of the people they saw just glanced at the two of them, their eyes sliding past without the slightest shock that Schuyler had a real sword strapped to her hip. *Neat trick*, she thought.

Grand Central Terminal was a big tourist hot spot. People came to admire the architecture, like the Whispering Wall, where one could stand in a specific spot in an alcove and hear conversations happening across the cavernous room. Or they came to gape at the painted constellations on the ceiling stretching far above the glowing clocks and the departure and arrival boards for commuters coming into and out of the city. Schuyler rarely had an excuse to visit. A native New Yorker like herself got tired of having to navigate around groups of tourists stopping dead in their tracks in the middle of the walkway to snap photos. But now Schuyler was more concerned that these same tourists were going to be in danger.

Jack gently touched Schuyler's hand, sending a spark of electricity up her arm.

He swept her around, shielding her with his body. "Silver Bloods."

Schuyler used all the skills she had acquired acting in plays and put her hand on the back of Jack's neck. It was easy to pretend to be having an intimate, quiet moment with her boyfriend, but this time she used the pause as an opportunity to peer over his shoulder. Sure enough, she saw a cluster of Silver Bloods—four of them in total—surveying the crowd. They were trying to act normal and blend into the mass of people, but they were doing a pretty lousy job of it. All of them were male, looking to be in their thirties, and muscular. They were glaring at anyone passing by; one of them was leaning on the wall, looking sour. But every so often, when their eyes turned away, Schuyler spotted the telltale flash of silver in their pupils. She could have sworn they looked hungry.

For them, being around so many Red Bloods at once was like sitting at a buffet, unable to eat.

"I count four," she whispered.

"Make that eight," Jack said, his head lowered, his baseball cap keeping his face obscured. Behind them another group of Silver Bloods was marching up the promenade. Schuyler tried not to let fear get the best of her. She put her lips to Jack's, hiding both their faces from sight, as the Silver Bloods passed.

It worked. The Silver Bloods made their way through the larger concourse, no doubt patrolling the perimeter, looking for targets, completely oblivious that Jack and Schuyler were there.

"All these innocent people are in the way," Schuyler said.

"The Silver Bloods are using the presence of so many mortals to their advantage. They'll be human shields. These guys know that we won't fight them if it means that people will get hurt."

Schuyler pulled Jack into a small alcove by a drinking fountain. A pair of police officers and a K-9 unit walked by. Human police wouldn't be able to stop anything from happening. It was up to Jack and Schuyler to think of something, and quick. They were running out of time. Schuyler looked at the clock. Aoife and Max must be getting close to the bridge by now. The other Paladin teams were no doubt already setting up their sigils. She worried that there would be Silver Bloods at those locations too.

Jack sent a quick text to Max and Aoife, warning them of the situation.

Meanwhile, Schuyler caught sight of something across the room. Something that might help. Her face brightened.

"I know that look," Jack said. "I love that look. What are you thinking?"

"It's super illegal, but I have an idea," Schuyler said. "I know how we can get all the innocent people out of here while also making sure we don't draw attention to ourselves as we do some minor vandalism on a city's historic site."

Jack blocked her from view again, turning his back as another group of Silver Bloods walked by. He and Schuyler were just a pair of teenagers, nothing to worry about. Sometimes looking innocent was their best weapon.

"Okay, what's the plan?" Jack asked with a smile.

"It'll be kind of like what I did at the museum. If you set off the fire alarm, everyone will have to evacuate the building. It's basic safety protocol. And if any Silver Bloods remain, we can kill them."

"If we weren't surrounded by enemies right now, I'd kiss you for real," Jack said.

Schuyler liked that idea very much, but there were more important things to attend to first.

Jack moved to go. "I got this. Stay here. I'll be right back."

"Promise?"

"Promise."

He left Schuyler leaning against the wall and disappeared into the crowd, melting into anonymity. No matter how hard Schuyler looked for him, he was nowhere in sight. She tried not to worry. The best warrior she knew could handle himself against a couple of Silver Bloods, so she kept an eye on the cluster in the concourse and tried to track their route. As the minutes stretched on, she spotted a third group of Silver Bloods, also composed of four men, making another loop around the station. That made at least twelve Silver Bloods. Aldrich Duncan had an entire army looking for Schuyler's crew. Schuyler's heart started to pound.

She jumped when a shrill alarm cut through the station. Immediately, people started looking around, concerned. The fire alarms blared, and their bright flashing lights were hard to miss. Everyone hurried to the exits; some grumbled about travel delays, but still they went. Schuyler stayed out of sight, peeking around at the Silver Bloods, who, just as she expected, were the only ones who remained. They looked agitated and confused.

Now was the perfect time to move.

The main concourse seemed even more massive now that there weren't hundreds of people packed into it. Painting the sigil would be so much simpler now. All that was standing in Schuyler's way were a dozen Silver Bloods on high alert.

From the backpack, she pulled out one of the many cans of spray paint.

The fire alarm still rang, echoing in her ears. They only had a couple of minutes until the fire department showed up and realized there wasn't, in fact, an emergency. Schuyler needed to stay out of sight. She made sure the sword was still strapped to her hip and rushed for cover behind the Hudson News stand.

The Silver Bloods' voices carried as they argued about what to do.

"Should we leave?"

"Aldrich said to stay put."

"It could be a trap."

From above, Jack leaped down right into the middle of their group. The Silver Bloods looked at him, completely stunned. He was in his element, the beautiful Jack Force, Gabrielle's sword gleaming in his hand.

"Evening, fellas," Jack said.

He grinned at them as their shock wore off, and they brought out their own weapons from underneath their coats or from their waistbands. It was twelve against one.

And then they attacked.

Jack expertly parried and dodged, fighting with all he was made of, and Schuyler moved into the main concourse, keeping low and moving through the wooden benches where passengers would normally wait for their trains. The fight was loud, shouts and curses and metal clanging, giving Schuyler the perfect cover. From her coat pocket, she pulled out the piece of paper detailing the sigil she needed to draw. It was an intricate design, made of swirls and loops, and she needed to make sure she got every detail right or it wouldn't work. She shook the paint can furiously and uncapped it just as a body slammed into the far wall. Jack had thrown a Silver clear across the room, creating a crack in the wall from the force of his blow. Schuyler ran over to look at the downed Silver Blood, who locked eyes with her. His pupils flashed, and he bared his fangs. Schuyler sprayed him right in the face with paint and he howled in pain.

With a swift strike, Schuyler plunged the blinded Silver Blood through the heart with her sword. The emerald gem in the hilt glowed with a spark of magic and the vampire turned to dust right before her eyes with a ferocious scream. Guinevere's sword really was magical. Schuyler had never seen anything like it.

Unfortunately, however, the Silver Blood's death drew the attention of the others.

"Uh-oh," Schuyler said.

Jack was busy fighting off three vampires as the ones who were still on their feet stalked toward her. They were battered and bruised, thanks to Jack, and they looked hungry. Becoming Silver had made their hunger insatiable, and Schuyler was the next dish on the menu.

She scrambled away but they were unstoppable, running up walls to gain ground. One stepped in front of her, his feet blocking her path, and Schuyler slashed out with her blade. She cut across her attacker's ankles and he fell to the floor. She lashed out again and the vampire turned to dust, his fangs the last part of him to dissolve.

Someone grabbed her around the ankle and yanked, dragging her backward. She kicked out with her other foot. The Silver Blood's nose gave a satisfying crunch as her boot met his face. Schuyler tried to swing her sword, but another Silver Blood grasped her tightly around her wrist in an effort to wrench the weapon loose.

With her free hand, Schuyler chucked the spray paint can as hard as she could and it nailed the Silver Blood who was holding her ankle right in the head, stunning him enough to let her go. She lifted her hips up, grabbed the other Silver Blood's throat, and pulled herself backward, flipping over onto his shoulders. She twisted her sword arm out of his grip and stabbed him in the side of his neck. When he crumbled to dust, she rolled with the fall and came up underneath to stab the next Silver Blood in the gut.

A heavy boot connected with Schuyler's back and she went flying forward. Her sword fell from her hand, and she gasped for breath. Her eyes watered. She couldn't breathe. The wind had been kicked out of her and she could only watch as a giant Silver Blood, whose muscles bulged under his coat, huffed like a bull. His heavy footsteps thudded as he stalked toward her.

Schuyler scrambled back, weaponless. The Silver Blood was about to strike, but suddenly Schuyler saw the tip of Gabrielle's sword pop out from his chest. His face, frozen in pain, looked shocked. He swayed and then toppled sideways. Jack stood behind him as the body fell to the ground, dead. Schuyler looked around for the next attack, but the rest of the Silver Bloods were gone. Jack had killed them all.

"Are you okay?" he asked. Silver blood was smeared on his cheek, remnants of his battle. He held his hand out to her. She took it and got back on her feet.

"I am now!" She looked at the giant clock in the middle of the concourse. "We don't have much time. The others should already be finishing up their sigils if they haven't run into trouble."

"Then let's get to it."

Jack took another paint can from Schuyler and together they worked, spraying the sigil onto the marble floor.

Before Schuyler could finish, a shrill laugh echoed around the concourse. All the hairs on her neck stood on end. She knew that laugh. Jack readied his sword.

Laughter seemed to be coming from everywhere at once, cold as the bottom of the ocean.

"Jack, cover your ears!" Schuyler yelled. Doing so would make him unable to fight, but what else were they supposed to do? He clamped his hands over his ears and looked at Schuyler with wide, frightened eyes.

Schuyler readied Guinevere's sword and spun around, scanning the empty concourse. The last time she had heard that laugh, a building had almost crushed her to death. The siren was back.

Water shimmered on the floor, moving as if on its own volition toward them, and both Schuyler and Jack rushed back. Schuyler put herself in front of him as the siren took shape, materializing out of the water before them.

"Oh, Jack." Harmony the siren sighed. "Why are you shutting yourself off from me?"

"Don't listen to her!"

"Thought you killed me, did you? Thought you could steal from me, did you?" The siren looked at Schuyler with a sneer before turning her eyes on Jack. "I've been looking all over for you, my love. Jack . . . come back to me." She held out her arms toward him.

"Stay away from him," Schuyler said. She gripped her sword tighter. She had no idea if it would work against a siren. She remembered the *Liber Monstrorum* saying that sirens were weak against iron and fire, but iron wasn't the sort of metal this sword was forged from.

But she'd already lost Jack once in another world. She wasn't about to let it happen again in this one.

The siren smiled, rows of fangs glinting in the light. "Try and stop me."

THIRTY-FOUR

MAX

The Brooklyn Bridge was always busy, teeming with cars careening down the five lanes of roadway, and tonight was no exception. The suspension towers were already lit up against the setting sun, adding to the sweeping view of lower Manhattan. It was picture-perfect, one of the best views in town, and the exact opposite of what Max and Aoife needed right now.

They stood on the pedestrian sidewalk above the road to catch their breath. Not only was the bridge packed with cars, it was also packed with people. The walkway above separated pedestrians from traffic, and it would have been easier to stop people from walking where they needed to work. Unfortunately, the walkway wasn't big enough for them to draw the sigil properly. Max would need to do it on the road. He frowned at the passing cars traveling beneath their feet.

"We need to get everyone off the bridge," Aoife said. "If Lucifer's minions try to stop us, we could be putting all these innocents in harm's way."

Tourists were taking photos with the suspension tower in the background, and folks were walking their dogs, and couples were holding hands . . . It was going to be difficult, but Aoife was right. No one here was ready for what was to come. Max had gotten a text from Jack saying he and Schuyler had run into trouble, and he knew it was only a matter of time before he found proof of Lucifer's Coven here too. He scanned the area for Silver Bloods, but so far no one looked familiar. Either Aldrich's loyalists were good at hiding, or Max had gotten very, very lucky. He highly doubted the latter.

Aoife too didn't seem convinced that this was going to be an easy job. She shifted her weight from one foot to the other in nervous anticipation. "I've got a bad feeling about this."

"Same." Even though he wasn't a vampire anymore, Max could feel danger in the air. It was too quiet—aside from the traffic noise. But they couldn't let it stop them now.

"I'm about to do something very stupid," he said.

Aoife glanced at him. "Have fun!"

They shared a quick smile as she took off toward the bigger tour groups and Max vaulted over the pedestrian guardrail. He landed on the hard pavement and darted out into traffic.

Cars heading toward the city screeched to a halt. Max held out his hands, yelling for people to stop. Horns blared at him, but he ignored them. He waved people away, even as they got out of their cars to yell at him. Max wasn't willing to let a few expletives stop him.

"There's an emergency! The bridge is closed!" he called. He shook the spray paint can vigorously.

As people watched, Max started working on his sigil, spraying the lines on the pavement. He heard Aoife shouting at pedestrians to get off the bridge, that it wasn't safe. Unfortunately, it seemed to have the opposite effect. People thought she was putting on some sort of staged performance and clustered around to get a better look.

Soon enough, the whole bridge was in a state of gridlock. Cars and buses honked, but Max paid no attention to them. No doubt someone was calling the police to come arrest him. He had a limited amount of time in which to paint the sigil and disappear before the police would carry him off in handcuffs.

But his luck ran out sooner than he expected.

"Stop right where you are! Put your hands up!"

Max froze. A police officer stepped toward him, hand on his belt, on his gun. Max slowly raised his hands but didn't drop the spray can. He'd been caught, literally, red-handed.

The cop pinched the radio at his shoulder and said, "Yep, I've got him." Max spotted Aoife, who was leaning over the guardrail of the pedestrian walkway to get a better look. He shook his head, warning her not to attempt to help him.

Max put on his best smile and turned his attention back to the cop. "You've got the wrong guy, Officer." A blatant lie, but one that Max was willing to commit to. He needed time to think of a way out of this and he was slowly running out of options.

The cop pulled out a pair of handcuffs from his belt, and Max's heart lodged in his throat. A few months ago, he might have laughed at the idea of being arrested. What kind of mortal handcuffs could contain an angel of the Apocalypse? But now . . . If it was his fault that their mission failed, he might as well throw himself into the river and spare the others the effort. But then the shield on his back started vibrating, like a phone on a silent ringer.

The shield sensed something and was trying to warn Max.

Max took a hesitant step backward, and the cop paused too. Max stared at the man's face, but he didn't recognize him. He wasn't a Silver Blood. *Unless . . .* "Don't come any closer," he said.

The cop's mouth split into a too-wide smile, a familiar smile. "Max . . . Come on, now. You wouldn't want to resist arrest, would you?"

Max narrowed his eyes. "Leviathan."

The mutatio melted away and the figure before him morphed and reshaped into the face Max had seen all too often in his nightmares. Onlookers shouted and gasped, unsure if what they had just seen had really happened. If people were smart, they'd start running right now.

Standing in the cop's place was a man dressed in a dark purple suit made of crushed velvet. When the light hit the fabric, it looked like it was coated wet with an oil slick, as viscous as his smile.

"I've been waiting for you to show up," Leviathan said. "I'd heard you died when they took your power. Now look at you. You're like a cockroach, finding new ways to crawl your way out of the filth."

"Guess I just don't know when to take a hint."

Leviathan sighed. People around them stared. Like his brother, Leviathan despised mortals. It rocked Max to think that one day, he and Jack would have been shaped into taking Lucifer's and Leviathan's places, brothers inheriting a legacy. It would be an unending cycle causing more pain and suffering, successive avatars of the titles of Lucifer and Leviathan passing down the abuse again and again, to their own sons. If he had remained in Leviathan's service, all Max would have brought into the world was more pain.

No. No more.

Max was going to break that cycle.

"I should have killed you then," Leviathan said. His features shifted and morphed once more, taking on their demonic form. His skin turned to coal, glowing from within like lava, his eyes red as a furnace. Someone screamed, then someone else. People began to panic and flee. "I won't make the same mistake twice." His voice was barely more than a growl, and he was growing taller. From his back, great, leathery, batlike wings unfurled.

Max's fear glued him to the spot, but he wouldn't give in to it and run. He would use it to bring about something greater than himself. He pulled his shield from his back.

Leviathan's power swelled and a shock wave of energy blasted cars away. Some of them slid right over the edge of the bridge, plummeting to the black water below and giving Max and Leviathan room to battle.

Aoife shouted Max's name, but she was too far away for him to hear it. Everyone wanted to get as far from the monster as they could, and she was fighting against a huge flow of people. Max didn't have the luxury of trying to escape. He'd been waiting for this moment for a long time.

Max readied his shield.

THIRTY-FIVE

SCHUYLER

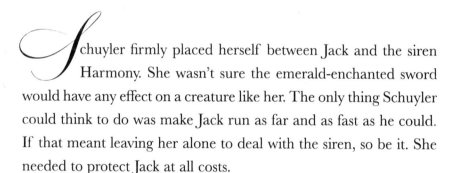

*S*chuyler firmly placed herself between Jack and the siren Harmony. She wasn't sure the emerald-enchanted sword would have any effect on a creature like her. The only thing Schuyler could think to do was make Jack run as far and as fast as he could. If that meant leaving her alone to deal with the siren, so be it. She needed to protect Jack at all costs.

Harmony seemed to find all of this so amusing. She didn't make a move to attack. She simply stood, facing Schuyler with a smile that sycophantic adults reserved for amusing naive children. "I've been in his head for too long," Harmony said. "My control over him is almost complete. One more song from me, and he'll do whatever I want him to do."

"Don't you dare."

"He can try to fight all he wants, but my lure is irresistible. Men have written stories about me and my sisters, warning each other of what awaited them in the farthest reaches of the ocean. And all this time I only had to wait for the right man to cross my path to know true happiness."

Schuyler got the sense that Harmony was a lot older than she let on.

"I can't forget someone as special as him," the siren said. "We were made for each other."

Schuyler immediately thought of Jack's hallucination that he had killed Schuyler. Harmony had made him see his worst fears come to life, and the siren could make this one happen for real. She'd make him kill Schuyler. He'd be powerless to stop himself. Even though their love spanned universes, it could still come to an end. Schuyler had seen Jack die in another world; in this one, his face might be the last one she ever saw. Anger burned hot in her chest.

"Jack! Run!" Schuyler screamed. He understood and took off for the exit awkwardly, his hands still firmly planted over his ears.

Harmony threw out her arms and let out a vibrato note that sent a chill down Schuyler's spine. It was perfectly pitched, and one of the most beautiful notes Schuyler had ever heard. It had no effect on her, but she could still hear what Harmony wanted her to hear. Like watching a movie in her mind, free from the hypnosis but all the same, able to understand. She heard promises of a long life with Jack, getting married to him, starting a family with him, living together as partners. No wonder Harmony's illusions could keep people trapped. They were too good to be true.

What Jack heard made him stop dead in his tracks. All Schuyler could do was watch in horror as his hands dropped to his sides. Harmony's song was too strong to resist.

"You're mine now, my love," Harmony said, victorious.

He turned, his gaze distant and unfocused.

"Jack, no." His sword was still in his hand, and brandishing it, he moved toward Schuyler. The blade glinted in the light, and Schuyler imagined the way it would flash as it sliced across her throat. Harmony slithered like water across the floor, sliding behind Jack and wrapping her arms around his chest. Her eyes flashed purple as she glared at Schuyler, hiding herself behind Jack's body.

"She's the only thing standing between us, my Blue Blood," Harmony sang. Her lips brushed against Jack's neck, and he didn't even flinch. He was under Harmony's spell. It was like he was sleepwalking. No matter how Schuyler pleaded, he was lost in his mind. Even if he realized what was happening, it would be too late.

Schuyler backed up as Jack stepped toward her.

The siren's smile was wicked.

Thirty-Six

MAX

Max hit the pavement like a rag doll for the tenth time. His whole body screamed at him to make the pain stop. His ribs were broken, making every breath agony, something in his ankle had popped, and his lip was bleeding, but still he wasn't going to give up.

Even though he had the shield, Max didn't have the speed or the strength to battle fairly, and Leviathan relished the fun he would now have. He could have easily killed Max if he wanted to, but instead he was playing with his food. He wanted to see Max suffer, wanted to watch him cough up bright red blood, to feel every bruise and strike, to remember what it felt like to be mortal for a moment longer before it was all over.

Every time he fell, Max wiped his mouth with the back of his wrist, smearing the red on his pale skin, and got back to his feet. His legs felt like Jell-O, but this only reminded him that he was still alive. There was still breath in his lungs, even if it hurt like hell to breathe.

Leviathan marched toward him, grinning with his rows of sharp fangs. His claws tore up the pavement as he loomed over Max and raised his hand. But a golden whip wrapped around Leviathan's wrist. Aoife's whip! She'd come back for Max.

For a moment, Leviathan looked amused. Then Aoife shouted, "Ignis!" and holy fire ripped down the length of the whip and blinded Leviathan. He roared in pain. Her Banner's fire burned Leviathan's arm, and for once he looked surprised—surprised that a mortal could hurt him.

If Max wasn't in so much pain, he would have laughed.

Aoife readied the whip again, snapping it in the air, and the sound was thunderous. She drew Leviathan's attention away and Max took a moment to gather his wits, ignoring his injuries. He knew they were running out of time. If Leviathan's whole plan was to keep them occupied, he was achieving it. Aoife needed to stop worrying about his maneuverings and focus on drawing the sigil. It was the only way they could hope to get rid of Lucifer once and for all.

Leviathan's smile was a snarl as he looked at Aoife. "Mortals always think they can stand up to gods."

Aoife locked eyes with Max. "This is the thing that killed Kingsley?" she asked.

Max nodded. "Ugly, isn't he?"

Leviathan's arm was drenched in golden blood thanks to Aoife's whip, and he looked angry. He unfurled his leathery wings and pounced on Max, digging his claws into Max's chest and pinning him to the hood of a car. The weight of Leviathan crunched the hood with a metallic groan, and then, with a pump of his wings, Leviathan took to the sky, clutching Max tight.

"Max!" Aoife's voice was swept away as the wind drowned her out. Max tried to pull free of Leviathan at first but quickly realized it was a stupid idea. The black water of the river churned below them, and if he dropped now, he'd surely drown. Instead he held on for all he was worth.

Leviathan laughed at the look of fear on Max's face. The cold of the air sliced across Max's skin, and he kicked reflexively. Leviathan growled. "You want to be free? As you wish!"

Max's stomach flew into his chest as Leviathan let him go. He yelled out and flailed, then he slammed hard into the top of the suspension tower on the bridge. Stars danced before his eyes. Max had never hurt so much in his life. His whole body felt like it was made of mush, and yet he still managed to get to his feet. It's what Kingsley would have done.

Leviathan landed in front of him, giving the pathetic mortal a chance to rise. He turned his back to Max as he looked out over the city, his wings spread wide, his arms held out as if embracing it in its entirety.

Max was pretty sure his shoulder was dislocated and he wavered on his feet. Pain blurred his vision, and he shook his head. He was amazed he was still standing at all. If he wasn't fueled by pure revenge at this point, he would have fallen over the edge of the tower and plummeted to his death, sparing Leviathan the satisfaction of finishing him off himself.

"This city has no idea what I've done for it," Leviathan said. "These people run in fear of me because they're no smarter than the apes they evolved from. They should be kneeling at my feet, thanking me for my mercy. They know nothing of power . . . They build monuments to what?" Leviathan spread his arms wider and the wind howled around them.

Max spat, and blood splattered on the stone at his feet. His tongue was coated in something that had the taste of iron. He was running out of ideas, and his brain was starting to get foggy. His shield hummed beneath his arm. It vibrated with the magical energy of the Paladin who had wielded it before him. Aoife had mentioned time and time again how objects could be imbued with certain powers. The one who had carried the shield before Max took possession of it had once slain a dragon . . . A spark of an idea blossomed behind Max's eyes. A dragon . . . Another name for a leviathan.

Leviathan took a deep breath of city air, his wings stretching, and he turned to Max. In the blink of an eye, he lashed out and grabbed Max by the front of his coat. Max barely had time to recognize that his shoes were hitting nothing but air. Leviathan had lifted him off his feet. He knew if Leviathan threw him, he'd fall thirty stories down to the water below. A watery grave, anonymous in death.

"My brother was so foolish to think his legacy could be passed down to a simple boy. Stupid, foolish, alone. You have nothing, no one left to defend you. You're an embarrassment to your kind and your name. You're nothing," Leviathan growled.

Max had called himself those things and much worse, so hearing Leviathan say the words aloud had little effect on him. He'd been so self-hating for so long, and he'd tried to patch himself up with more self-deprecation because he thought such bravado was what would make him strong. But he knew it wasn't true. He knew he wasn't alone. He had people who loved him, who cared about him, despite everything he'd done. He'd asked for forgiveness, and he was still working to deserve it. Leviathan's words only made him angrier.

He bared his teeth and managed to sputter out, "So what?"

Max struggled to get down to solid ground. It was infuriatingly close, but Leviathan held him up to keep his feet from touching.

"Take one last look, Max," Leviathan said. He turned Max's face toward the city. "You're going to die for this?"

A calm washed over Max as he looked at the city. It was always so beautiful at night. This was his home, the only place he could call home. His angelic spirit had barely remembered Paradise, but Manhattan was the only home he had ever known. It wasn't perfect in the slightest, far from that, in fact, but it was his. Seeing the city now, at what looked like the end of his life, wasn't the worst thing he could do. The island and the people in it were worth fighting for. He thought of Schuyler, of Stephen and Aurora, the Paladins, of Jack and Kingsley. Max couldn't help the smirk that came to his face.

He raised his shield, defying the pain screaming through his arm, and turned the dragon's face to Leviathan. The dragon's eyes began to glow and the metal shook on Max's arm as the power built up. He knew he had only one shot, and he wasn't going to waste it.

Leviathan's surprise couldn't be masked. He thought mortals like Max were below him. His underestimation was his downfall.

A glowing inscription on the back of the shield told Max everything he needed to know. He said the word through clenched teeth.

"Ignis."

Holy fire burst from the dragon's mouth, blasting directly into Leviathan's face. His skin melted, his blood boiled, and he screamed in agony. He dropped Max and tried to put out the fire, but it was too powerful, even for a demon from hell.

"NO!" he howled, clawing at his face as fire ate away at his body.

Smoke filled the air, the heat unbearable even as Max tried to scramble back.

With a final roar, Leviathan exploded in a shower of sparks and ash, the very cells of his body destroyed. The shock wave threw Max backward and he rolled as helplessly as a tumbleweed in the desert. At the last second, he lashed out and grabbed hold of the limestone edge before he rolled over the side of the tower. Pain in his shoulder blinded him and he cried out, but he held on. Max's feet dangled helplessly. He tried not to look down, but he couldn't help it. His fingers could barely hold on to anything; they burned, bearing his whole weight. He was slipping. He didn't have any strength left.

Max was going to fall.

THIRTY-SEVEN

SCHUYLER

This was Schuyler's worst nightmare.

Jack approached her, his sword extended, and she raised her own. Her knees shook. Her palms were drenched in sweat. Her lungs burned with the urge to cry. She didn't want to do this.

"Jack," she whispered.

"Kill her, my love," Harmony urged. She stood behind Jack, peering over his shoulder, her smile victorious.

Jack paused in front of Schuyler, his sword raised with both hands, ready to strike. Schuyler steeled herself for the hit. Then Jack smiled.

She didn't know how to react. But then Jack tapped his finger on the bracelet around his wrist. Schuyler met his summer-green eyes again and he winked. She knew what to do.

"Now!" she screamed.

Jack stepped to the side just as Schuyler swiped down with her sword.

Harmony didn't realize what was happening until it was too

late. Schuyler lopped her head clean off her shoulders. The siren's head rolled on the floor, finally coming to a stop and staring in shock at Schuyler for a fraction of a second before her eyes turned white like sea foam, and her body crumbled to the floor.

The siren's cry echoed as she turned into a pile of flotsam, dead fish, and seaweed, and the purple mist of her song faded into nothing.

This time the siren was dead for sure.

Schuyler stood, panting, and glanced at Jack, who stared down at what was left of the creature. The look on his face could only be described as relief. He took Schuyler's hand and squeezed as he let out a shaky breath. His nightmare was over, and Schuyler had saved him once more. She leaped into his arms and kissed him deeply.

When she pulled away, returning to solid ground, she reared back her fist and punched him in the arm. Jack let out a small yowl. "That's for scaring me!" she shouted.

Jack massaged the spot where she'd hit him, his cheeks pink. "I'm sorry! It was the only way I could get her close to you."

"A little heads-up beforehand would have been nice." She wasn't truly mad at him, but heat rushed to her face. A whirlwind of emotions made her head ache.

"You're right. I'm sorry. I won't scare you anymore, I promise."

She knew he meant it. "How did . . . The siren song—"

"The bracelet you made," Jack said, holding his wrist out. "It must have protected me. Aoife has always said that the mundane can become magical."

Of course, Schuyler thought. She had unintentionally imbued the bracelet with her love as she thought about Jack while making it. She'd saved his life without even knowing it. "I thought I'd lost you. *Again*."

"You'll never lose me, Schuyler. Not even if you try."

Schuyler allowed herself to smile. "Since when did you get so cheesy?" she asked.

"Since we were running out of time." His eyes went to the giant clock. "We need to finish this."

Together, they finished copying the sigil. Schuyler closed the final loop and stepped back. She waited a breath, then another. Nothing seemed to be happening. She checked the image of the sigil on her paper, making sure they had copied it correctly.

"Did we do something wrong?" Jack asked.

"I don't—" But as Schuyler spoke, the lines on the floor started to glow with a soft white light. "It's working!" she gasped.

Flashing blue and red lights filled the concourse, followed by the telltale howl of a fire engine siren.

"Great," Jack said, "because we need to get the hell out of here." He grabbed her hand and together they ran through the station, fleeing the scene into the cool night.

THIRTY-EIGHT

SCHUYLER

The charity concert was in full swing by the time Schuyler and Jack arrived, but Aldrich hadn't yet begun the final phase of his plan. They caught their breath and remained out of sight, hidden in a small copse of oak trees and tall bushes, watching the crowd of concertgoers moving to the beat of the music. The whole place was crawling with Silver Bloods, mixed in with thousands of humans. Schuyler searched, but there was no sign of Aldrich, or Oliver, for that matter. Not too long ago, he'd asked her to go to this concert with him. Had he known what was to come? Did he want her to have a front-row seat?

"Paladins are ready," Jack said, nodding at a pair who gave a small salute to his and Schuyler's hiding spot. Hundreds more were in the crowd, waiting for the signal. "Now all Aldrich has to do is show his face."

Schuyler's heart had made a home in her throat. She struggled to swallow around it. It was almost time. "Where is everyone?" she asked.

Almost as if on cue, Theo and his team arrived, followed closely by Ruby, who was nursing a bleeding arm. They came crashing through the underbrush, breathless and pink-cheeked.

"It's done," Theo said. He grabbed Ruby's arm and healed her, then asked Schuyler and Jack, "Are you two okay?"

"We're fine," Jack said.

"Damn vampires," Ruby hissed. "It was bad. Rockefeller Center was crawling with them. We almost didn't make it. One of the Silver Bloods tried to radio for backup, but we killed them before they could."

"Do we need to change our approach?" Theo asked Jack.

"No, stick to the plan. We're waiting for the last sigil."

Theo gestured to his team, signaling them to get to their positions. They fanned out into the crowd.

Schuyler nodded toward the stage. "They're not even hiding it." The Enochian machine stood on the stage beneath the open sky. The concert lights and thumping music couldn't distract her from her awareness of the storm that had started to gather overhead, growing more intense as the machine's strange writing glowed with it.

"Everyone thinks it's just part of the set," said Theo.

"Where are Max and Aoife?" Jack asked.

Schuyler scanned the crowd. "They should be back by now." Her heart sank with each passing second as Aoife and Max failed to appear. Their sigil couldn't be inactive. If only three out of the four sigils were active, their plans would abort. It would bring their mission to a grinding halt. If they didn't activate the resurrection sigil soon, they'd miss their only chance.

"Something's wrong," Schuyler said. "I have to go find them."

Jack grabbed her hand and stopped her, his face pale. "Look."

The band had finished their set and left the stage, and Silver Bloods started filing into place. The crowd stirred with anticipation, expecting Mayor Aldrich Duncan to appear at any moment. Meanwhile, the sky swirled darker. The wind kicked up, and a chill composed of something more than just the cold made the hair on Schuyler's arms stand on end.

"He's powering it up," Jack said. The machine was fully glowing now. Its symbols were almost blindingly white, glowing with ancient power. The concertgoers thought it was part of the show and applauded for more.

Just then, a spotlight hit the stage, shining on Aldrich Duncan. He waved and smiled to the crowd as he stepped up to the microphone. The cheers grew louder, the ground shaking with the noise. He was their hero mayor, leading them through times of hardship. Everyone loved him. Schuyler's whole body felt like it was going to snap with tension.

"Aoife, Max . . ." Jack whispered. "Come on."

They were running out of time. Schuyler's heart hammered painfully.

Aldrich's voice carried across the Great Lawn, booming through the speakers, strong and proud. "Ladies and gentlemen, thank you! Thank you! What a turnout! There's so many of you, you can feel the energy in the air." The crowd applauded. "We have a great show lined up for you tonight."

Schuyler's stomach felt like it dropped to her feet when Oliver stepped up to the stage. He was shirtless despite the cold, wearing only white pants and Azrael's power around his neck. He walked straight shouldered, his head held high. He was ready. Aldrich was there with him, speaking to him in his ear, and then Oliver took his place on a small dais etched with Enochian symbols. People murmured to one another, wondering what was going on. Azrael's power glowed against Oliver's chest. It seemed to thrum with the pulse of the ancient symbols, like it was eager to be set free from its cage.

Schuyler closed her eyes. All her memories of the years she'd spent with Oliver as her best and only friend, in this world and the last, forced themselves into her head. She remembered how deep their friendship was, how he'd made her laugh, how he'd shared his heart with her. She loved him, more than he ever knew, and she wanted to hold on to those happy memories. They were real to her and that's why she needed to fight for him. The Oliver who was standing up on that stage now wasn't the same Oliver she had known. Her Oliver wouldn't be doing this. There had to be some way to get to him and talk reason before it was too late.

When she opened her eyes again, she saw Jack looking at her, his mouth pulled into a small frown.

"I know," he said. Jack had almost let his brother slip through his fingers. Max had come so close to succumbing to Lucifer's temptation to acquire ultimate power. Jack must have felt the same helplessness and grief that Schuyler was going through. "You'll stop him," Jack said.

Schuyler nodded stiffly. "I'm the only one who can."

"Citizens of this great city," Aldrich cried into the microphone. "I ask you, bear witness. You are the first, and the last. Thank you for your sacrifice."

The crowd didn't know what to make of these words. People

glanced around at one another, shuffling nervously. The air was humming with something new; the storm was growing impossibly darker. Some people started to break away from the crowd, anticipating the arrival of the freezing rain.

"This is wrong," Jack said. He took a hesitating step forward. "This is . . . everyone, fall back."

"Jack?" Theo asked, fear in his voice.

"I said, fall back!" Jack's eyes flashed with panic.

Crrrrack.

It sounded like the sky itself had broken open. A white light, made of pure energy, shot from the machine and into the dark purple clouds churning overhead.

The machine worked to tear into the fabric of reality.

First it was one drop, and then another, and then the storm descended. Freezing-cold rain drenched the spectators almost instantly but despite the water, the Enochian symbols only glowed brighter.

Without the final activation sigil, Schuyler's team wasn't ready. If she confronted her enemies now, she'd be fighting without a plan. Her heart raced with anxiety.

The air felt thick and heavy, charged with electricity, and the symbols continued to flash like lightning. At first, Schuyler didn't know what was happening. But then she heard the screams. That was when she noticed the bodies. One by one, every time the machine flashed, a person dropped to the ground, dead. Aldrich was stealing their souls to generate the power to collapse universes.

"Don't get near the stage!" Jack screamed. "Stay back!" He braced his arms in front of Theo and Ruby.

The machine glowed brighter yet with each new soul it harvested, and the storm roared overhead. The sky looked about ready to burst. Screams carried across the field. Schuyler wanted to run toward them, but she couldn't. If she got too close, the machine would kill her too. All she could do was watch in horror as things unfolded.

Once it looked as if the machine couldn't handle any more souls, Aldrich nodded. Oliver snapped the pendant of power from its leather cord around his neck and held it firmly in his hand. The glow from Azrael's power leaked through his fingers. His chest heaved with the thrill of what he was about to do.

Schuyler wanted to scream out to stop him, to do something, anything. But Oliver tipped his head back and drank all of Azrael's blood. When the charm stone was empty. he dropped it at his feet, and it shattered like glass.

THIRTY-NINE

MAX

*M*ax couldn't hold on much longer.

The storm was pummeling him. Thunder rolled through the sky and the rain made the stone slick in his grip.

Baring his teeth, he willed himself to hang on for a millisecond longer, but for what? He was just delaying the inevitable. No one was coming to save him. He'd killed Leviathan, and he'd killed himself in the process. At least he could die knowing he'd avenged Kingsley, even if he couldn't resurrect him at the end. Maybe he could join Kingsley in Purgatory. He didn't expect to go to Paradise, or even to the underworld. He'd done so many horrible things in his life, he imagined that they had canceled out whatever good he might have tried to do in such a short amount of time.

Max's fingers slipped.

For a moment, nothing happened, and then gravity took hold; it felt like everything was moving in slow motion. As if the ledge was falling away from Max instead of the other way around. He reached out, but the distance was too far. He dropped.

In the span of a heartbeat, he knew he was going to die. When he'd been the angel of death, he'd never feared dying. He knew he would always be reborn again and again.

Being mortal meant this was the end.

Nothing awaited him. And that was okay. He wished he could say goodbye to Jack. He didn't want his twin to mourn him forever, but still, he did want Jack to think that he'd been a good brother.

Then, in another heartbeat, Max had the opposite thought. He didn't want to die. He didn't want all of his efforts to be for nothing. He wanted to keep going because his work wasn't finished yet. He still had more to give to the world, more for once to give rather than to take.

He reached out, stretching his fingers toward the tower again. He let out a yell, one final plea to whoever was listening, a plea that his fight wasn't over. He needed to live.

A whip appeared at the edge of his vision then wrapped around his wrist. He grabbed on.

Max barely had time to realize what was happening before he slammed to a stop, dangling by a rope. Bewildered, he looked up and saw Aoife standing atop the tower, gripping tightly to her Banner, teeth bared with the effort. She let out a growl, her arms shaking with the weight of him.

She'd saved him.

"Don't say anything in Latin!" Max screamed. The last thing he needed was to be set on fire.

"I know!" Aoife howled back.

Fist over fist, she pulled him up. Max scrambled up the vertical face of the tower, using what purchase his sneakers could catch on the slick limestone, until he reached the ledge once more. Aoife fell backward as Max collapsed on solid ground. They lay together on their backs, breathing heavily, staring at the storm as it rained down upon them. Max's whole body ached with exhaustion and pain, but he was alive. He had been given another chance.

He looked over at Aoife. Her eyes were closed, and she was panting with exhaustion. She'd climbed all the way up here to help him. He didn't think he could ever repay her. In a way, she reminded him of Schuyler.

All this time he'd been searching for a family to fill the hole left by the one he'd lost. But in that moment he realized that Schuyler's dad, Stephen, was right. Family was about choosing who to love. That's all it had to be.

"Thank you," he said. He let out a small whimper of a laugh, relief and terror mixed in a confused ball of emotion in his throat. Then the laughter turned more hysterical. He hurt everywhere, but he was so damn happy. Max put his hands over his face and let himself go for a moment.

"Max," Aoife said. The surprise in her voice shocked Max out of his fit of laughter. She was looking at him like he'd grown a second head. "Your wrists."

He sat up straight and stared. Tattoos had appeared on his wrists, two circles interlocked—the marks of a Paladin, just like the ones Aoife had. He had been chosen.

Max could hardly believe it. He stared at his wrists, then at Aoife. She grinned at him.

"You did something to impress someone," Aoife said.

The shield at Max's feet seemed to glow brighter when he looked at it. The dragon slayer's shield. His shield.

Slowly, he got to his feet. His body felt new. He was stronger, his injuries healing; he could tell he was faster. Max had become a Paladin.

But his newfound hope was short-lived.

A deafening explosion made both him and Aoife duck as a huge pillar of fire shot into the sky, coming from Central Park.

A shock wave rocked the bridge on which Aoife and Max were standing; they grabbed on to each other for balance. Cars and trucks honked. The whole city was the epicenter of what felt like an earthquake, but Max knew it was something else.

Azrael's power had been freed.

"We're too late," he gasped. "The end has begun."

PART FOUR
ENEMIES & LOVERS

FORTY

SCHUYLER

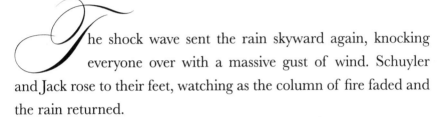

The shock wave sent the rain skyward again, knocking everyone over with a massive gust of wind. Schuyler and Jack rose to their feet, watching as the column of fire faded and the rain returned.

And in the next moment, everything was still.

Oliver's body glowed from the inside, veins of white light streaking across his skin. He'd always been skinny, but now he looked like he'd been training at a gym for years. For the first time ever, a mortal had become something more. Everyone was struck by his beauty, even the Silver Bloods, especially Aldrich. No one dared to speak or move. . . . It was like time had stopped.

Oliver looked at his hands, seeing the power circulating beneath his skin, and he threw back his head. As if he'd finally gotten everything he ever wanted, he laughed at the storm above him and relished the moment. He was so powerful, the rain never touched him. It just rolled off the invisible aura surrounding him, glistening in the stage lights.

He had become more powerful and awesome than Schuyler could ever have imagined, and she was terrified.

The glow faded from his body, and he turned his eyes on the nearest Silver Blood. His new fangs emerged, and he attacked the Silver Blood in a swift move, draining the unfortunate soul in seconds. Aldrich only smiled, pleased with his latest creation. Oliver had taken upon himself the Silver Legacy, just as Aldrich had wanted Max to do. Oliver had become a perfect weapon.

He gasped with ecstasy as the Silver Blood dropped to the stage floor, dead, and he licked the last of the demon's blood clean from his lips. His eyes, now liquid gold, flashed with even more hunger than they had moments before. He wasn't as yet satisfied. Schuyler doubted he'd ever be satisfied. Azrael's power craved death, and Oliver was going to give death to him.

Schuyler's whole body shook with a mixture of rage and fear. How could they kill the angel of death?

"I have to stop him before he summons Michael's sword," Jack said, stepping forward.

"Wait," Schuyler said. "We're too late. Let him do it."

"What!" he cried over the rain, bewildered.

"We can't get the sword unless he summons it from the ether! He's the only one who can control it now! Trust me!" Max had lost Azrael's power forever. His claim to the sword had ended. This was their only chance.

Jack realized that Schuyler was right. "Gabrielle's sword is the only weapon that can match it."

"Then use it," she said. Who else could face the angel of death but the angel of destruction?

The storm above had turned into a kaleidoscope of light.

Schuyler knew the effect wasn't just the result of lightning. There was something moving beyond the clouds, something obscured like it was hidden behind fogged glass. The multiverse was starting to open. The souls powering the machine were pushing the worlds closer together than ever. The shrieks and growls of monsters and creatures from other worlds echoed through the sky. Everyone in the entire city would hear it, but no one would know what to make of it. It was too late to turn the tide. The monsters were coming. Everyone was in danger.

The Enochian machine whined loudly, as if it were screaming with pain. The energy pouring out of it kept the different realities open. From the sky, giant fireballs streaked toward the earth, falling like meteors. When they crashed into the ground, monsters emerged from the smoke and ash. Snarling, howling, hissing, a variety of hideous, horrifying creatures took their first steps in this new world.

Schuyler recognized some of them from drawings in the *Liber Monstrorum*. Others were unrecognizable except from her nightmares.

Anyone who could flee, fled.

Paladins started gathering their weapons in hand.

The Apocalypse had begun.

Oliver paused for a moment and looked out across the grass, watching the monsters as they landed, but it was as if he was looking for something, or someone, specific. His eyes had turned from honey to gold and his gaze landed right on Schuyler's hiding place.

He smiled, his fangs catching the light. He was beautiful and horrible all at once.

Through the glom, Schuyler felt tendrils of thought reaching out to her like a thousand whispers. They came in Oliver's voice, surrounding her. *Schuyler . . . I know you're here. . . . Do you see me now?*

Schuyler squeezed her fists so tightly, her fingernails drew blood from her palms. She closed herself from the glom so Oliver wouldn't sense her rage.

At that moment, Aldrich hurried to Oliver's side and put his hands on his shoulders. Oliver stood taller, prouder, his chest heaving with emotion. "My son . . ." Aldrich said. "I've been so blind to your potential, yet here you stand. Make me proud. It is time. Use Azrael's power." Aldrich's voice boomed over the chaos in the park. "Tear all the worlds down."

Oliver smiled.

He summoned Michael's sword to his hand. The golden blade shone like the sun against a storm. A sword of the Apocalypse, wielded by the one who ended all things. And his name was Death, and hell followed him.

In a flash of blinding light, Oliver transformed into Azrael and took to the sky, streaking upward like a rocket, Michael's sword in his hands.

"Jack, stop him!" Schuyler cried. In response, he transformed into Abbadon and gave chase with Gabrielle's sword.

Schuyler turned to the other Paladins and unsheathed Guinevere's sword.

"Kill as many monsters as you can," she told them, "and save as many people as you can as well. Together, we can save this city. Leave Lucifer to me."

FORTY-ONE

MAX

he end of the world was at hand, and Max and Aoife still needed to finish copying their sigil.

"Hurry!" Max shouted.

"I'm going as fast as I can! The rain is washing away the paint!"

She was right. Every time they laid down a line of red, the rain made it run, like blood. They had to keep going over the lines to make sure there were no gaps. Fully healed now, Max hurried over and helped Aoife, and together they laid down enough paint that when they connected the lines, the sigil began to glow.

"I think that's a good sign," Aoife said.

"It better not be too late."

Fireball meteors were dropping from the storm cloud circling over Central Park and this could only mean one thing. Max could hear people screaming and crying, fleeing on foot across the bridge and into Brooklyn. To him, the scene looked downright biblical. Fire raining down from a storm of mirror images of Earth, pressing upon them like a great glass prism. The worlds were colliding.

A sudden, deafening screech sounded seconds before a meteor crashed into the bridge where Aoife and Max were standing. The two had to cling to each other to stay on their feet. From the crash site, a lion emerged, stamping its great talons and spreading its wings. It snarled at people trying to escape, its fangs dripping with venom. Its tail was a living snake, the head as big as a bowling ball, hissing at anyone who came near.

"It's a chimera!" Aoife shouted.

"What's a chimera?" asked Max.

She gritted her teeth. "You don't want to know."

The monster whipped its snake tail at a passing cop car, and the hood crumpled under the blow. The siren on the car wailed pathetically before it completely died, and the snake hissed in satisfaction.

Max and Aoife jumped from the tower, leaping from suspension cable to suspension cable, back and forth, all the way down until they reached the street. There, Aoife snapped her whip at the lion, and Max rushed forward with his shield. Aoife's Banner cracked with lightning and the chimera snarled at her, reeling back, leaving enough room for Max to flank it and bash his shield into its head.

The sound of screeching tires sounded behind them and a red 1969 Ford Mustang drifted across the pavement, kicking up gravel and smoke as the rear of the car slammed into the chimera, knocking it off the bridge with a great roar. Max knew that car.

Behind the wheel was Stephen.

He rolled down the window and called to Max and Aoife: "Get in!"

They didn't need to be told twice. They threw themselves into the backseat, and Stephen took off before Max could even close the door.

"How'd you find us?" he asked, breathless.

"Just followed the sound of chaos," Stephen said. He drove the car expertly through the mess, avoiding stopped vehicles and fleeing pedestrians like he was a professional stunt driver.

Max and Aoife glanced at each other, impressed, and Aoife grinned. Despite the circumstances, she looked like she was having fun.

"Where's Aurora?" Max asked.

"She'll meet up with us."

Max's teeth clacked together as Stephen hopped a curb to avoid a crashed truck. Max perched on the two front seats and asked, "Do you know where to go?"

"Central Park! Just sit back, put on your seat belt, and hold on."

Stephen threw the car into another gear. Max fell sideways as Stephen took them into a hard turn around a corner. With his face pressed up against the window, Max got to see a streak of light shooting into the sky through the swirling vortex of clouds. He knew that light because his soul had hosted that raw power. It was Azrael. The angel of death, unleashed.

A horrible sinking feeling weighed down Max's stomach. Oliver had consumed Azrael's power. Max would never get it back now, though he realized he didn't mourn losing it anymore. He only wanted all of this to stop.

Stephen floored it and the car growled with more speed.

Through gaps in the passing skyscrapers, Max spotted another streak of light taking to the sky to meet Oliver.

"Get him, Jack," he whispered.

FORTY-TWO

SCHUYLER

*T*he battle was furious.

Monsters and Paladins clashed in the open meadow. Magic lit up the darkness, beasts roared, and weapons rang out. Schuyler fought, always keeping an eye on the sky. Clouds blazed with lightning, monsters attacked, but she still pushed toward the stage.

She needed to destroy the Enochian machine. It their last chance.

But at that moment, a different kind of light caught her eye from the direction of the Brooklyn Bridge, and her heart leaped at the sight. The final sigil had been activated. Max and Aoife had done it. But was there still time to save Kingsley?

Schuyler couldn't risk not finding out. She rushed to the steps of the stage, sword in hand.

Aldrich's attention was entirely fixed upon the eye of the storm as it churned overhead. As if he were enamored of the sight, his icy-blue eyes captured the light of the multiverse, all the images pressing down upon them like a kaleidoscope of mirrors. It was only the two of them, Schuyler and Aldrich, alone. She had him exactly where she needed him to be. Schuyler stepped forward, cautiously, but Aldrich was too struck by the grandeur unfolding above them to track her movements. She didn't know if he even noticed her, wondering if the torrential rain and tumultuous thunder from above drowned out her footsteps, or if he even cared that she approached, but when he spoke, all her questions were answered.

"It's beautiful," he said, his smile bright. "Look at all the possibilities, Schuyler. Millions of worlds, all for the taking."

The only world she cared about, though, was this one. It was the only one that mattered right now. If she distracted Lucifer's attention long enough and Jack obtained the sword from Oliver, there was still a chance. Her eyes darted to the machine, which was currently teeming with souls. Maybe, if she was able to destroy it, she could stop everything altogether. She looked at Aldrich Duncan once again, her face hard with determination despite the weakness in her knees. "This ends now," she declared.

Aldrich looked at her and smiled. It chilled her to the bone. He squared his shoulders as he faced her, cool and calculating. Horrified, Schuyler realized that perhaps confronting her had been his plan all along. He had wanted her to be here. Jack and Max had said he was an expert manipulator and strategized to the umpteenth move. It was she who was now seeing his vision fully realized. "No, child," he said. "This time I will not fail."

He sent her sword flying off into the distance with a simple twitch of his finger. Everything was moving so quickly. Her empty hand felt cold.

"Look at it, Schuyler," he said as he pointed to the sky. Schuyler recognized faces from the other world, the old world that belonged to another Schuyler, a different version of her life. She saw Bliss, the red-haired cheerleader whom the old Schuyler had called a friend. She too had been Lucifer's daughter.

"Look at what I had," he said.

"That's not your life."

"No, but it could have been. And that is the real tragedy. To know what I could have had, and what I could have done . . . I can remake the universe. But first . . ." He raised his hand. Schuyler took a step back, but Aldrich said, "Come here."

Schuyler couldn't stop her own feet from moving toward him. He compelled her to obey. The mortal half of her couldn't resist. He made her stop close enough to permit him to wrap his arms around her, turning her toward the battle unfolding on the lawn.

"You really are something special," he said, his lips uncomfortably close to her ear. "You are different than the others. I can see it now. A half-blood. The only way that's possible is through *her*. Gabrielle. Where is she?"

Schuyler's whole body strained against his hypnotic question. Every muscle in her body was set to explode as she tried to move by her own will, but his words were impossible not to obey. Sweat on her brow mixed with the rain and she shook with rage.

Schuyler hissed through gritted teeth, "She's not here."

Aldrich smiled coolly.

"Enough, Aldrich."

One moment the space was empty in front of the stage, and then it burst into a dazzling array of color and ghostly music. Once it faded, a silhouette stepped into the light. There stood Aurora, Gabrielle—the Uncorrupted.

For the first time, Schuyler noticed surprise on Aldrich's face. "Gabrielle." For all his planning, all his calculation, he could not believe his eyes. "You're . . . You've come back."

"Let my daughter go."

Aldrich's grip on Schuyler's shoulders tightened, and she hissed in pain. *Mom, run! Get away from here!* But Aurora ignored her warning in the glom.

"*Your* daughter." Aldrich's voice was tinged with hurt. "You've been hiding from me all this time, shielding your power from me, denying your truth. But you come running when your *daughter* needs you. Where were you when I needed you in Paradise? Were we not family once? Bondmates? Does that mean nothing to you?"

"Yes," Aurora said, standing proud and tall. "And I broke those ties to you. They weren't bonds, they were shackles. I made my choice a long time ago, I won't change for you now."

"Of course, Gabrielle. You've always been the best of us. The favorite."

Schuyler pushed harder against his power, but her strength was failing. Sweat rolled down her back, and she knew she couldn't fight much longer.

"This doesn't have to end this way, Aldrich," said Aurora. "When did you lose your way?"

"You denied me that family. You denied me a daughter. Schuyler should be *mine*." He snarled that last word, his teeth bared. His fingers gripped Schuyler's shoulders tightly once more. Tears of pain pricked her eyes. She was helpless to stop any of this.

"Instead of being with me," Aldrich went on, "you chose this life? You threw it all away for this?"

"There's still time," Aurora said. She took a step forward, but Aldrich yanked Schuyler even more closely toward him. It made Aurora stop, daring not to come any closer. "You can still choose the right path."

"Let's see who makes the real decisions here." Aldrich pulled on Schuyler's shoulder and whipped her around.

Schuyler found herself standing in front of a still sea, alone. The sand underneath her bare feet was black, cold, and dry. Around her, there was only silence, darkness. All sounds of the battle had stopped. The sky above her was dark except for a single star. It took her a moment to realize where she was.

This was Lucifer's glom, just like it had appeared in her dream.

One minute the sea was empty and the next Aldrich stood in the middle of the still water, his back turned to her, the water at his bare feet rippling gently. His white suit stood out against the pure darkness. The Morningstar. Together he and Schuyler watched the sky as a new dawn rose. The sun melted the darkness away, but there was nothing to shine upon. All was empty, all was black. Lucifer had become a king of nothing.

"I failed you," Aldrich said. His voice reverberated all around Schuyler. "This whole time, I could have been there to guide you, to see your true potential. You should have been my daughter, my heir. I could still do that for you. I can still show you how."

Schuyler could feel the pressure building up painfully in her chest, like she was going to burst from within. His words seemed to suffocate the life out of her. But at the same time, she saw the truth in what he said, visions of possibilities as real as the sea in front of her.

He turned to face her then. His handsome visage, full of kindness and compassion . . . and love. "The world is an imperfect place. Famine, disease, poverty, all of it designed by a flawed hand . . . But it can be repaired. You are a child of both these worlds, mine and mortal. You can be the bridge that mends the break. You can make the world better. I'll give you the same choice I gave your mother when my family cast me out of Paradise. Join me. Save them all."

FORTY-THREE

JACK

The power of Abbadon felt like lightning in a bottle. It was a power that needed to be tempered and tamed, used only when he must. And now he must.

He chased the boy who was once the Oliver he'd known from school, the one who laughed easily, offered help, cared for Schuyler. And all this time he'd been hiding a secret desire for power that Lucifer had taken advantage of. Jack pushed himself faster, burning more of his energy, determined not to give up yet.

If Azrael's sword broke the physical barrier keeping the universes apart, Oliver would end everything in all of existence. Jack willed himself to go faster, the wind and rain rushing past him as he flew like a missile upward. He was gaining on Oliver, but was it enough? Oliver was almost there, his sword out. He stretched toward the glasslike window to another world, the tip of his blade a hairbreadth away.

At the last second, Jack grabbed him by the ankle and ripped him down. Oliver plummeted earthward but caught himself in midair, furious. He flew at Jack, Michael's sword blazing. Schuyler had asked Jack not to kill Oliver, but his promise didn't stop Oliver

DE LA CRUZ

from trying to kill him. Jack unleashed Gabrielle's sword. The twin blades connected, the sound of thunder and lightning colliding as they flew past each other, battling it out in the sky, high above the war raging below. To mortal eyes, they looked like they were teleporting, disappearing in one place and reappearing in another. It was a dance of death and destruction as chaos unfolded.

Azrael's power was unstable, flickering and stuttering, as Oliver pushed himself too hard too fast. He attacked with such ferocity and hate, it took everything in Jack's power to keep up. He parried and countered Oliver's sword strokes, trying to distract the boy from his mission, but Oliver tried to get past him. When Jack cut into his flesh, light spilled out. Oliver roared in pain, clutching his arm.

Oliver looked at the golden blood coating his hand and grimaced, his features contorted in agony. "What makes you so special?" he howled. "Why? Why did Schuyler pick you?"

Jack could hear the pain in his voice. He couldn't answer for her. Instead he said, "She asked me not to kill you. She still loves you."

"Not the way I love her!"

"Ending the universe will not make her love you."

"I have to do this! I need to be like her, like you!" Oliver's voice cracked.

"Let her go, Oliver," Jack said. "If you really love her, let her go."

"You stole her from me!" Oliver charged at Jack again, screaming, Azrael's power blinding. Jack dealt one final blow with his sword, knocking Michael's sword and Oliver from the sky. Oliver began to fall. With a thunderous crash, he hit the ground like a meteor, churning up dirt and grass as he slowed to a stop in a smoldering crater. He didn't get up.

Abbadon's power began to fade, fully spent, and Jack floated to earth, just as Max, Aoife, and Schuyler's father, Stephen, arrived. When Jack's feet touched solid ground, his pain snapped into reality.

He was bleeding. Michael's sword had cut him sometime during the fight, and he'd barely noticed. Now his blue blood was flowing. He pressed his hand to his side and wavered on his feet. His blood was warm and thick between his fingers. Max caught him as he fell, propping him up. Without him, Jack would have keeled over.

"I've got you," Max said. "I've got you."

It felt like Jack could finally breathe again. "The sword, where . . ." The fight had taken a lot out of him, too much. He could barely move. He needed to feed if he was going to use his power again. But Michael's sword was nowhere to be seen.

He searched the battlefield for Schuyler too. It was a mess of monsters and men, dueling in what was turning into a pit of mud. His voice cracked when he called out, "Schuyler . . . Sky!" But she wasn't there. He couldn't see her anywhere in the sheets of heavy rain; neither could he discern Aldrich. They'd both vanished. Where did they go? Jack needed to find them, but his knees gave out and Max held him tighter to keep him from falling.

"I have to find the sword," Jack said. "I have to get it to Schuyler."

"We'll find it!" Aoife said. She and Stephen rushed into the fray, but Jack knew he couldn't join them. He needed to regain his strength, but all his thoughts were centered on Schuyler. He couldn't lose her now. With the painting of the last strokes on the Brooklyn Bridge finished, the resurrection sigil was ready. But without the sword, it was useless.

Max tensed at Jack's side and Jack realized why.

Oliver had finally reappeared, emerging from the hole in the ground, crawling on his hands and knees in the dirt before slowly rising to his feet. Golden blood covered half of his face like a veil. He could barely stand. Like Jack, his power as Azrael had been spent, but his mortal form looked like it could barely remain standing. He stood like a rag doll, his limbs all sharp angles and his body slumped like a great weight was bearing down on him. His skin looked molten, like cracks in lava, radiating Azrael's light. Azrael's power was consuming him from the inside out, searching for every last drop of Oliver's essence to summon up more energy. His mortal form could only hold him together for so long.

If Max were to try to take Azrael's spirit back now, even if he figured out a way to do it, it would be impossible. The angelic power was as volatile as a nuclear bomb, primed and ready to eliminate everything in its path.

As Oliver's golden eyes fixed on the two brothers he took lumbering steps toward them. His face was pulled into a mask of pain and anguish, and fury, but Jack also saw fear and sadness. The human part of Oliver was struggling to stay in control. Azrael's power had driven him mad, yet even the fury of madness could not make him stop. He would fight until he didn't have a body any longer.

Jack barely had the strength to clutch Gabrielle's sword in his fist, but he did it anyway. He had promised Schuyler he wouldn't die again, he wouldn't leave her alone like he had in another world. He was going to keep that promise. He didn't want to let her go on without him. He wanted that family with her, he wanted a life with her, he wanted all of the things he thought he didn't deserve. He wanted to be happy with her, *for* her. She had chosen to love him, even when he'd given her every reason not to. She could have seen that he'd been raised as a tool by Lucifer and given up on her feelings, let him drown in his own fate. But she'd reached in and pulled him out.

Oliver was almost upon them.

"Max, run," Jack cried. "Take Gabrielle's sword and find Schuyler. It's our last chance."

"Shut up!" Max yelled. "I'm not leaving you!"

Oliver ignored the battle that was raging all around him, barely reacting to the sudden appearance of a giant bird—the size of a school bus—crashing through the air with arrows sticking out of its wings. His focus stayed glued on his targets.

That was when Jack spotted Michael's sword buried in the mud between him and Oliver.

FORTY-FOUR

SCHUYLER

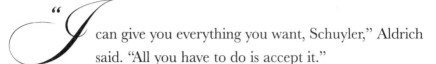

"*I* can give you everything you want, Schuyler," Aldrich said. "All you have to do is accept it."

In the glom, Aldrich made images appear in her mind. These images flooded her thoughts, drowning out her own internal voice. He showed her a Paradise on Earth. Everyone alive, and happy. Her parents smiling, Jack and Max laughing in the sun, Aoife and Theo and all the other Paladins able to put their weapons down. Aldrich showed her a future that awaited her if she threw aside her hesitation and pounced on the opportunity he offered. At his side, she could save herself and all her friends.

The worst part of it was that Schuyler was actually considering his offer.

What if she did join him? In another world, she had let Jack die so everyone else could live. What if this time it was different? What if she could save all the worlds by giving herself over to Lucifer? What would she become? She could remake the world on her own terms. No one would have to suffer ever again. She could save Oliver, safely remove Azrael's spirit from him.

No, it's not true! a small part of her cried out, a candle in the dark.

Aldrich walked toward her, barely disturbing the water beneath his feet, and showed her the truth laid bare. He was the angel of enlightenment, the bringer of light.

"How do I know you're not lying?" Schuyler asked. "How do I know you'll let everyone live?"

"I am merciful. I am also a reasonable man, and I know a good deal when I see one. Surely you can see it too. You know that our conflict has only led to pain and war, and it can all be over. You're the one who can end all wars forever."

"You'll stop this madness? You'll stop the collapse of the worlds?"

"If that is what you want, so long as I know you're at my side. Together we can save them. I promise." He put his hand over his heart and bowed his head. "All you have to do is say yes."

Schuyler couldn't breathe. Could it really be so easy? To save the world, to save all of her friends? Could she merely utter one single word and the battle would be over? No more bloodshed, no more chaos. She could finally end this. She could finally rest.

"What will I become?" she asked.

"What you're destined to be. Now there won't be anyone to stop you. They'll love you for saving them. They'll fall to their knees when they see you. You will be the next bringer of light, my child."

"I don't want people to fall to their knees. I just want peace."

"If that is what you wish it to be. The world can be remade for you. Join me, make it real."

Schuyler's chest swelled. She unclenched her fists and took a deep, steadying breath. This was it. This was all she ever needed to do. She'd been fighting against fate for so long, and now it was time to choose. This was the moment everything had been leading up to.

This time Jack wouldn't die. This time she could save him.

"All you have to do is say yes," Aldrich said.

The dawn was bright behind him. He shone like light itself, and Schuyler remembered why she was here. Kingsley, Max, Aoife . . . All of them needed her. She couldn't betray them, even to save them. Her parents, Jack, her life. It had been hers all along.

A heavy weight materialized in her hand, and she wrapped her fingers around the hilt of a sword. Michael's sword.

She was Gabrielle's daughter, the daughter of an archangel, but she was also the daughter of mortals. She would not be a king for anything.

In a blink, she slashed Michael's sword and Aldrich's smile fell.

His right hand fell to the water, disappearing into the still ocean at his feet.

The glom dissolved.

Schuyler blinked and she was back on the stage, all the sound rushing in like a great wave. The storm, the battle, the monsters . . . Michael's sword was still in her hand.

Aurora was in the middle of the battlefield, standing among Max and Jack and Oliver. She had grabbed the sword when it fell and threw it to Schuyler.

Aldrich screamed, clutching his bleeding stump to his chest. The heavens shook.

"I mark you for exchange, my will be done," Schuyler said. She held out her sword, pointing it at him now. "I send you to Purgatory, Aldrich Duncan."

All four points of the sigil that made up Manhattan began to glow, like spotlights shining from within heavy clouds.

As Aldrich's blue blood pooled at his feet he bared his teeth at Schuyler. His fangs emerged as his true form, his form as Lucifer, began to take shape. Then a portal of chaos symbols illuminated the spot beneath his feet. Schuyler stepped back. She was standing in the middle of the circle. The symbols spun around them and the ground shook as a hole opened underneath.

FORTY-FIVE

SCHUYLER

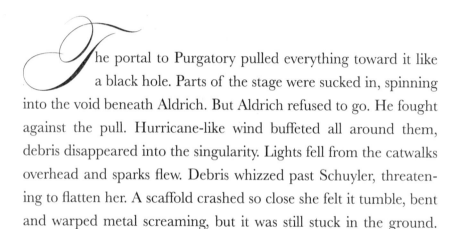

The portal to Purgatory pulled everything toward it like a black hole. Parts of the stage were sucked in, spinning into the void beneath Aldrich. But Aldrich refused to go. He fought against the pull. Hurricane-like wind buffeted all around them, debris disappeared into the singularity. Lights fell from the catwalks overhead and sparks flew. Debris whizzed past Schuyler, threatening to flatten her. A scaffold crashed so close she felt it tumble, bent and warped metal screaming, but it was still stuck in the ground. Like a lifeline, Schuyler held on to the steel. She barely had enough strength left, but terror made her hang on, just for a little longer.

Aldrich too threw himself at the scaffold, and he grabbed her wrist. She struggled to break free, but his grip was too strong. She cried out, feeling like she was being split in half. Aldrich's voice carried above all the chaos, vibrating through the glom. "I will not go alone."

He was going to drag her into Purgatory with him.

Nothing could escape the portal. Schuyler could feel her fingers slipping. The stage disintegrated around her piece by piece, disappearing into the deep black hole. Schuyler's strength started to give width:969px; height:1556px;

out. She wondered if she would even realize she was in Purgatory, or if she would remember this world once she was gone.

Schuyler could see Jack trying to get to her, but he was weak. He collapsed and tried crawling toward her, but Max held him back. They needed to stay away. She couldn't let them get any closer. Their mouths moved silently. Her name was on Jack's lips as he pleaded for her, his words stolen by the wind.

The portal ripped apart the Enochian machine, tearing it to bits like a sheet of aluminum foil. The scaffold collapsed in upon itself, the metal twisting and grinding.

In the chaos, Schuyler spotted another figure.

Oddly calm in the frenzy around him was Oliver. He watched her. She reached out into the glom. *Ollie . . .*

His golden eyes regarded her with a softness she hadn't seen in them in a long time. He looked like a cracked porcelain doll. His skin was almost all light now. Her Oliver was still in there somewhere, beneath the roiling light of Azrael's spirit as it fed his determination to break free. She knew it. It couldn't be too late.

Ollie, help me. Please.

Oliver's voice echoed in her mind. *This was the only way we could be together forever. . . .*

Ollie, listen, she pleaded. Her fingers burned with the effort to hang on. She was sure they'd break. *Please. Help me. I can't hold on.*

Oliver blinked and looked at the chaos swirling around them. It was as if he were seeing it for the first time. If the portal remained open, it would consume everything in existence. Monsters and humans alike were fleeing.

Oliver's hair was buffeted around his face, and he looked more broken than before. The tips of his fingers glowed as his body started to disintegrate. He looked at his hands, realization setting in.

Schuyler cried out. Her forearm burned. She couldn't hold on any longer.

A shadow lifted from Oliver's face, and he ran toward her. With a leap, he wrapped his arms around Aldrich's body. Lucifer's grasp on Schuyler's wrist broke.

"No!" Schuyler screamed. "Oliver!"

Schuyler met Oliver's gaze as he pulled Aldrich into the portal with him. He gave her the small boyish smile she'd known all her life. Then he and Lucifer disappeared into the void. Aldrich's scream of rage was the last thing anyone heard.

There was a second of silence and then . . .

BOOM!

The portal exploded like a supernova.

A giant shock wave rolled out from the middle of the stage and flattened everything around it. Schuyler was blown backward and buried beneath the stage. Trees fell, huge boulders crushed monsters as they tried to get away, people ducked and covered their heads. It was as if the world were coming to an end. Darkness fell.

A ringing silence settled over the city as lights flickered back on in skyscrapers and car alarms wailed endlessly. The images in the storm above flickered and faded and the clouds parted. Rain stopped hammering down and calm returned to the city.

It was over.

Lucifer was gone.

Oliver had saved them.

FORTY-SIX

MAX

*M*ax's ears wouldn't stop ringing. He opened and closed his mouth a few times, convinced his eardrums had exploded, and when he groaned, it sounded muffled, like he was speaking underwater. Jack shifted above him. He'd thrown himself on top of Max to protect him from the blast. They were both alive, but dazed. Max shook the dirt from his hair and looked up. Where there had been a stage was now a crater in the middle of Central Park. Everything within a fifty-foot radius had been destroyed. The ringing in his ears faded and now he could hear the commotion of everyone around them.

"Schuyler," Jack gasped. He rushed to his feet and dashed toward the crater. He tripped and fell but scrambled to his feet again, still holding Gabrielle's sword. Schuyler had been in the middle of the blast, but she was nowhere in sight. Max joined him, grabbing on to the back of Jack's coat to keep him upright, and together they rushed to the crater's edge. Had it worked? Or had it all been for nothing? A ridiculous pipe dream?

Max's stomach dropped when he saw a figure standing in the middle of the crater, his body steaming in the cold.

Long, dark hair; chiseled jaw; dangerously intense eyes—unmistakable. He looked around in shock, panting, like he too couldn't believe his eyes. There was no denying the person standing there. His body had been restored, his soul returned . . . he was as whole as he'd been on the day he'd died.

"Kingsley," Max gasped.

Kingsley Martin turned and his expression softened. "Max!"

Max slid down the crater wall and threw himself into Kingsley's arms. Kingsley wrapped him into a tight hug, and their knees buckled as they fell to the ground together. Max buried his nose into the slope of Kingsley's neck. He was solid and real and Max never wanted to let him go.

She'd done it . . . Schuyler had brought him back from Purgatory.

With strong, familiar hands, Kingsley brushed the back of Max's head. Tears fell when Max squeezed his eyes shut trying to cement this memory in his mind forever. Time was all he'd ever wanted.

"I've been searching everywhere for you," Kingsley said with a smirk.

Max pulled back and looked him straight in the eyes. This was the same Kingsley who Max had thought he'd hated so deeply, he'd wanted to kill him. Then Max kissed him, saying everything he wanted to say. He could feel Kingsley's smile against his mouth as Kingsley kissed him back and cupped the sides of his face. His hands were so warm and strong. After a moment, Kingsley kissed the tears from Max's cheeks and brushed his hair away from his forehead, getting a better look at him and at his warm, dark eyes. Max knew he was a mess, with monster blood on his clothes and his bruised and broken face, but Kingsley didn't seem to care. His smile never wavered.

Max kissed him again, and Kingsley sighed into his touch. They were together, and that's what mattered.

They only broke away when Jack's voice cut across the air, desperate and ragged.

"Schuyler! Where are you? Schuyler!"

Something was wrong.

FORTY-SEVEN

JACK

*J*ack couldn't find Schuyler anywhere. He searched with his eyes and in the glom, trying to find any trace of her, but all he found was a hole in the ground and a heavy quiet. Distantly, he heard shouts and calls from Paladins checking on one another, but he couldn't understand their words. His fight with Azrael had taken too much out of him, and his head felt like it was swarming with hornets. He could barely manage to put one foot in front of the other. Every time he called her name, it rang hollow in his ears.

The spell had worked—Kingsley had been saved, Aldrich Duncan was gone. They'd all been freed from his control. All of the worlds had been saved once again. But in the end, had Schuyler fallen with Lucifer? Desperation and panic gripped Jack's throat. He tried to swallow the feelings down, but doubt and anguish twisted his gut.

As the seconds passed, his head started to clear. His voice grew stronger. Schuyler had been so close to disappearing into the void, but he wasn't ready to believe that she had been trapped in Purgatory. He couldn't begin to imagine a world where she wasn't at his side.

At the sound of rubble shifting, he turned. A giant pile of debris sat nearby, and a hand was visible beneath a giant slab of rock. "Schuyler!"

Jack yanked the slate off her, sending the rock flying like it weighed nothing.

But she didn't move, not even when Jack brushed dirt away from her face. His hopeful smile fell. "Schuyler?"

She lay still, eyes closed, her mouth slightly open.

"No," he gasped. He put his hand to her cheek, but she didn't stir. He couldn't feel her heart beating. His own heart stopped. "No, no, no." He scooped her up into his arms, and her head lolled listlessly into his chest. She was so light.

"Help!" he cried. "Over here!"

Max and Kingsley rushed to his side to help him ease Schuyler's body down on flat earth.

"Schuyler," Jack whispered. He knelt over her body, clutching her hands in his, willing the warmth to come back to her fingers. "Schuyler, you did it. It's over. Lucifer's gone. Kingsley is here. Come on, open your eyes."

"I'm here, I'm here," Kingsley said, smiling.

Max cut his wrist open and his red blood began to flow. He held up his arm to Schuyler's mouth, letting her drink, but when he took it away, his blood pooled in the corners of her lips, untouched.

All of them went quiet. No one even dared to breathe.

Not like this, please. Not like this.

Grief washed over Jack. His heart beat, and then beat again, reminding him that time was hurtling forward, even when he didn't want it to, not without Schuyler at his side. In an instant, everything he had ever cared about had been taken away from him. Just like that.

Numb.

His whole being felt weightless and immensely heavy at the same time. His worst fears, realized.

He refused to let go of her hands.

He had the vague sense that her parents had arrived behind him. Slowly, they seemed to realize what they were witnessing. Kingsley and Max stepped back, giving them room.

Aurora knelt, gently lifted her daughter's head, and placed it in her lap.

"Save her," Jack whispered.

She looked at him, eyes shining with a million unsaid things, and something inside him broke. He couldn't bear it anymore. He dropped his forehead and let the tears flow. No one spoke as Jack silently wept. He gripped her hands tightly, praying he could do something, anything to get her back. But all was quiet, all was still. Then a voice cut through the silence.

"I think I should be dead . . ."

Jack lifted his head, choking on tears. She was looking at him, slits of blue behind half-lidded eyes. He almost thought it was a trick of his imagination, a hallucination, born of desperation, but then Schuyler smiled at him. His heart leaped.

It couldn't be . . . No way.

"Jack, is that you?" Schuyler said.

With great effort, she sat up and Jack embraced her. He held her close, repeating her name over and over again in her ear, rocking back and forth. She groaned in pain, and he released her, but she laughed. Aurora stepped back, smiling behind her hands as she moved to rejoin her husband. Kingsley and Max watched in awe. Aoife and the other Paladins arrived just in time to see the miracle for themselves.

How it had happened, Jack didn't know. Schuyler had died, but she'd been brought back to life. The impossible had been made real. Her presence here was impossible in so many ways.

Jack kissed Schuyler's fingers, pressing her knuckles to his lips, and closed his eyes, vowing to protect her until the end of time.

Schuyler pulled him in and kissed him as dawn rose once again, new and bright.

PART FIVE

THE END IS JUST THE BEGINNING

FORTY-EIGHT

SCHUYLER

*S*chuyler opened the curtains in the sitting room of the Force mansion and looked out across Fifth Avenue, smiling in the soft sunlight that warmed her face.

It had been several days since the battle in Central Park. Of course the events of that night had been all over the news. No one could ignore the swirling vortex of folding dimensions that had borne down upon the city for a whole night, let alone the resounding explosion that knocked the power out in half the state. Despite the devastation, the world was starting to return to normal. Most people chalked it up to a mass hallucination, despite the thousands of hours of video evidence that had been taken by terrified onlookers.

Experts and analysts all agreed: It was better to leave some questions unanswered.

As she gazed through the window, she observed people ambling along the sidewalks, cars rolling steadily down the street, and clouds slipping across a deep blue sky. The day was bright and promising. Schuyler threw open the window for good measure, letting in a gust of fresh air. At the same time, it felt like she was letting something out, making way for the new. The room was stuffy and in desperate need of a dusting. It looked more like a hunting lodge than a mansion. She'd been told it was Max's office when he was Lucifer's Venator, but everything inside had been burned. Piles of ash and debris were all that was left of Max's tenure as Venator. Aldrich had tried to scrub their existence off the face of the earth, and yet the Force boys were as stubbornly persistent as ever. Just like everyone else in New York, they had been changed, but they too were moving forward.

Schuyler's heart ached as her gaze settled on the Met across the street. Steady streams of visitors walked up the stairs of the building, heading in for a day of enjoying the exhibits. She missed doing that very same thing . . . with Oliver. She doubted she'd ever be able to look at the museum and Central Park beside it and not think of him.

"Hey," Jack said softly from the doorway. She turned around and smiled at him. He was holding a stack of singed books that had somehow escaped Aldrich's vengeful depredations. Even though she smiled, she couldn't mask her grief well enough. Jack came to her side and rubbed his hand on her arm as he too looked out the window. "Do you want to talk about it?"

Losing Oliver was like losing a limb, the memory still raw and bleeding. She knew it would heal, but it needed time. She took a breath. "No, I'm okay."

Jack kissed her forehead, and she breathed in his scent. Him simply being near her made her feel better. She didn't remember dying, but she knew that she had. She wasn't sure how she'd managed to return. Even though Azrael's power, along with Oliver, was in Purgatory, everyone doubted that that power was the cause. Just because the angel of death's power was gone didn't stop death from happening. Something else had brought her back, but she didn't care to speculate about what it was. All that mattered was that she had another chance to live a life with Jack.

Faintly, Schuyler could hear Paladins working on the rest of the mansion, moving debris and destroyed furniture out of the building, calling and laughing with one another, playing music over the speaker system to pass the time. Everyone pitched in to help clean up and rebuild, working together to put new life back into the grand old home.

"Does anyone need help?" Schuyler asked.

"No, it's all taken care of." Jack smiled. "I can't remember the last time I had this many people in my house. I'm still getting used to the commotion. It's nice."

Both Max and Jack had agreed to open the doors of their home to Paladins who needed shelter, turning the once empty and dark mansion into a Paladin headquarters of sorts. Little Megan and some other younger Paladins who'd been orphaned by monsters moved into a more permanent residence in the west wing. The Force mansion had once again turned into a family home. In the end, Jack had gotten what he wanted. His and Max's isolation had finally been broken with their adoptive father's sudden and mysterious disappearance.

No one knew what had really happened to Aldrich Duncan. Never before had a sitting mayor of New York gone missing, and it was national news for a while. His office and the members of his administration had completely vanished overnight after his disastrous charity concert. But the mystery would remain unsolved. New Red Blood candidates for the office were already campaigning for a special election to fill Duncan's seat. The city was slowly but surely readjusting and moving toward a future—one without Lucifer.

Jack took Schuyler by the hand. "Come on," he said. "Kingsley's almost done making lunch." He led her toward the back of the mansion.

For too long the mansion had stood like a mausoleum, a repository of the old; now there were sounds of children running through the halls playing with each other in the sunlight coming through the grand arching windows. It was as if the building itself could breathe a sigh of relief after being locked in the dark for so long.

Schuyler stepped out of the way as a swarm of tiny children came sprinting down the hall, led by a cackling Megan, grinning through her missing front teeth.

"'Scuse me, Miss Schuyler!" she called as she whizzed past.

Whatever they were up to, Schuyler would let them have their fun. She couldn't help but smile at their antics.

Megan's visions and sleeping spells had stopped almost entirely since Lucifer had met his fate. Occasionally, she would wake up in the night with a new prophecy that needed translating, messages from beyond, but she'd mostly turned into a bubbly, bright child who was up to no good most days.

The kids disappeared into the sparring room, where Theo was healing the scraped knee of a young Paladin who'd tripped on the carpet, his eyes still watery with tears. Theo comforted him with a pat on his head.

"Coming to lunch, Theo?" Jack asked.

"In a bit! These kids are determined to keep me busy." He sounded exhausted, but he still smiled.

"Come down when you're done," Jack said.

Theo gave them a casual salute as Schuyler and Jack headed downstairs. Paladins were busy moving what was left of Jack's library out the front door. The Silver Bloods had wrecked it, shelves and books alike. Jack had been helping them all morning, fixing it up to its former glory. They planned to add desks for the kids and newer books to the collection. He'd said he'd been meaning to update the catalog for a while, and now he had a good excuse, including adding some more chaos magic resources on the shelves. It might come in handy again someday.

They found Ruby in the great hall, struggling with the giant oil painting of the Force boys that Aldrich had destroyed. Jack and Schuyler rushed forward and helped her maneuver the portrait through the door. It was a tight squeeze, but they did it. Outside, a few Paladins put the painting in a large truck and headed off to the dump.

"Thanks, guys," Ruby said.

"No, thank *you*," said Jack. "You've all been so helpful."

Ruby waved her hand dismissively.

"Hungry?" Schuyler asked.

"If Kingsley's cooking, you know I'm there," she said with a grin. "Let me get cleaned up, then I'll meet you."

Conversation was coming from the kitchen and they soon found Aoife, Max, and Kingsley standing around the island counter, plates and glasses already set out for a meal. Kingsley was in the middle of serving up steaming bowls full of rice for everyone in the house while Max and Aoife were leaning over an iPad, reading together. It struck Schuyler just how casual everyone looked, including herself, standing around. They were a patchwork team.

Aoife pushed up her glasses when she looked at Schuyler. "What do you know about strigas?"

Schuyler shrugged, same as Jack. "No idea," she said. "Why?"

Max said, "Apparently there's been a few sightings in Miami, some disappearances and midnight attacks. Couldn't hurt to take a trip to see what's going on. I'm all ready to go."

Even though Lucifer's world-ending machine had been destroyed, monsters still managed to get through. No one was sure how many had gotten stuck on this Earth, but the Paladins expected they were going to be dealing with a lot more cases in the future. Silver Bloods were rumored to have gone into hiding in all corners of the world. The Paladins' work was far from over. And now that Max had joined their ranks, he'd settled into his position as one of them.

"You're never going back to Duchesne?" Schuyler asked him.

"Call it a sabbatical. I wouldn't say never."

Aoife asked Max, "You think you could handle it on your own? We've got a Paladin stationed in Atlanta who might help, though I'm not sure how busy they are with their own cases."

"I'll manage. Besides, Kingsley could use a vacation."

Kingsley snaked his arm around Max's torso; coming up behind him, he rested his chin on Max's shoulder and hummed. "Miami. Beaches. Cocktails. Monster hunting. What's not to love?"

It seemed like everyone could use a vacation. Max had repaid Schuyler's parents' generosity and kindness with a much-needed trip to Hawaii. He'd said it was the least he could do. Stephen and Aurora, while humble, didn't turn him down. A free vacation to an island resort, sipping on mai tais and lounging on the beach, was exactly the kind of respite they needed.

Max leaned into Kingsley, smiling. He looked happier than he had ever looked before, a man remade. Theirs was a relationship that was stronger even than that between soul mates, for theirs was forged in the fires of sheer willpower. They were inseparable. Kingsley would follow Max to the ends of the earth, and vice versa.

"I hear the nightclub scene is particularly fun," Max said, grinning at Kingsley.

"You can take over the training sessions while I'm gone, right, Young Blood?" Kingsley asked Schuyler, using his favorite nickname for her.

Schuyler flushed and smiled nervously. "I guess. But I'm not nearly as good at teaching as you are."

"Nonsense, you're a natural." Kingsley had taken over the sparring room, designating it as his new classroom to replace the one he'd lost in the Repository. He'd become a mentor, taking up the mantle of leader once more as he taught the younger generation of Paladins everything he knew about monster fighting and hunting. He'd march up and down the rows of students like a drill sergeant, much to the amusement of Schuyler, Jack, and Max, who watched from the wings; despite his sternness, he seemed to truly enjoy passing on his knowledge to eager students.

When he wasn't teaching, he cooked up some of his favorite meals for anyone staying in the house, using recipes he'd memorized during his adventures across the world, while singing his favorite sea shanties from when he'd had traveled the seas as a pirate in the 1700s. Hearing his voice accompanied by the smell of food was just another reminder that the group was moving in the right direction. Kingsley had settled nicely back into the world of the living.

Just then, there came a gigantic crash from the floor above, shaking the pendant lights and raining dust on their heads. Max shielded the food as best he could from a dusting of drywall.

With a sigh, Kingsley said, "It would seem that Megan found the candy stash." There were shrieks of laughter coming from the second floor.

"*That's* a candy raid?" Jack asked, aghast.

"Chaos magic can only hide so much from a determined little girl with an insatiable sweet tooth." Kingsley vanished into the hallway, calling up the stairs: "You little gremlins need to be using chaos for good, not evil!" Screams of laughter echoed as he ran up the stairs to chase after them.

"Well then," Aoife said, with an amused sigh. "We've still got a lot of work ahead of us."

Jack's fingers interlocked with Schuyler's and she squeezed his hand. He'd been welcomed into the Cervantes-Chase house with open arms. The future was bright, and she wanted to bask in it as long as she could.

"Nothing we can't handle," she said, beaming. "As long as we've got one another."

Lucifer was gone from this world. Schuyler was a daughter of Heaven and Earth and the world wasn't perfect, but it was good, because there were still people who wanted to protect it. And that was enough.

Acknowledgments

Massive thanks to my incredible editor, Kieran Viola, and the whole amazing team at Disney, which has been home to my Blue Bloods for two decades. Thank you to Richard Abate and Ellen Goldsmith-Vein, my "dad and mom" in the biz. Thank you to Mike and Mattie always, everything is for you. Thank you to the Blue Bloods faithful.